Praise for *Saving Mrs. Roosevelt*

Full of intrigue and historical detail, Patterson brings to life the little-known women's SPARs who deserve to have their story told as part of the Greatest Generation. Drama and faith seamlessly blend together with just the right amount of romance to delight any WWII fan.

—J'nell Ciesielski, bestselling author of *The Socialite*

In *Saving Mrs. Roosevelt*, Candice Sue Patterson has crafted a home front story of WWII that will satisfy fans of Lynn Austin and Amy Lynn Green. Filled with intrigue and drama, the hero and heroine must work together to infiltrate a spy ring that is determined to harm Mrs. Roosevelt. Along the way you'll enjoy the setting and supporting characters. This is an engaging story with a layer of romance that I enjoyed.

—Cara Putman, bestselling, award-winning author of *Flight Risk* and *Lethal Intent*

≡ HEROINES OF WWII ≡

SAVING MRS. ROOSEVELT

CANDICE SUE PATTERSON

BARBOUR
PUBLISHING

Saving Mrs. Roosevelt © 2021 by Candice Sue Patterson

Print ISBN 978-1-63609-089-4

eBook Editions:
Adobe Digital Edition (.epub) 978-1-63609-091-7

All scripture quotations, unless otherwise noted, are taken from the King James Version of the Bible.

This book is a work of fiction. Names, characters, places, and incidents are either products of the author's imagination or used fictitiously. Any similarity to actual people, organizations, and/or events is purely coincidental.

Cover Photograph © Joanna Czogala/Trevillion Images

Published by Barbour Publishing, Inc., 1810 Barbour Drive, Uhrichsville, Ohio 44683, www.barbourbooks.com

Our mission is to inspire the world with the life-changing message of the Bible.

ecpa Member of the
Evangelical Christian
Publishers Association

Printed in the United States of America

In memory of
Seaman Joseph Franklin Patterson,
United States Navy
(Grandpa Joe)
and
Seaman Turner Lee Ridge,
United States Navy
(Grandpa Turner)

You are missed.

⚎ CHAPTER 1 ⚎

Lubec, Maine
December 1942

Shirley Davenport was a breath away from dying.

Of boredom.

She lowered the newspaper to her lap. Why did men get to have all the fun?

Brows arched, Daddy looked up from the boat he was cleaning and held out the scraper. "I'm sorry. Did you want to remove the layers of crust? I wouldn't call it fun."

Embarrassed, Shirley bowed her head. She hadn't meant to voice her thoughts aloud, but she did that sometimes.

"I was speaking of the war, Daddy."

The heater surged beside them, warming a small bubble of space in the massive barn. The scent of hay and dust and kerosene wasn't a pleasant one, but she'd rather be working in a cold dank barn any day than in a stuffy kitchen.

Her father winced and stood from his crouched position, hand bracing the pain she knew lived in the curve of his back. "I know."

A gust of winter forced its way between the cracks of the old structure. Christmas was over, and a new year awaited. While two of her brothers were scattered across the globe, fighting for freedom and justice, she was stuck in a little town by the frozen sea, doing the same things she'd done since childhood.

And would probably do every year for the rest of her life.

Daddy's footsteps shuffled remnants of straw on the dirt-packed floor. Easing onto an upturned bucket beside her, he grimaced. As much from exasperation with her as from the pain, no doubt. "War is never fun, Shirley Jean."

Guilt pricked her as she recalled the gruesome stories of the World War he used to tell her and her brothers while they lounged by the fireplace after dinner. They'd hung on every word. Their mother didn't care to hear the tales, but she'd told Shirley it helped him to talk about them. Her mother would hum church hymns to block him out while she mended clothes on the other side of the room.

Shirley had liked the gory parts as much as her brothers, not understanding everything her father recalled. Older, she understood now. "I'm sorry. I only meant that I'm left here, helpless to do anything for the cause, while men all across the country are free to sign up and fight."

He frowned at her, bulging his auburn walrus mustache threaded with gray. "They called the draft. Not all men were willing to go."

His comment was beside the point. She passed him the newspaper. "Have you read about the Doolittle Raid? It's amazing."

He pointed his nose to the rafters and closed his eyes. "Sure, there's great victories. But there's also death and destruction. When war is over, nothing's the same. *Nothing*."

Restless, she stood and toed a pile of straw. "I can't sit by and do nothing either. It's my country too. There's got to be something I can do to help."

"There is. You can ration, write to your brothers, sew blackout curtains, get married, and have children. Maybe then you wouldn't be so discontented."

She pointed to the newspaper curled in his grip. "I'm restless because I want to be with them. I hate sewing, I already write to James and Thomas once a week, and all the young, decent men are off fighting."

The man she'd spotted in town yesterday sprang to mind. Younger than Daddy, he was much older than Shirley but still handsome enough. The interested way he'd looked at her, almost as if he could see inside her, had made her nervous.

Shirley plopped down beside Daddy and noted the frayed hem of her trousers and her scuffed boots. "Even if there were eligible men my age, they'd not want me."

"Hush now." His big hand landed on her shoulder. "When it comes to young ladies, you're the finest kind."

She refrained from rolling her eyes. "That's not true, and you know it. I don't possess one feminine skill. All I know is fishing and lobstering, boat repair, and how to build a fire. Hardly duties that will help protect my country. Or catch me a husband."

Her dearest friend, Joan, had once told her boys liked girls who were approachable, weaker. Girls who looked soft. Not girls who could keep up with them in a boxing match.

Daddy nudged her with his elbow. "Someday the right man will come along and appreciate your resourcefulness."

The pathetic description was accurate. Resourceful, never desirable. Not that such a thing mattered to her. Well, it did. She wanted to be soft. She wanted to be wanted. To marry and have children someday. But first—before she spent the rest of her life cooking meals, cleaning house, and changing diapers—she wanted to do something grand.

Over the course of time, she'd seen the young women in this town fade beneath the weight of homemaking and childbearing, like Mama. Shirley loved her mama, but she didn't want to *be* her mama. Shirley had ambition and a desperate need to make her mark on the world. She wanted to live in a world where she was free to do so. Was that too much to ask?

If nothing was the same when war ended, then she hoped after this one such a world for women would exist.

She looked up at Daddy. Deep lines etched his weathered skin and traced a path into his gnarly beard. She smiled, showing teeth, the way she had when she was a child trying to persuade him to her way of thinking. "Assembling airplane motors and stuffing bullets is resourceful too."

He chuckled and pulled her to his side. "Shirley Jean, your patriotism is honorable. I understand your need to help. I truly do. But you're my little girl. There's no need for you to go traipsing off to the big city for a factory job. You're taken care of right here. Aid the effort like the other local women until this is all over."

Twenty-two hardly qualified as a little girl.

"I want to go to Washington too, Daddy."

He crossed his ankles. "I know you do. My word from last week stands firm—if you go, you're getting there on your own. I'll not take part."

Disappointment settled like a boulder in her chest. Hundreds of women were flocking to Washington, DC, upon hearing Eleanor Roosevelt's request for clerical workers and switchboard operators. Shirley didn't have enough money saved to sustain her travel and living expenses for more than a few weeks. Until she saved enough for at least a month—in case finding a job was harder than she thought—she'd be scraping boat bottoms, hauling pots, and building fires.

She reached for the scraper in the front pocket of her daddy's overalls and began scraping where he had left off. Dried barnacles and crusted algae fell to the floor.

Daddy released another sigh and rubbed his forehead. She didn't mean to be so exasperating. It came naturally, according to her brother Walter.

The barn door burst open behind her, sending a cold shock to Shirley's backside.

Joan stepped in and tried to tug the door shut, but the cantankerous hinges didn't like winter any more than Daddy's joints. Daddy waved her into the barn and tugged the door to seal them in.

"Thanks, Mr. D. Have you seen this, Shirl?" Her best friend held out a crumpled paper in her red glove. Joan's cheeks were nearly the color of her scarlet coat, and clouds of breath escaped from her mouth and nose.

Shirley took the paper and smoothed the edges. A colored printing of a woman in a dark blue uniform raising an American flag stared back at her. *"Enlist in the Coast Guard SPARS. Release a man to fight at sea."*

Joan's radiant smile almost reached her ears. "It's a new female-only reserve of the Coast Guard. The president approved its establishment last month. We'd be taking over duties on the home front to release the men to fight."

"We?" Shirley's heart raced at a pace that made her dizzy.

Joan shook her arm, rattling the paper. "This is what we've been waiting for," she whispered.

The advertisement trembled in Shirley's hand. She looked to Daddy, who shook his head and turned away.

Eleanor Roosevelt's words from her last "My Day" column played in Shirley's memory. *"Do what you feel in your heart to be right—for you'll be criticized anyway."*

Joan raised a brow at her, clearly confused as to why Shirley seemed torn after months of their dreaming of an opportunity like this. She took the paper from Shirley, turned it over, and pointed at the writing. "A Captain Webber is going to be recruiting single females or married women whose husbands are not members of the Coast Guard at the town hall in Machiasport tonight at six. If we really want to help our country, here's our chance."

A rhythmic *scritch* filled the silence that followed. Daddy had retrieved another scraper and gone back to work. Shirley didn't want to abandon her family or defy Daddy's wishes, but she was a grown woman. The independence that had been pounding at her heart's door since childhood shoved forth into the light.

For herself and for her country, she'd be the first in line for Captain Webber or perish.

≡ CHAPTER 2 ≡

Captain Leonard Webber's anger ran as red as the sun setting against the harbor. Machiasport Town Hall was stifling, unlike the frozen tundra outside. His breath made the glass fog, hindering his view of the water.

The thought of water brought his brothers to mind, and his stomach seized. Lonnie had loved the ocean from the moment he'd first spied it on their trip to Bridgeport, around the age of five, if Leo remembered correctly. That would've made Leo ten. Watching the sheer joy on Lonnie's face was like Leo experiencing it for the first time himself.

Donald had been the opposite. He'd feared the powerful waves but had loved the music and attractions of Pleasure Beach. Leo's younger brothers may have been identical twins, but where one left the womb ready to take on the world, the other had a cautious, sensible nature.

How he missed them.

Leo swallowed down the memories and stepped back to let the fog on the window dissipate. The vapor was so light, so thin, yet it had the power to completely obstruct the beauty lying beyond.

Like the disaster at Pearl Harbor. A vapor of false security, of assumption that the blip on the radar screen was only a group of American B-17s arriving from California and not two hundred of Japan's best pilots flying loaded.

Leo's hands balled into fists. More than half of the country's Pacific Fleet had been moored in that harbor. Why hadn't someone been more vigilant? Why had Japan's alliance with the Germans come as a surprise to the United States? Why hadn't American informants discovered that the Japanese were modifying their torpedoes to navigate the shallow waters of Pearl Harbor and sent warning?

Despite what men said, there were no rules to war. Mistakes were made, sometimes people betrayed their countries, and there were times when the other guy won.

He rubbed away the pressure that built behind his eyes. The pain was too fresh, and his thoughts were too loud in the silent room. A room that would soon be filled with exuberant women lining up to serve their country.

Women.

Not that he was against their help. By all means, they were just as capable as the men—in some respects more so—but hadn't they suffered enough already by sending their loved ones to war? By taking over the running of the household? By answering the knock at the door where a telegram awaited that would alter their lives forever?

Like his mother.

Three children out of four deceased. His sister—stillborn. The navy was doing its best to make sure Leo remained alive. The reason his superior had pulled him from commanding his own ship and landlocked him recruiting women for the SPARs. The government didn't wish to rob a mother of all her children. Honorable, but the enemy had poked a sleeping bear when they'd murdered his brothers, and Leo lusted after justice.

Something touched his elbow, yanking him from the dark path his mind liked to travel of late. Commander Dorothy Stratton frowned. "Captain, are you all right?"

"Yes, yes, of course. Got a little lost admiring the view, is all."

She peered out the same window he'd been blindly gazing out for who knew how long. "Yes, that's. . .quite a sight."

Said view was nothing more than a giant stack of lobster traps, ropes, and spare boat parts covered in a layer of snow tinted orange by the sunset.

She studied him a moment longer. More questions were simmering beneath the surface, but thankfully she wasn't the prying type.

"Recruits should start arriving within the hour," she said. "Everything is set up and ready to go. Do you need anything? The secretary has coffee, tea, water."

Leo blinked away the remaining haze of memories. "Coffee. I'll get it myself though. Thank you."

She tilted her head to an acute angle. "I'll fetch it for you, Captain. You enjoy your. . .view."

The commander retreated on sturdy shoes, spine as straight as a flagpole. Though he hadn't been thrilled with his reassignment, he'd been impressed with Commander Stratton from the day they'd met, when she'd been a lieutenant commander in the WAVES, the Navy Women's Reserve. The former dean of women at Purdue University had a repertoire to rival any man's. A bachelor of arts degree, a master of arts in psychology, and a doctorate in philosophy. Every accomplishment made her uniquely her and the perfect woman to direct the SPARs.

It was her psychology degree that made him uncomfortable, however. He was proud of his ability to tuck away emotion. To do what was needed without feeling. Feelings could be processed later. Stratton had the ability to see straight to his core and spot every worm that feasted on his rotting insides.

That scared him to death. Like a bulldog, she also smelled fear, which was most disconcerting.

If even a handful of the women enlisting were as intuitive as Stratton, the coalition's chances of winning this war would skyrocket. That's what he prayed for—victory for the United States and her allies. Victory for all who valued human life.

If all the death and destruction and evil in this world made Leo this sick, it must make the good Lord vomit.

The squeaky leather of Stratton's shoes warned him of her return. "Here you are, Captain."

He took the offered mug and watched the swirls of steam curl as they lifted into the air, then disappeared. So like life. A vapor.

Leo pasted on a smile. "I hear Mainers are a hearty breed. I look forward to seeing who enlists."

The corners of her lips twitched. "I wouldn't speak such thoughts in front of the recruits, Captain. No matter how tough or resilient we may be, remember, at the end of the day, we're still women and would like to be thought of as such."

Her scolding was soft and every bit as effective as his mother's. He supposed she was right. He'd been around men for too many years to recall the sensitivities of the female nature. His dreams of a wife and children had burst like a torpedo with the declaration of war.

And the loss of his brothers.

Stratton mimicked his stance at the window. "A view, like beauty, is in the eye of the beholder. My grandfather used to write to me at college and tell me what a beautiful view he had from his hospital window. Glorious sunrises and sunsets, lush green fields with cattle dotting the pasture. After midterm exams, I caught the fastest train I could home to visit him before he passed. By the time I arrived, I was too late. What shook me more than his death was his view from that window."

Leo waited while she reminisced.

"There were no windows in the room, Captain. All my grandfather could see from his bed were the painted brick walls."

The declaration hit him square in the chest.

She smiled. "Hang in there, Captain. For one day, our view will be much different."

⅀ CHAPTER 3 ⅀

The excitement surging through Shirley's veins created enough friction that she barely felt the sting of Old Man Winter frosting her father's Buick. He'd insisted on driving them to Machiasport, even though Shirley knew well how to navigate a vehicle. He'd made it clear his gesture was not in support of her endeavor but for protection since she insisted on going. She only hoped the old car didn't let them down the way it did last fall on their way to Boyden Lake.

Her father turned into Joan's driveway and parked in front of the house. Light glowed in every window, casting pale reflections in the yard. Joan was the oldest of six children, and the Fischer house was always abustle.

"I'll hurry." Shirley left the car and tiptoed through the icy patches to the front porch, not wanting to twist an ankle. Not that a twisted ankle would keep her from enlisting, but it wouldn't make the greatest first impression.

Laughter and childish squeals emanated from the home. Shirley pulled off one glove and knocked hard enough to be heard over the noise. A few seconds later the door opened. Joan's little brother Maxwell peeked his head out, revealing his toothless smile.

Shirley bent to inspect his mouth. "All four?"

"Ayuh. *Daed* says it must be an omen to lose all my front teeth at the same time right before a new year."

Shirley didn't think baby teeth held any kind of prophetic significance, but the tiny white nubs poking through Maxwell's gums definitely made him look more impish than usual. "Is Joan ready?"

Maxwell shrugged and then yelled, "Joan, are you ready? Shirley's here."

"*Ach*," his mother scolded and opened the door wider. "Stop yer yelling afore your *daed* takes a spanking to ya." She shooed him down the hall. "Come in, Shirley, come in."

"Thank you, Mrs. Fischer." Shirley stepped on the faded rug and closed the door behind her. "I'm here to pick up Joan. Is she ready?"

"*Ach*, you know that girl. She thinks she has to look exactly like that Carole Lombard woman before she can leave the house. She'll be at least another hour."

Joan had been unnaturally shaken by the actress's death announced earlier that year—a plane crash while on tour helping raise money for war bonds.

Shirley looked at her watch. "If we don't leave now, we won't make it in time. May I fetch her?"

Mrs. Fischer looked down at Shirley's wet boots and backed away. "You stay here. I'll hurry her along."

The woman swayed down the hall and ascended the stairs. A high-pitched scream ripped through the house, followed by stomping. "Give me that," a little voice yelled.

Boyish laughter filled the next room, and then Ike plowed into Shirley as he ran backward, taunting his little sister by holding her dolly out of reach. Shirley steadied the boy by his shoulders.

Ina, all of four, balled her hands into fists and punched them onto her hips. Her little mouth screwed into the meanest face Shirley had ever seen. Ina flared her nostrils and breathed heavily for intimidation. "Give me back my dolly, you yellow-bellied, one-eyed snake."

Shirley covered her chuckle with a cough.

Ike shook the doll in the air. "Come and get it, you gimpy shrimp."

Ina's mouth dropped open.

Incensed that Ike would attack his sister's handicap, Shirley grabbed the boy's wrist and wrestled the doll from his grip. Her gaze flicked to the movement in the corner. A man entered the room.

The man she'd seen in town yesterday.

The handsome one with the dark eyes that seemed to probe inside her soul. Her presence appeared to take him by surprise as well, but he recovered quickly.

He nodded.

Shirley passed the doll to Ina and scolded Ike for picking on someone younger than himself. Ike stuck his tongue out. The man rattled off something in German that made the boy wince.

Ike turned regretful eyes to Shirley. "Sorry."

"Thank you. I accept your apology. Now apologize to your sister."

The man silenced Ike's protest with raised brows and a tip of his chin.

Ike sighed. "Sorry, Ina," he mumbled.

The man said something else, and both children left the room. The hallway seemed to shrink under his watchful stare. She wondered what he'd said to the children, but her German was limited. Her family had migrated to America nearly a hundred years ago, and the language wasn't spoken in her home anymore.

Smiling, the man took a step toward her. She fought the urge to back against the door. Warning alarms blared inside her. She was being silly. He wouldn't be allowed inside the Fischers' home if he wasn't a nice man. Still, she couldn't shake the cornered-animal feeling.

Joan bounded down the stairs. "Sorry to keep you waiting."

She grinned at Shirley and palmed her perfect pin curls secured with a pearl clip. "What do you think? Do I look like I belong on the big screen?"

"Uh"—Shirley looked from Joan's brown hair to her clasped hands to the man across the hall—"yes. Very Hollywood."

Joan grabbed the lapels of Shirley's coat and spread them open. "Oh, my dear, you're not wearing that."

Shirley assessed her loose fabric overalls and striped shirt. "What's wrong with my clothes?"

They were clean, even if a bit worn.

"We're trying to convince military officers we're the right women for these jobs. Part of our duties will be to boost morale. Nothing lifts a man's spirit like beautiful, well-dressed women!"

A grunt ensued from the corner. Joan turned. "Uncle Ernst."

She tugged the man by his elbow closer to Shirley. "Tell my friend Shirley that she'll have a much better chance wooing an officer in stockings and heels than she will a pair of overalls with dried lobster guts on the knee."

Shirley kicked out her leg for inspection. "It's a turpentine stain, and my overalls are clean."

Uncle Ernst mumbled something in German that made Joan laugh.

Uncomfortable, Shirley reminded her friend they needed to leave. "We're not going to woo officers. We're going to be of service to our country. Besides, if the purpose of a SPAR is to free the men to fight, there won't be anyone to woo."

"They're not all leaving the country. And what greater service is there to mankind than procreation?" Joan slipped her arms into the coat her uncle held out for her. "Being attractive helps to set it in motion."

Heat filled Shirley's face. Her friend's obsession with the Hollywood elite had also made her brash. Joan reasoned her behavior by saying that everyone should take the artists' cue in forward thinking and speaking, that it was a more honest approach to life.

Shirley believed in honesty, but she also believed in tact.

Shirley caught the man gawking at her, and she hastened to button her coat. Joan stood on tiptoe to kiss his cheek. "Goodbye, Uncle Ernst. We'll talk later."

She hooked her arm around Shirley's elbow and pulled them through the door. "No time to worry about your appearance now. Just smile like I taught you, the way that makes your dimples more pronounced, and you're sure to win them over."

Joan slipped on frost coating the bottom step. Shirley kept her upright. At least one of them had worn sensible shoes. "If I didn't know better, I'd think you were embarrassed to be seen with me tonight."

"Nothing could be farther from the truth." Joan tightened her hold on Shirley's arm as they approached the car. "I'm proud to know you, Shirl, you know that. But if we're ever going to get out of this town and do something *really* great, we have to use every tool at our disposal. Allure is one of those tools."

"Huh?" Shirley reached for the door handle.

Joan shoved her hand away. "Appeal. Magnetism." She tipped her head to the side. "You have been taught about the birds and the bees, haven't you?"

"Of course I have. I'm just failing to understand what it has to do with the Coast Guard." Shirley moved her friend's hand, opened the door, and gestured for Joan to slide in first.

Halfway in, Joan stopped and looked at Shirley. "It's how we get our foot in the door in a man's world. *Then* we stun them with our intellect."

Did Joan ever consider that the abuse of feminine wiles might account for the reason men didn't take women seriously from the start?

After Joan was settled next to Daddy, Shirley got in and closed the door. "What's the way in the door? And what door?" Daddy asked as he drove away.

Shirley cringed. She was not discussing sex appeal with her father.

"Food." Joan nudged Shirley's arm and offered Daddy her sweetest smile. "The fastest way to a man's heart."

Daddy nodded his approval. "Have you found a young man?"

"Me?" Joan laughed. "Not around here. However, I'm sure there are plenty of eligible men in Washington." Her sigh was long and dramatic. "As Shirley was so practical in pointing out, though, we'll be far too busy for such things."

"I didn't know you had an uncle Ernst." Shirley unbuttoned her coat and relaxed for the long ride. "When did he arrive?"

"Oh, he isn't really my uncle. He's. . .well, it's complicated. He's been here for a couple of weeks now."

"Who's this?" Daddy turned onto the main road leading to Machiasport.

Joan adjusted her floral dress over her knees. "Ernst Schultzheimer. He's a relation ten times removed or something like that. He's from Germany and staying with us for a while until he can find a permanent place to live."

"I'll have to come over and introduce myself. Have him over for dinner soon." Daddy swerved to avoid hitting a hole, sending Joan straight into Shirley.

"I'm sure he'd like that." Joan readjusted her clothing. "He's looking for work, and Miss Neilson has agreed to teach him English."

"Sounds like he plans to stay then," Daddy said. "We'll make him feel most welcome. Won't we, Shirley Jean?"

"Of course," she mumbled. Though she'd avoid him as best she could until she was sure what she thought of the tenth-removed relation.

Joan went on to talk about the latest *Life* magazine and an article about Clark Gable's effort in the war. She mentioned a few actors who were suspected of being spies. Actors Shirley had never heard of before. Shirley enjoyed going to the movies as much as the next person, but she didn't get into the glitz and glamour of the Hollywood lifestyle. The way she saw it, at the end of the day when all the costumes and stage makeup were put away, the actors were average, everyday people too.

An hour later, they parked at the curb of the Machiasport Town Hall. Women of various ages in various states of dress milled along the street and sidewalks, all heading in the direction of the enlistment site.

Sweat dotted Shirley's upper lip and her pulse raced. Joan nudged her. "Come on, Shirl. What are you waiting for?"

What was she waiting for?

Stomach clenching, Shirley eased open her door so as not to hit a group of three women walking past.

The cold air was a relief. Women chattered. The door of the town hall groaned with every push and pull.

Joan's heels clicked on the pavement. She looked at Shirley and arched her perfectly sculpted eyebrows. Not wanting any more disapproval over her appearance, Shirley met Daddy's steady gaze from behind the wheel.

"I'll wait there," he said, and pointed to the parking lot at the side of the building. Dread mingled with pride shone from the gray depths.

Joan prodded Shirley with her purse. With one last glance at her current surroundings, she shook off the guilt Daddy's sad eyes produced and helped Joan maneuver over the snow mounded against the sidewalk. She opened the door to the town hall, and together they stepped inside.

⟨ CHAPTER 4 ⟩

Leo was shocked by how many women attended from Machiasport and the neighboring harbor towns. Crammed in like sardines, many stood against the walls and in the corners of the town hall. More had been turned away with the promise of another opportunity to enlist tomorrow.

The sight was overwhelming. Of course he'd seen thousands of working women in DC—code breakers, switchboard operators, secretaries, nurses, office assistants—many of whom were born in big cities and came from privileged families. The women who now sat before him had probably never traveled farther than a few counties from home. From what he'd heard about Mainers, they stuck close to home, and the majority of families had genealogies dating back to the area since the Revolution.

These were strong women, resilient women who'd lived through hard things, who knew how to survive. He could see it in the hard angles of their faces, the determined set of their chins, the eagerness in their eyes.

He held up a hand. "May I have your attention, please?"

The commotion slowly waned to silence. "I'm Captain Leonard Webber with the United States Navy, former commander of the USS *Adams*. You may be wondering why the navy is recruiting for the Coast Guard. The Women's Navy Reserve known as the WAVES has been so successful that we're helping build that same foundation for the Coast Guard using the navy's most competent female officers.

"I'd like to thank you for your willingness to serve your country. War isn't just fought and won overseas. It's an everyday battle that must be challenged and withstood on the home front by willing and brave individuals such as yourselves. It takes all of us working together to withstand the enemy.

"We need you, your talents and abilities, to join with us—the US military branch of the Coast Guard—in a new, female-only based reserve known as the SPARs. I encourage you to search your hearts tonight. If liberty is what you desire for yourselves, your future children, and grand-children, then join us. Together, we will win this war."

Clapping nearly shook the rafters. Leo appreciated their enthusiasm, but he silenced them with another show of his palm. "I introduce to you Lieutenant Commander Dorothy C. Stratton, director of the SPARs."

As noise once again filled the room, Stratton stepped forward and offered a placating smile. "Thank you, Captain, for that very *rousing* speech."

Had he said something wrong?

Shushes echoed. Stratton cleared her throat. "*Semper paratus*, 'always ready.' This is the very essence of the SPARs.

"Originally our division was nicknamed WORCOGS, short for Women's Reserve of the Coast Guard. I explained to my superiors that the name sounded too close to warthogs, and no woman in her right mind would volunteer to become a warthog."

The crowd laughed.

"I was granted permission to change the name to SPARs in honor of the Coast Guard's motto—*Semper Paratus*, 'Always Ready.'

"Our mission is to train you to be always ready. Train you for posi-tions on the home front in order to free our men for combat. But the SPARs will also offer you a chance at self-improvement, advancement in a field where you already possess skills, an opportunity to travel, and a little excitement and adventure.

"You must be at least twenty-two years of age, be willing to leave the comfort of your homes, and participate in rigorous testing before graduating to your positions. Your positions will not be permanent. This women's reserve is only active during war. But the skills you refine and memories you create during your time with us will last a lifetime.

"If the SPARs are for you, please form a line and sign the recruit-ment sheet provided at the table before leaving."

She pointed to a small table in the back corner.

She went on to introduce herself and her credentials, told about her former work in the WAVES, where she'd come to know Captain Web-ber, and how she'd become the director for this new reserve of the Coast Guard. "Are there any questions?"

Multiple hands rose. Some women had dressed in their best, com-plete with fancy hairstyles and cosmetics. Others appeared to have come less polished but more prepared for what the title entailed.

Leo fought the urge to tug at his collar. The temperature in the room was suffocating. He thought of the frozen harbor outside and imagined how wonderful it'd be to step into the night.

For what felt like hours, Stratton answered questions and allayed fears. Throughout it all, Leo studied the women, their appearance, their body language, their expressions. They were here with the desire to serve their country. A desire for which he was grateful. Freedom was not free, and victory could only be obtained by the combined efforts of all.

But he was also not naive.

Citizenship didn't always equal loyalty. Extremist beliefs, conspiracy theories, spies, and defectors of all kinds had taken root like weeds at the start of the war. A group had been arrested and detained just yesterday for their underground efforts to aid Hitler. Was the heart of every woman in this room pure, or would someone among them prove corrupt?

The line of women enlisting snaked around the chairs of the town hall. Shirley and Joan had been waiting for an hour already and still had several more women ahead of them until they reached the registration table. Shirley shifted positions. Daddy was either about to blow a gasket or he was frozen to his seat. She'd never imagined it would take this long.

Joan made a whiny noise that had grated on Shirley since the line formed. "These shoes are killing my feet."

Joan braced herself using Shirley's shoulder and shifted her weight from foot to foot, rolling circulation into her ankles.

"Questioning my wardrobe choices now?" Shirley smirked.

"Actually, yes." The line moved forward and so did Shirley, causing Joan to teeter sideways before catching her balance.

Joan scowled. "How can I possibly regret looking my best when someone as handsome as Captain Leonard Webber is about to shake my hand and welcome me aboard?"

Shirley loved her friend like a sister despite the theatrics, but the girl was exhausting sometimes.

For the next twenty minutes, the line crept forward while Joan babbled about which position she hoped to gain and if the captain was single. "I don't see a ring," she whispered in Shirley's ear.

"It doesn't matter if he's single or not," Shirley hissed back. Handsome or not, his intense, serious demeanor was intimidating and borderline scary. "He's a captain. He cannot and would not disgrace his position over a relationship with—"

"Miss?" A male voice with a rich tenor sizzled over her like sea foam left behind from a retreating wave.

Shirley turned and fell into the greenest eyes she'd ever seen. Vibrant green, like the pines that lined the shoreline, rimmed in warm brown that reminded her of—

"Your name?"

His lips were working but her brain wasn't. A jab to her spine jump-started her synapses and she managed an "um."

Joan snickered behind her.

Mortification doused Shirley's body. "Davenport." She cleared her throat. "Shirley Davenport."

The captain's dark, wild eyebrows formed a V over his mesmerizing eyes. "Well, Miss Davenport. Do you solemnly swear to support and defend the Constitution of the United States against all enemies, foreign and domestic?"

"Yes, sir." Why had her voice come out as more of a squeak than an affirmation?

"Very well." Captain Webber held out a pen. "Please leave us your information so we may contact you regarding an interview and aptitude test."

With a shaky hand, Shirley took the pen and bent over the paperwork lying on the table. While she filled out her name and address, she mentally berated herself for acting like an imbecile just because the captain was the best-looking man she'd ever seen. Good grief, if she didn't know any better, she'd think she was turning into Joan.

She didn't have time for a silly schoolgirl crush. And neither did the captain, if his stiff manner toward Joan's attempt at flirtation was any indication. Commander Stratton relieved him of social niceties when she asked Joan to join her side of the table.

At the section on the paper that asked Shirley to list her skills, she hesitated. She thought back to the conversation with her father in the barn earlier that day and decided that knowing how to successfully build a fire wasn't a skill set worth bragging about.

Especially to the Coast Guard.

The captain pointed to the paper where her pen was poised midair. "Here is where you'll list any nursing, clerical, technology, or mathematical skills."

Another flash of embarrassment surged through Shirley. Should she leave it blank or write *none*?

The captain cleared his throat. "Communication skills? Leadership? Artistic?"

Shirley laid down the pen and shook her head.

Captain Webber frowned. He picked up the paper and read it. "Fourth-generation fisherman of herring and lobster. Boat repair."

She sounded like such a boy.

"Truth is," she sighed, "other than patching and painting boats, fishing, and knowing the best places to catch a lobster dinner, I don't have skills to speak of. But I'm a fast learner, and I'm eager to serve my country. Sir."

His jaw flexed and the lines on his forehead grew even deeper. He studied her and she studied back, noting his dark five o'clock shadow and a slight bump on the bridge of his nose. To a decorated man like himself, she was no doubt wholly inadequate.

She lowered her gaze to his polished black shoes.

"Fast and willing learners are exactly what we're looking for."

She lifted her head. She looked for any untruth in him but found none. What she did discover—attraction, swift and deep. So immense it nearly swept away the steady ground beneath her, one-sided though the attraction may be.

Joan looped her arm through Shirley's and bounced on the balls of her feet. "Shirley's a loyal friend and very talented. If worse comes to worst, she can always rustle up a fine seafood platter for the crew."

Oh, Joan. The perfect example of misguided good intentions.

"Next." Commander Stratton pursed her lips and gave Joan a look of warning.

"Uh. . .I'll meet you at the car, Shirl." Joan sashayed toward the exit, having long ago perfected the art of catching a man's attention with a few simple steps.

But to Shirley's surprise, Captain Webber's gaze wasn't following Joan. It was fixed on Shirley. "Sign here, please."

He pointed to the bottom of the paper.

Lips parted in surprise, she lifted the pen and signed her name on the corresponding line. As she straightened her posture, the hurried scratches of male penmanship caught her attention. On the part where she was supposed to have written her skills, he'd written *marine exploration* and *nautical restoration*. She smiled at the flattering exaggeration.

She couldn't say for sure, but she thought she spied a crack in his sober demeanor. He leaned slightly forward as if sharing a secret. "Don't underestimate the importance of a good meal."

Before she could fully process his words, he raised to full height and motioned his fingers for the next woman to step forward. Shirley walked away, too stunned to do anything else.

The room began to sway, her head and heart woozy. Was this what it was like to be smitten? Sure, she'd had boyfriends and had fancied herself in love once, but this. . .this was a hurricane of conflicting and delightful emotions.

The frigid air outside added to the blissful feeling. Daddy had parked beneath a streetlamp alongside the curb. Vapor steamed from the tail-pipe. The shadow of Joan's head could be seen next to Daddy's through the back window.

Shirley opened the door and got inside. "Sorry you had to wait so long."

Daddy didn't move to drive away, just sat staring out the windshield. "You signed up, then?"

Her conscience walloped her good. "I did."

His throat worked before he put the car in DRIVE and pulled away. Joan reached over and squeezed Shirley's hand. The giddiness of her encounter with Captain Webber dissipated.

"You did the right thing," Joan whispered.

Unease anchored deep in Shirley's gut.

She sure hoped so.

CHAPTER 5

Two weeks later, Shirley closed her eyes against the blinding light dangling from the ceiling. A man in a white medical coat leaned over her. "Open wide, please."

Dental tools poked and prodded every tooth. She flinched when his hand slipped and metal jabbed her gums. She worked to not gag at the metallic taste that followed. Dr. Graves spoke to the nurse in medical language foreign to Shirley, while the nurse made marks on the paper secured on her clipboard.

"You may close now." Dr. Graves raised the back of her chair and turned off the light.

Purple spots swirled in her vision, and she blinked them away. She'd already suffered through an eye exam, a hearing exam, and an extensive interview about her education, marital status, family history, character, and mental strengths. The whole process was still far from finished. Vulnerable and exposed described her well.

"You've passed your physical examination." The doctor held out a hand to help her from the chair. "Perfect age, healthy stock, good teeth."

Shirley was beginning to feel less human and more equine by the second. If she'd dressed in more glamorous and less practical clothing like Joan, maybe she'd have gotten a gentler response.

"Um, thank you." Shirley tucked her hands into the pockets of her wide-legged pants.

The doctor pushed up the glasses sliding down his nose, signed a paper, and gave it to the nurse. "Follow me, please," she said and left the room.

Smothering a yawn, Shirley traced the nurse's steps, passing a dozen other women under examination. The scent of rubbing alcohol mingled with voices and the squeak of rubber shoes on tile.

She vaguely remembered her brothers talking about their exams upon enlisting, but she'd grown to ignore the vulgarity that sometimes came with a houseful of males. This time, however, they hadn't been exaggerating.

The nurse took her to a room filled with school desks. The stern-faced woman behind the teacher's desk at the front of the room took over. She handed Shirley a packet of papers and a pencil and told her she had one hour to finish the exam. When the schoolmarm turned her back, Shirley sat and released the yawn she'd been holding.

The government had paid her expenses to Bangor, home of the nearest navy recruiting office. She, Joan, and at least twenty other women had arrived yesterday evening in just enough time to eat dinner, settle into the motel, and sleep. Shirley had always struggled to sleep away from home, not that the opportunity came often. The motel bed was extremely uncomfortable, and Joan had insisted on talking most of the night. Joan's nervous jitters had robbed Shirley of precious sleep, and it was catching up with her.

The print on the pages began to blur as Shirley fought to stay awake. Her thoughts traveled from arithmetic to how comfortable her pillow was back home, how soft her mattress, how warm her blankets.

A deep male voice drifted along the fuzzy edges of her conscience. She recognized that voice. Rich and smooth like butter and maple syrup on hot pancakes. Her stomach grumbled. She heard the man say *meal*, or at least that's what she thought he'd said, and her brain jolted to attention.

Captain Webber.

The schoolmarm was turned sideways at her desk reading a book. Shirley leaned back in her chair to get a better view of the male voice. Across from the open doorway, she could see through a narrow gap into the room across the hall. A tall, masculine form trimmed in a navy officer uniform stood talking to one of the doctors, his profile defined and strong. As if he sensed her watching him, he turned and looked right at her. His brows knotted above his nose.

Seconds ticked by. As the doctor continued to speak to Captain Webber, he nodded to Shirley in acknowledgment and then turned his back. Disappointment bloomed in her chest. Silly woman. What did she expect him to do, burst into the room and declare his undying love?

Ugh, she'd been listening to Joan's theatrics too much lately. This was war. Captain Webber had a job to do, and he certainly had no interest in a mousy tomboy from the easternmost corner of the country. Dashing in his decorated uniform, he was meant to be paired with a classy Vivien Leigh look-alike.

The scrape of a chair against the wood floor jerked Shirley's gaze to the schoolmarm. The woman stood and glared over the top of her glasses, the gold chain attached swaying like a pendulum. "Focus, Miss Davenport."

Shirley lowered her head and forced herself to concentrate on her exam instead of the elusive Captain Webber. This was her one chance to leave Lubec and be an independent woman. She *had* to pass this exam and become a SPAR. If she didn't, her only choice would be to go back home and continue lobstering with her father until she could marry a local boy after the war. If any returned.

If that was her fate, she'd eventually shrivel in the salty water and evaporate on the breeze.

Leo had been shocked and pleased to see the woman from the recruit meeting the other night. He couldn't remember her name. He'd seen so many women in the past week. He did recall, however, her blond hair and brown eyes, and the pink in her cheeks when he'd asked her to list her skills on the enlistment card and she'd claimed to have none. He'd worded a few things on the card to help her out, but she'd claimed to be an eager and fast learner, and he believed her. All he did was give her a chance to prove herself. The rest was up to her. But she was young, had comported herself sensibly, unlike her friend, and had a sweetness in her smile that reminded him—despite all the evil in the world—there was still some good.

"Thank you, Doctor." Leo took the proffered papers. "I'll get these to Commander Stratton right away."

Leo tapped the rubber seal on the envelope containing a stack of medical records and a list of names of those who'd passed all their examinations.

Dr. Graves ran his thumb and forefinger down his mustache. "I'll have the rest of today's cadets ready for you by four o'clock." Leo knew by *cadets* he meant records and names of the remaining women who'd passed their exams.

"Much appreciated."

He left the doctor and stepped into the hall, glancing into the next room at the woman who'd been staring at him minutes earlier, now bent over her test, pencil moving with great speed. He passed the doorway, then paused midstride. A clipboard hung on a nail outside the examination room. He lifted it and scanned the testing times and the names of the women currently testing.

Shirley Davenport.

That's right. He recognized her surname because it reminded him of the old general store he liked to shop in as a kid, Davenport Goods & Hardware.

Hadn't she mentioned lobstering that night? He realized how far away breakfast had been and decided a lobster dinner sounded like heaven. It had been ages since he'd eaten lobster.

He dropped the clipboard and listened to the ping of it connecting with the wall as he walked away. He wished Miss Davenport all the best.

The air in his temporary office was cold and musty. Leo turned on the light and turned the valve wheel on the radiator. It knocked and clunked in the small space. He tossed the envelope on his desk and loose papers underneath scattered. His eyes burned. He needed food and sleep. Except sleep was always haunted by images of better days or the horrifying scenes of his brothers' last moments.

Leo rubbed his eyes and sat in his chair. He still had to finish his paperwork before he delivered the day's records to Stratton.

The phone rang. He picked it up and pressed the cold receiver to his ear. "Webber."

"Grant."

"Admiral Grant, sir." He started to stand at attention, then called himself an idiot and sat back down.

"How are the recruits?"

"Very promising, sir. The majority have passed their examinations."

"Good. Good. Do you have plans for this evening?"

Images of his seafood dinner revived his hunger pangs. "Uh, no, sir. Nothing specific."

"Good. You're needed in Washington right away. Code breakers just deciphered a threat against the president."

⚎ CHAPTER 6 ⚎

Bleary eyed and in serious need of coffee, Leo walked into headquarters. There wasn't a decent cup to be found in the city due to rationing, and he'd rather go without than drink the watered-down version the pretty secretary had offered. Coffee should be strong and bold like sailors, not brewed with one part ground beans to fifty parts water.

He rubbed his thumb and forefinger over his closed eyelids, then yawned before entering the office. Admiral Grant stood hunched over his desk, examining a document.

Leo stood at attention. "Reporting for duty, sir."

The admiral passed him a fleeting glance. "At ease."

Leo relaxed and worked the kinks from his shoulders. The overnight train had been long and uncomfortable. His uniform was creased in spots, and he was certain he didn't smell his best. But as soon as he'd received the admiral's phone call in Bangor, he'd rushed to tie up any loose ends on his assignment, then boarded the first available train.

"Look at this." The admiral jabbed his thick finger at the paper on his desk.

Leo's shoes squeaked against the wood floor. He bent over the desk cluttered with papers and files and scanned the scrambled letters on the page. "It's a cipher."

"Cracked by Chief Yeoman Dyer and her team of code breakers." Admiral Grant pointed to the corner.

A young lady sat erect in a chair in the corner, her navy-blue skirt cascading over her knees. She didn't look a day over fifteen, but she'd have to be much older than that to work for the government. Her pale skin, blondish hair, and innocent eyes reminded him of Miss Davenport.

He mentally kicked himself. "Thank you for your services."

She blushed. "My pleasure, sir."

Upon further inspection, dark smudges tainted the skin beneath her eyes. It was obvious she'd been working round the clock. The admiral was the best of men, but he exacted more from others than they sometimes had to give.

Leo focused his attention on the paper and its rushed pencil strokes. *Bullseye. Get ER get CC.*

A bull's-eye was always an intended target. The president was known as the commander in chief, so ER was likely to refer to Eleanor Roosevelt.

"Who and why?" Leo asked.

"We don't know." The admiral frowned. "This cipher isn't like the others. It's in shorthand and appears to have come from somewhere within the United States, but we can't trace back the signal."

Treason.

"Whoever this is"—Admiral Grant picked up his full mug of light brown water—"their intelligence is one step ahead."

Anger stewed inside Leo. America was the greatest nation on the planet. The greatest in all of history, in fact. Who would dare turn their back on this country? Bite the hand that fed their freedom? "We've got nothing?"

The chair creaked as Miss Dyer stood. She wrapped her arms around herself like a scolded child. "No, sir, but my team is working on discovering the origin. Messages are coming in faster than we can keep up."

Miss Dyer's nose turned red, and her chin wobbled. Leo wanted none of that. She was a strong woman to have gained this position in the first place, but exhaustion would break down even the toughest of men. Miss Dyer needed a good meal, a comfortable bed, and at least ten hours of sleep.

"Admiral, has Miss Dyer or her team gotten any rest in the last forty-eight hours?"

"Rest?" Admiral Grant's white eyebrows folded over bewildered eyes while he considered Leo's question. "I suppose not."

Leo perused Miss Dyer's appearance. One side of her collar was turned up and her sweater was one button off. Both made her look adolescent and lopsided. Leo was certain she was neither.

She scratched her cheek. "We've been taking short naps in our office, Captain Webber."

"Admiral?" Leo laid his palms flat on the desk. "I propose that if

Miss Dyer can round us up a couple of Cokes, we allow her and her team to go home and rest until their next appointed shift."

The admiral looked at the clock and nodded, as if mentally calculating how long of a break that would be. "Very well, Miss Dyer. We'll see your team again at the start of your next shift."

Her body wilted in relief, and the wobble in her chin became more pronounced. "Thank you, Captain Webber. Admiral Grant."

She gave a little bow and left the room, the click of her heels growing fainter as she retreated down the hall.

Admiral Grant raised a brow at Leo, one side of his mouth angling down. "You're too soft."

"You're too hard."

"War is hard."

"Which makes the soft moments all the more necessary."

Admiral Grant chuckled. "I've known you since you were a babe. It isn't like you to wax poetic." He started to sit, then stopped. "Have you started seeing a woman since I saw you last?"

Heat prickled the back of Leo's neck, and he shoved away the image of Miss Davenport before it had a chance to fully form. It didn't make sense that his mind kept conjuring the image of the little tomboy with dimpled cherub cheeks.

Leo picked up the cipher and read it again. "I don't have time for women. We have a traitor to catch."

———————≈———————

Shirley stood in the middle of the kitchen, nervous energy snowballing in her stomach. The envelope from Coast Guard headquarters trembled in her hand. What if she hadn't passed the written examination? What if she had to stay in Lubec and fish for the rest of her life? What if she never saw Captain Webber again?

That last thought raised her ire. How ridiculous. She wasn't one for silly crushes and sappy romance, and even if she did pass the fifty tests they'd put her through, it was doubtful she'd run into the captain once she was sent for training.

Joan's attempt at the recruiting center to make Shirley look less pathetic still thrummed a somber chord in her chest. As if the captain would ever be interested in her as a woman. She didn't have glamour or good looks or charm. She was plain and simple and practical.

Resourceful.

Mama held out the silver letter opener. "You've been waiting for over a week. Are you going to stare at it all evening, or are you going to open it?"

Shirley took the letter opener and sighed. "I'm scared."

"You? You've never been scared of anything in your life."

"I'm scared of this. I'm scared of. . ." *Being stuck here when I've come so close to freedom.* "I'm not good with numbers. Never have been. Where I'm confident I passed the other exams, the written aptitude test is the one I'm unsure of."

Mama brushed Shirley's hair back over her shoulder. "I'm sure you did fine. Either way, I'm proud of you for having the courage to try. It's good for a young woman to expand her horizons."

"Really?" Mama was a model example of wife and mother for *Good Housekeeping* magazine, but she'd never tried to do anything remotely exciting in her life. Shirley had assumed Mama thought women shouldn't venture outside the home.

"My desire to serve doesn't make you angry, like Daddy?"

Mama offered a small smile, fanning small age lines around her eyes and mouth. "He's not angry. He's afraid."

"Of what?"

"Losing his little girl."

"I'm not a little girl anymore."

"He knows that." Mama untied her apron. "That's what he's afraid of. You see, he enjoys having you on the boat with him every day. Enjoys still being your protector. That's his responsibility until he passes your hand to a husband, you know."

If she ever married. But she couldn't live with her parents the rest of her life either. She had to gain some independence.

"If you leave him without the protection of a husband, he has to worry about your well-being."

"Marriage doesn't equal safety, Mama. I could be a bride and still get hit by a speeding car while crossing the street."

Mama's eyebrows quirked.

With a deep breath, Shirley sliced the opener through the flap of the envelope, pulled out and unfolded the paper. Her eyes landed on the Coast Guard insignia at the top, two crossed anchors beneath a circle stating the branch and the establishment date. She visually traced the border of twisted rope around it all, avoiding the words below.

"Well?" Mama nudged her arm.

Shirley dropped her gaze to the first sentence and sucked in air. "I made it!"

"Ah!" Mama hugged her waist and laughed. Light and tinkly, like bells.

Shirley's mind reeled. She was a SPAR! One of the first-ever females in the Coast Guard. Tears sprang to her eyes.

Daddy walked in bringing the briny scent of saltwater and fish with him. "What's all the commotion?"

A chair scraped against the vinyl floor as he pulled it out.

Shirley held up the letter. "I did it, Daddy. I'm a SPAR!"

Halfway to sitting, he froze. His expression turned mournful. Shirley looked to Mama, whose excitement had turned sober. The oxygen leached from the room as Shirley waited.

Please say something. Please be happy for me.

Daddy's overalls finally reached the chair.

Mama licked her lips. "Winston?"

He picked up the folded newspaper sitting on the table from where he'd left it that morning and snapped it open. He propped his elbows on the table. "What's for dinner?"

Shirley's spirit plummeted. Her head drooped. Mama reached over, put her finger beneath Shirley's chin, and lifted it high. *Hang in there*, her eyes seemed to say.

She tried to smile but failed. "May I go see if Joan received her letter yet?"

"Don't stay long," Mama whispered.

With weighted steps, Shirley went to the front door and shrugged into her coat. She jammed her feet into her boots and walked out into the frigid evening. The biting wind froze the tears of disappointment on her cheeks.

≡ CHAPTER 7 ≡

The Fischer household was boisterous as usual. Music and laughter emanated from the house so forcefully it was as if every window and door was open to the frigid winter night. The light spilling through the panes of glass proved otherwise. Shirley stood where the road met their front yard, watching the warm glow. Listening to the celebratory sounds.

So unlike the Davenport residence.

No doubt, Joan had been accepted too. Joan had been the top student in their one-room schoolhouse and excelled in math and science. Excelled so well that she'd been invited to attend extra classes at Whiting High School, ten miles away. After graduation she'd taken classes at the University of Maine for marine biology, while Shirley wished she'd tried harder in school so she had other options besides fishing.

Joan had returned home after one semester. Homesick, she'd said.

Possible, but knowing Joan, the story went much deeper than that. But Shirley never pressed. Joan would tell her when she was ready.

Now they both had their second chance. Together.

Well, hopefully. Shirley had never considered being accepted and Joan not. What then?

The celebration inside was too lively to follow a rejection, so Shirley walked the rest of the way to the house, her boots crunching the snow.

She knocked. Seconds passed, but no one answered. Shirley knocked louder. Her breath formed clouds around her head as she waited.

Nothing.

Shirley considered going back home but knew they weren't answering only because they couldn't hear her. The doorknob gave a full turn in her hand, so she stepped inside.

"Hello?"

Fiddle and harmonica played a lively tune, and clapping hands accompanied. Shirley smiled, her mood lifting. She loved watching Mr. Fischer play the harmonica. After slipping off her coat, she hung it on an empty hook, then removed her boots, leaving them on the rug to dry. In stockinged feet, she padded toward the music.

The parlor furniture had been rearranged by the fireplace so there was a makeshift stage in front of the audience. Joan's father played the harmonica, while Uncle Ernst played the fiddle. Quite brilliantly.

Maxwell kept the beat with a set of spoons. The women sat on a small couch in front of the musicians, clapping. All except little Ina, who was swinging arm in arm with her brother, Ike. At least they were getting along tonight.

Maxwell was the first one to catch sight of Shirley leaning in the doorway. He smiled, showing a big hole where all his front teeth should be, and lisped, "Shirley!" over the music.

The women turned.

"Shirley!" Joan sprang from the couch, ran over, and twirled her friend.

Dizzy, Shirley broke away and placed a hand on her forehead. "Did you get in?"

"Of course. You?"

"I made it."

"Ah!" Joan wrapped her arms around Shirley and squeezed. The action momentarily stole Shirley's breath.

"Oh, my friend, this is it," Joan said. "We're going to change the world."

Change the world? It was an optimistic thought, but she'd settle for changing their futures. Judging by the tilted bow in Joan's hair, her rumpled dress, rosy cheeks, and bloodshot eyes, Joan was tipsy on both the good news and Mr. Fischer's German lager.

The Fischers didn't celebrate a hangnail recovery without lager.

Once Joan's headache wore off in the morning, she'd once again see things in perspective.

"A toast," Joan said. "We need another toast."

The music stopped, and Mr. Fischer stood. "*Ja, ein* toast."

The yeasty scent of warm beer filled the room as Mr. Fischer poured the dark homemade liquid from a small barrel into tankards. Joan pressed one into Shirley's hands and yelled, "To our heritage, to the SPARs, to the victory that will be had in this war. To us!"

Joan threw back her head and downed at least half the tankard. Shirley simply stared into hers. She'd tasted beer one time when she was younger and immediately spit it back out. Her family were temperance people anyway.

Ernst stared at Shirley over the rim of his cup, his blue eyes dancing. She squirmed, sloshing liquid over the rim and onto her hand.

"Drink up," Joan urged. "We're celebrating."

There were better ways to celebrate in Shirley's opinion. Ways that wouldn't be followed by nausea and a wicked headache in the morning. Still, it smarted that the Fischers were proud of their daughter. So proud they couldn't contain their joy, and it spilled out into music and dancing and laughter.

While Shirley's father stewed at the kitchen table without so much as a "congratulations", a smile, or even a simple pat on the back.

———— ≈ ————

Cold wind snapped the flag behind the group of women standing before Miss Dorothy Stratton—Lieutenant Commander Stratton. Shirley was going to have to get familiar with using titles. After all, as soon as she said the oath, she'd officially be a SPAR.

The sun chose that moment to peek from behind the clouds. Warmth radiated over Shirley's shoulders and seeped into her wool coat. Snow sparkled in a happy reply. For a winter day at the end of January, they couldn't complain. At least they'd held off the ceremony until the nor'easter had passed.

The West Quoddy Lighthouse stood guard beside them, its red and white stripes vibrant and patriotic. It was the perfect location to welcome thirteen women into the Coast Guard for the first time in history. Dozens of other women across the nation would be taking their oaths in the coming days, all pioneering the way for females in the future.

Pioneering. Roughing the wilderness to blaze a trail for those to come. Leaving their footprints on history.

Wouldn't it be something if someday women were able to hold the same occupational positions as men?

Commander Stratton turned her back to the SPARs and addressed the audience. "The journeys on which these young women are about to embark are of the upmost importance to our country. They will celebrate victory and they will endure heartache. But they will first and forever be a SPAR."

Shirley's father stood with his hands in his pockets, gazing around the landscape as if he'd rather be anywhere but here. Her mother's bottom lip quivered. A pool of tears filled Shirley's eyes. She'd miss her parents terribly—and the comforts of home—but she wasn't sad to leave. She just wished her father was supportive and that her mother wasn't afraid to show him that *she* was.

The commander spun to face the SPARs. "Raise your right hand."

Palms went up immediately.

The commander's voice echoed off the lighthouse. "Do you promise to support and defend the Constitution of the United States against all enemies, foreign and domestic, freely without any mental reservation or purpose of evasion?"

One at a time going down the line, they each said, "I do."

With a spin on her heel, the commander addressed the crowd once again. "On this day, January 30th, in the year of our Lord 1943, I present to you the SPARs of Washington County, Maine."

Applause erupted.

Shirley smiled as a proud tear rolled down one cheek. She was now a member of the US Coast Guard.

Ceremony ended, the ladies dispersed to their waiting families and friends. Shirley maneuvered through the throng toward her parents but stopped when a man blocked her path.

Ernst Schultzheimer. A cigarette dangled from his lips.

Attempting to be polite, Shirley smiled and tried to sidestep him. He caught her arm and tugged her away from the crowd. "*Ich muss mit dir sprechen.*"

Her mind reeled trying to translate the German muted by the cigarette. Why was he wanting to speak to her without anyone overhearing?

She tried to pull her arm away. "I need to find my parents. Please, let me go."

His grip tightened. Not hurtful, but the urgency in his blue eyes was evident. He yanked the cigarette from his mouth and held it in two fingers. "*Unsere familien werden sich vermischen. Vereinen.*"

Oh, why hadn't she been more diligent in learning her native language? Because she'd been born in the United States, therefore English was her native language. German was her heritage.

"I. . .uh. . ." His lips twisted in frustration at his limited English, revealing a faint scar along his mouth and chin. "*Familien.*" He raised his hands and tapped the ends of his fingers together. "*Vereinen.*"

Families. . .

He huffed. "Uh. . .b–end." He shook his head. "B–l–end."

Families blend?

She reared back. He wasn't proposing marriage, was he?

Panic set her heart to racing. She looked in every direction for her parents, who seemed to have disappeared in the crowd. Was this Daddy's idea? His way of getting her to stay?

Whoever's idea it was, she was *not* getting married. Not to Ernst anyway. Good-looking or not, he was too old for her, and she had a life of independence to experience before she settled into marriage.

A hand touched her elbow, and she turned. "Mama."

Desperation dripped from Shirley's voice. Mama must have noticed because she looked at Ernst and frowned. "Is everything okay?"

"Of course." Shirley's giggle sounded fake to her own ears. "Ernst was just—" But Ernst had already turned and was walking away.

"Ernst was what, dear?" The groove was still marring the skin between Mama's brows.

"Never mind." Shirley took a deep breath. Daddy walked up behind Mama, squinting at Ernst's retreating back. Neither held the look of an anticipated marriage proposal. How silly of Shirley. The man could hardly speak English and likely used the wrong word for what he was trying to convey.

Shirley had been spending too much time with Joan, and her friend's dramatic nature was rubbing off.

Mama wrapped her arm around Shirley's. "Let's go home, dear. My feet feel like blocks of ice."

Shirley's did too, now that she gave it thought.

The entire ride home, Shirley sat in the backseat and worked on pushing the sound of Ernst's voice from her mind. She'd never had a man pull at her like that and keep her from walking away if she wanted. The whole thing had taken her by such surprise that she hadn't considered if she'd truly been in danger. What if he'd meant her harm? Would her instincts have guided her?

She'd have to think critically from now on. If she was going to live independently, she would have to be able to protect herself. She was a SPAR now. From this day forward, she was *Semper Paratus, Always Ready.*

Leo had thought being summoned to Washington meant a reassignment. That's what he got for thinking.

Chief Yeoman Dyer and her code-breaking team had deciphered many messages over the last week, but none were related to the original threat against the president and First Lady. They had, however, received word that Germany had destroyed a section of Britain in an air raid the night before.

Admiral Grant looked up from the map spread across his desk and pinned his gaze on Leo. "You're going to Iowa. We need you to assist Lieutenant Commander Stratton in advancing a nucleus of enlisted WAVES into SPAR officers and see that the reserve runs smoothly and efficiently. This is the first training, and there will be bumps along the way. See that Stratton has everything she needs. After the first training graduation, the navy will pull out and leave it wholly to the Coast Guard."

Iowa? What would they use in defense training, cows and pigs? Leo crossed his arms behind his back, biting back a growl. "Yes, sir."

Admiral Grant leaned back in his chair. "Miss Dyer?"

The slip of a woman stood against the wall so quietly Leo had forgotten she was there. Her gaze bounced between the two men. "Yes, Admiral?"

"Thank you for bringing this to our attention." Admiral Grant held up the telegraph she'd brought. "Our prayers for Britain."

Miss Dyer nodded and left the room. Her color was better than when Leo had first met her, as he'd been making sure her team received proper breaks for rest. Her eyes were clear, and her sweater was now buttoned to perfection.

"Close the door." The admiral's face turned to stone.

Leo obeyed.

"Colonel Farnum informed me this morning that foreign agents, both male and female, have penetrated the coast of Maine via the Grand Maran Channel and are investigating shipping prospects. Others, they believe, have filtered across through the Canadian border. Our citizens are sitting ducks."

The admiral leaned over the map.

"What can I do, sir?" Energy tingled along Leo's spine.

"Iowa. The majority of Maine's SPARs are training there. With men freed up to fight, it's our women who will secure our borders. No one knows these communities like the women who've been born and raised there. Work with Commander Stratton to see that they're properly trained. The ones that excel—use them. I want a list of graduates in six weeks. I'll work with Captain Cook of the Coast Guard on getting them stationed in Eastport."

The admiral pointed to a little town near the Canadian border.

Six weeks was a long time in terms of collateral damage and espionage. "In the meantime?"

The admiral rubbed his forehead. "I'll take care of *in the meantime.* You take care of Iowa."

The Midwest was not where he'd planned to aid the war effort. But at least now Leo had a mission.

⫶ CHAPTER 8 ⫶

The Grand Trunk Railroad Depot surpassed anything Shirley could've imagined. A clock tower stood sentinel at the center of the massive building, with smaller towers and gables branching out on both sides. The curved cathedral architecture inside was the closest Shirley would ever get to the Sistine Chapel. Polished granite comprised the walls and ticket booth, while dozens of wooden benches lined the deep pink carpet in the waiting rooms.

The main foyer was full of fellow SPARs and their families, along with the standard passenger traffic. This was their embarkation point, and the mood in the air was both joyous and somber.

Shirley's parents conversed with the Fischers several feet away. Ernst hadn't made any efforts to speak with Shirley since the day at the lighthouse, but he'd arrived with the Fischers to see Joan away. He'd blended into the throng, and Shirley hadn't seen him since.

She was relieved. This day was full of enough emotions without adding her strange feelings for him into the mix.

"Are you nervous?" Joan pointed to Shirley's white-knuckled grip on her suitcase handle.

Shirley's heart was pounding as if she'd run all the way to the station. She chuckled to downplay her anxiety and rested her suitcase on the floor. "A little. You?" She flexed the cramp in her fingers.

"A lot." Joan chortled. "Look at us. Finally leaving the nest, and we're scared to death."

"You're scared to death. I'm fine." Shirley bumped Joan with her elbow, grinning.

"It's a big responsibility. Saving the world and all." Joan studied the ornate ceiling.

"You're always so dramatic."

Joan shrugged. "I was born that way."

An overwhelming sadness bubbled up from deep inside. Shirley reached for her friend's hand. "I hate that we can't take this journey together."

Joan was being sent to Palm Beach, Florida, with other SPARs who excelled at science and math. Shirley was headed to Iowa State Teachers College in Cedar Falls.

"Me too." Joan turned Shirley by the shoulders so they faced each other. "But though we're apart, *together* we can do great things."

Joan's words were slow and calculated, as if sending a secret message. Shirley tried to make sense out of it, but then, Joan didn't always make sense.

Joan looked around and leaned closer. "Shirley, I—"

Behind Joan, Ernst appeared from a side room and moved toward the Fischers. His gaze locked on Shirley and held like a vise.

Joan turned to see what Shirley was staring at and tugged Shirley's arm. "He's smitten, you know."

"What?" The word escaped much louder than Shirley intended.

"He tried to tell you at the lighthouse, poor thing, but he still barely knows a lick of English."

Shirley opened her mouth but didn't know what to say. A man being smitten enough with her to fall all over himself was foreign to her. His demeanor since she'd met him certainly portrayed interest. It was the intensity of that interest that made it downright uncomfortable.

Borderline sinister.

Was this what Mama had meant when she'd said there were several boys who'd tried to pursue Shirley, but she'd been too naive to notice? Mama claimed Shirley had always treated them like brothers until they lost interest.

She'd had boyfriends, of course, but none for long. When it came down to it, she couldn't imagine living with any of them every day for the rest of her life.

"He's old." There she went, letting her thoughts slip out again.

"He's forty. Married once, but she passed away. Lost a child too. He's been through a lot, poor man. But Uncle Ernst is a good man, and he's from our home country." Joan squeezed her hand.

Married to a man eighteen years her senior? And America was their home country, not Germany. "Joan, ever since the war, you—"

A mustached man with a rotund figure walked among the passengers, a megaphone at his lips. "The train to Chicago is now boarding. Gather your belongings and make your way to the platform, please."

Her question to Joan would have to wait.

Goose bumps spread over Shirley's body. This was it. She picked up her suitcase, gripping it like a life preserver.

On the platform, steam rolled from the underbelly of the train. Passengers rushed to the open doors. Loved ones hugged. A woman sobbed on a man's shoulder. Shirley's parents followed close behind.

"Enjoy the tropical climate." Shirley steeled her shaky voice.

"Be safe. We'll write." Joan threw her arms around Shirley's neck and held tight.

A cry rose in Shirley's throat, but she swallowed it down. Through teary eyes, she saw Ernst standing in the entryway between the waiting room and the platform. He raised his hand in a wave. It sounded like the man had been through very tough times, and she hoped her aloofness hadn't added to his pain.

She waved back, sniffed, and released Joan. She captured her friend's radiant face in her mind to pull out later when homesickness set in.

Mama turned Shirley by her elbow.

"Travel safely." Her mother's lip trembled. "Eat properly, mind your manners, and make sure to dress for the weather."

Shirley nodded, not trusting her voice.

"I packed you extra underclothes," Mama whispered.

Chuckling through her tears, Shirley kissed Mama's wet cheek.

She faced her father. He stared into the distance as if completely unaffected, but the end of his nose blazed red. Her heart sank. The man never showed emotion, but she'd learned over the years that a red nose meant he was broken on the inside.

"Goodbye, Daddy." Shirley hated how timid and childish she sounded. She stuck out her hand in hopes of balancing it out.

Still refusing to make eye contact, his calloused fingers slipped into hers. Her determination to be tough caved. She pulled him close, rose on tiptoe, and clutched him tight.

He returned the pressure, patting her back. "Behave yourself." He cleared his throat. "Do me proud."

"Yes, sir." Shirley released him and brushed a stray tear with her knuckle. Enough of this. She was a grown woman, and it was time for her to make her own way in the world.

The smell of hot brakes and diesel fuel permeated the platform. A smell she'd have to adjust to for the next two days until she reached Cedar Falls.

"Last call for passengers to Chicago," the megaphone man announced.

On shaky legs, Shirley stepped toward the train.

"Wait!" Joan rushed to her. "I forgot to give you the note I wrote."

Joan reached into her coat pocket with a gloved hand and pulled out a lump of mismatched things. She tried to pull her other glove off with her teeth, when a man bumped into her and sent her items tumbling to the ground. Joan growled and bent to collect them.

"Last call for Chicago."

"Joan, I'm sorry, but I have to go." Shirley took one step onto the train.

"Wait. Here." Joan shoved all the items at her. "It's in there somewhere. Love you, Shirl."

"Love you too, friend. We'll write."

Shirley ascended the rest of the steps and made her way down the narrow aisle to an empty seat apart from the clusters of passengers. She settled onto the stiff bench by the window and laid her suitcase at her side.

A shiver stole through her despite the warmth of her wool coat and mittens. She shoved the tangle of items Joan had handed her deep into her pocket and huddled farther into her scarf.

Her breath fogged the glass. She rubbed it away with her coat sleeve and memorized the faces staring back. Mama dabbed at the corners of her eyes, her hair—so like Shirley's—mostly threaded with gray. Daddy searched the train windows. His head did a double take before he raised his palm. She pressed her hand against the window.

The train began to move, and a part of Shirley wanted to yell for them to stop the train. It was silly when she was finally getting what she wanted, but a beginning was hard when it came on the heels of an ending.

As the train moved farther down the platform, she saw Joan. She waved, but Joan was concentrating on Ernst a hundred or so feet away. Joan created movements with her fingers that looked much like the baseball signals her brothers used to throw during their games.

Or sign language.

The glass hazed over again, and the train picked up speed as it left the cover of the station. Shirley sat back, perplexed by Joan's actions. She knew nothing of American Sign Language, so she had no idea what Joan had been communicating. Come to think of it, she wasn't aware that Joan knew any sign language.

And Ernst? What were the odds that multiple family members knew it when none of them were deaf?

"Ticket, please."

The deep bass of the inspector startled her. She dug around in her purse and produced her ticket. The inspector glanced at it and handed it back. "Chicago's a long way to travel alone."

His brown eyes assessed her.

"It is."

"You look a mite sad, ma'am." When she didn't answer, he continued. "If I can be of any assistance to you, let me know. I'll do my best to watch out for ya. My name is Mervin."

"Thank you, Mr. Mervin."

He moved on to the next row of passengers and held out his dark hand for their tickets. She relaxed a little, knowing she wasn't alone on this journey and that someone cared enough to watch over her.

She adjusted the lapels of her coat to better cover her legs and dissected what she'd seen of Joan and Ernst. She could think of one thing Mr. Mervin could do for her—translate that display she'd just witnessed from the window.

CHAPTER 9

The mahogany walls of the small office were closing in on Leo. He needed windows and fresh air. Even if it was only five degrees outside.

Commander Stratton sat behind her desk in her half of the room, writing away. He couldn't believe the navy expected him to share a space no bigger than a matchbox. Stratton seemed quite content, which irritated him even more. He wanted the open sea. Since he was being denied, he at least wanted space to breathe.

"How do you stand it?" he asked.

"I thought I heard you grousing over there." She continued writing, never missing a beat. "I told myself that a navy captain wouldn't grouse and decided it was noise from the radiator."

He grunted, and she laughed.

Stratton set down her pencil and folded her hands in front of her. "I'm the daughter of a Baptist minister, God rest his soul. In all the places I've lived or traveled for work, my personal areas have been small. My father taught me many things, but one thing he lived as much as he preached was the perspective of the apostle Paul. 'In whatsoever state I am, therewith to be content.'

"This office is at least ten feet larger than the one they gave me when I started at Purdue. I had a lot of fun convincing President Elliot for a larger space, one more convenient for my students to find me."

Leo imagined Dorothy Stratton received anything she set her mind to have. He leaned his head against the wall, since his chair and desk were nearly flush against it, and rolled his neck from side to side. "I apologize for my temperament. Admiral Grant's code-breaking team deciphered a threat against the president and First Lady."

49

"I was informed." Her thin lips curled in a smile. "Putting myself in your shoes, I understand your disappointment. You want to be off fighting, and yet you're landlocked with a hundred women, eighty of whom have no military background or training."

Leo ground his back teeth together. She was uncanny at reading minds. More so than questioning his duties, he should be questioning why the secretary of war wasn't sending her overseas as a spy. With her talent for telepathy, she could communicate every enemy move ahead of time and the US military could end this war within two weeks.

"And you believe you can ascertain my thoughts and feelings simply by looking at me?" He turned from side to side to pop the tension from his back.

Her blue eyes sparkled behind almond-shaped lids. "I ascertain it by experience. I was born into a gender that hinders me from doing all the things I dream about. Don't get me wrong, I very much enjoy being a woman and all it entails. But I do wish I wasn't put into a box. Like you wish you weren't put into a box simply to keep you safe."

She knew, then. A tornado of grief and anger began to swirl in his chest. He'd been warned that she loved a good debate. Leo found himself enjoying debating with her. Until she dug deep enough to strike the roots of him, and then all it seemed to accomplish was putting him in a darker mood.

"I have the capability to break free of this box." He held out his arms to indicate the room. "At least for a couple of hours." He stood. "I'm going for a walk. Want to join me?"

"Thank you, but no. I've some paperwork to finish. The SPARs will be arriving soon." She tugged the sleeves of her sweater to her elbows. "If it's any consolation, Captain, what we're doing here is most honorable and will aid this country to victory. I dedicate my life to making sure these women are as well trained and efficient as any male members of the Coast Guard."

Leo paused with his hand on the door and winked, throwing her favorite phrase at her. "Maybe more so."

She chuckled and went back to her writing.

Leo escaped the stifling room and walked the hallways of the campus. For now, that would have to be enough.

Shirley stepped off the bus tired, ragged, and freezing. The heat hadn't radiated far enough to reach her seat, and her frosted window had not only hindered any view but also allowed cold air to seep into her seat. She bumped into the woman next to her and apologized.

Iowa State Teachers College was a mini-town within a town. The main building towered over her, more castle than college. All stone with paned windows and ornate wooden doors.

She'd never seen such richness.

Her stomach squirmed. This whole experience was far above any previous imaginings. Was leaving home and traveling halfway across the country too lofty a dream? Was she a strong enough woman for this?

"Are you going to go in?"

Shirley turned to the woman beside her with hair the color of a steamed lobster shell. "I. . ."

The woman giggled. "Pale as a ghost. First time away from home, eh? I'm Bridgette Hasler from Minnesota."

"Shirley Davenport, Maine. I gather this isn't your first time away from home?"

"Nah." Bridgette waved off the outlandish remark. "I've been away from home for a while now. The other girls are marching in. Best we follow."

Feeling silly for being callow, Shirley retrieved her suitcase and crossed the threshold of the massive doors.

They were shuffled into a room marked SOCIAL SCIENCES and told to fill all available seats. Shirley looked around the room at the various hairstyles, hair colors, and fashions that undoubtedly came with a mix of colorful personalities. The next six weeks would be a social science experiment of sorts, so they'd come to the right place.

She took a seat next to Bridgette and unbuttoned the lapels of her coat. Bridgette leaned closer and pointed to a stain on Shirley's blouse. "Butter?"

"Egg." Shirley folded her hands and covered the stain.

Bridgette held out one side of her sweater. "Gravy."

"I'm known to be a little clumsy when I eat."

"Perhaps we were twins separated at birth then. I also have a bad habit of biting my nails."

Shirley held up her fingers, revealing clean nails with squared white tips.

"Hmm. . . You don't. Guess we're not twins then." Bridgette giggled.

Shirley's toes began to thaw. She should've ditched the pumps Joan recommended she wear and opted for her fleece-lined boots. Good first impression or not, this was the military, not a fashion revue. From here on out, she was wearing warm, comfortable boots until they told her differently.

Commander Stratton moved down the aisle to the front of the room. Although Shirley didn't know the woman, it was reassuring to see a familiar face. Head held high, the commander had the poise of a woman comfortable in her own skin. Shirley admired that. She too had always been satisfied to be herself, though she was often criticized for not being like everyone else. Did the commander ever confront such issues? If so, how did she resolve them?

"May I have your attention, please?" Commander Stratton held up her palms. The chatter in the room ceased. "Thank you, ladies. You've overcome a major hurdle in your journey, and we're honored to have you here.

"You will occupy the dormitory rooms on the third floor. Each morning you'll be awakened at six o'clock by bugle. You will have thirty minutes to prepare yourself, tidy your room, and file into the cafeteria—aka mess hall—for breakfast. From there, your day will be filled with vigorous physical and mental training. In the evening, you will report to your rooms no later than eight o'clock sharp. Lights out by nine."

Commander Stratton went on to explain where they could find certain facilities and how they should conduct themselves. "Your uniforms will be brought around shortly. You have the rest of today to settle in and familiarize yourself with the campus. Please partner up and go choose your rooms. You're dismissed."

Shirley waited until most of the women exited before she followed. She was used to wide-open spaces and sea air. Large clusters of bodies beneath a flat ceiling made her claustrophobic. She stayed toward the back and watched the women funnel up the stairs like salmon swimming upstream.

The marble stairs beneath her feet felt. . .foreign. The only time Shirley had seen a stair railing this thick and polished was on a ship they'd toured while visiting the shipyard in Bath when she was sixteen. The amount of money it took to build this foyer alone was more than Shirley would ever see in a lifetime.

Murmured conversations turned to high-pitched excitement around her. Shirley stretched on her toes to see what the commotion was about. Women were tapping each other and pointing to the hallway below them. Shirley followed the direction of their stares and halted midstep.

Captain Webber.

Her heart picked up speed as she followed his movement down the first-floor hall. He ignored the women. Probably best since the majority were making a fuss as if he were some kind of celebrity. The fierceness with which he carried himself was impossible to dismiss, and she understood why nearly every woman on the stairs was fawning over him.

At least ten officers followed behind the captain, all mimicking the serious lines of his mouth and the clench of his fists.

"Hey, Shirley from Maine." At the tug on her arm, Shirley turned to the woman on the step below her. Bridgette grinned, emphasizing the freckles on her nose and cheeks. "You're clogging the line."

"Oh." Shirley started forward, embarrassed, once again, by the giddy reaction she had toward the captain. Giddy and completely inappropriate. But boy, had it warmed her cold insides fast.

Bridgette laughed. "Handsome, ain't he?"

"Who?"

"Who? Nice try. Hey, want to bunk together? I think we'll get along swell. I promise I don't snore. Too loudly."

With four older brothers, Shirley wasn't used to sharing a bedroom, but Bridgette was friendly enough. Shirley didn't want the hassle of finding someone to pair up with anyway. "I'd like that."

Since they'd been near the back of the line, they had to take one of the rooms at the very end of the hall. It held two beds, one window, and one chest of drawers and smelled of stale winter air.

Bridgette tossed her suitcase on the nearest bed and looked around. "Home, sweet home."

Sweet wasn't the word Shirley would've chosen to describe the dim, drafty space, but home it was for the next six weeks.

Sadness welled inside Shirley so strong it made her nauseous. Was this what they called homesickness? Never having been away from her family any farther than her brother Charles's house, Shirley hadn't experienced the emotion before. She blinked back tears.

Bridgette patted Shirley's shoulder. "Best to get it all out tonight, 'cause come tomorrow morning, you'll be too busy to be melancholy."

Shirley sank onto the adjacent bed and hoped Bridgette was right.

"It's not so bad." Bridgette sat beside her. "I've spent the last year serving in the WAVES under Lieutenant Commander Stratton. When they asked her to head up the SPARs, she brought me along with a few other volunteers. She takes good care of us. You'll be just fine."

Not trusting her voice, Shirley nodded. Bridgette walked to the radiator and worked on warming the room.

Shirley closed her eyes, inhaled a deep breath, and slowly released it through her lips. She could do this. She *would* do this.

Determined, Shirley unwrapped the scarf from around her neck, folded it into a neat rectangle, and stuffed it into her coat pocket. Her fingers grazed a papery texture, and she removed the contents of her pocket. The bundle of things Joan had handed her at the depot filled her palm.

She smiled at the bulky handful of unrelated items—a bobby pin, a candy wrapper, a hair ribbon, a receipt, pocket fuzz, and a wadded-up napkin. The napkin rolled out of her hand and landed at her feet.

Bridgette peeled back the drapes, allowing precious light to filter into the room. "You can have the top two drawers. I'll take the bottom two."

Shirley picked up the napkin and noticed black lines from a pen. She smoothed the edges of one side over her knee. The mark of red lips branded the papery fabric. Fire engine red.

Another wave of homesickness washed through her. Joan was the most eccentric member of their small community, insisting on looking like a Hollywood starlet in a harbor town that survived on practicality, but Shirley had always loved her for it. Joan knew what she wanted in life and wasn't afraid to pursue it despite convention.

Shirley had known what she'd wanted too but had always met resistance in one way or another. Fear was something she'd thought she was immune to, but here she was, living the dream, and it scared her to death.

"That a phone number for your fella?" Bridgette wiggled her eyebrows.

"Ha, hardly. Just trash." Shirley walked to the wastebasket and started to drop it in, when Bridgette stopped her.

"It's got something written on it. You sure it's not important? I'm notorious for jotting things down and throwing them away later, forgetting I'd used it as a memo. I've learned to double-check myself."

Shirley turned over the scrap of napkin. *Heidelberg Bakery, 101 Main Street.* The script was in Joan's slanted penmanship.

Joan knew where the bakery was located. It had been there since before they were born and was the only one in town. Why the need to write down the address?

"It's nothing important." Shirley crumpled the napkin and dropped it into the wastebasket. Joan had mentioned her uncle Ernst looking for work. Perhaps the directions had been for him.

Shirley shook off the dreadful feeling that followed. She'd promised Joan to consider a potential courtship with her uncle, but the idea always made her feel off balance. With any luck, Ernst would find interest in a female elsewhere while Shirley was away.

⅀ CHAPTER 10 ⅀

Leo folded the newspaper and slapped it on his desk. He imagined a window where there wasn't one and envisioned the sunrise beyond.

When God looked down on earth, what did He see? As a man, all Leo could see right now was evil, chaos, and death. How did God feel, watching His prized creation destroy one another?

The tepid coffee in his cup made his stomach roil, even though the roasted acorn and ground coffee mix they used here tasted better than the watery version he was accustomed to in DC. He pushed the mug away and rubbed his tired eyes.

Life hadn't always been full of turmoil. In fact, he'd had the best childhood possible. As a young seaman he'd worked hard to serve his country, taken pride in living as a law-abiding citizen and friend to all. He saw those same traits in others nearly everywhere he went—France, England, Iceland. Years later, as if someone had flipped a switch on human decency, the world split and nations collided.

What did God see?

His Sunday school teacher had once explained God's view of time much like a parade. When humans observed a parade, they only saw the sections marching directly in front of them, maybe a little farther ahead, a little farther behind. But God, being high up and looking directly below, saw the entire parade from front to back.

Knowing that God saw earth's timeline in such a way, what did He see? Would there be times of peace and prosperity and kindness again? Celebrations, innovation, progress?

Or was this the beginning of the end?

Sure felt like it.

Commander Stratton stepped into the office and went to her desk for pencil and paper. "The Soviets are gaining ground against the Germans. This morning's headline."

Leo's temples began to pound. The headaches had become more frequent, especially when he allowed himself to dwell on the statistics of war. The numbers threw his focus off. But once his brain started computing the thousands of lives lost, someone's father, son, brother—his brothers—it was hard to keep himself from disappearing into his hole of grief.

At his silence, Stratton frowned and perched a hip on the edge of her desk, bumping a clock that resembled a ship's wheel. "Does this not please you?"

"Of course it does." It would please him even more if the enemy would concede and end this war altogether. "I didn't sleep well last night."

Stratton buttoned her oversized sweater. "Ah, it's always tough sleeping in an unfamiliar bed."

That hadn't been the problem. He'd always been able to sleep anytime, anywhere. Even in the belly of a leaky ship in a wet hammock and sopping clothes. No, it had been memories of his brothers that had kept him awake. He needed to call and check on his niece, Grace, and her mother, Meredith. Send them some more money.

If only Leo had made a different choice, his brothers would still be alive. Donald would get to watch his daughter grow into a woman and see his wife grow old.

Chest burning, he stood and smoothed the lapels of his uniform. "Ready to teach these ladies how to march?"

Stratton stared at him a moment too long, then rose to her feet. "Right behind you, Captain."

Sunlight burst through the window and gleamed off the gold buttons of Shirley's uniform. The dark blue fabric backing the sparkling buttons made them look like stars in a midnight sky. Though she preferred not to wear a skirt unless the occasion called for it, the tailored cut fell perfectly midcalf, as if she'd been fitted ahead of time.

"Amazing, isn't it?" Bridgette joined her at the mirror. "Mainbocher is a genius."

"Who?" Shirley pulled back hair at her temple and secured the wavy strands with a bobby pin.

Bridgette snorted. "I thought I was raised in the backwoods. Main Rousseau Bocher, fashion journalist for *Vogue* and *Harper's Bazaar*? No? Anyway, he lives in Paris and designed the Duchess of Windsor's wedding dress. He designed the uniforms for the WAVES, which is now the same uniform worn by the SPARs."

"We wear the same uniforms?" Shirley secured the hair on the other side of her head.

"It was easier that way." Bridgette assessed her form by pivoting side to side. "It's the closest thing the majority of us will ever get to wearing couture fashions."

The statement was certainly true in Shirley's case. Especially considering she'd never used the word *couture* in her life. She bet Joan was ecstatic. No doubt her friend looked and felt like a celebrity starlet. If only they could've stayed together. Shirley would pay to see Joan's reaction.

The hall clock dinged. Shirley turned for the door. "We'd better go."

"Your cover."

Turning, Shirley took the hat Bridgette held out and placed it on her head. Bridgette stepped closer and twisted it to the side. "There. Now you look the part."

They stepped into the hall, and Bridgette closed the door behind them. Dozens of fellow SPARs emerged from their rooms, congesting the hallway as the line funneled to the top of the marble stairs. A quiet hum of conversation flowed, but the energy buzzing through the air made the little hairs on Shirley's arms and neck stand at attention. These were fellow American citizens, her sisters, and together they were going to fight this war.

On the ground floor they were ushered into the same room they'd met in the previous day. Ten officers of various ages lined the front wall, sharp and commanding in their navy blues. Bridgette squealed when a pretty blond waved from a few rows over and made her way toward them.

"Lucy, it's good to see you!" Bridgette threw her arms around the woman's neck, knocking Lucy's cover askew.

Lucy laughed and readjusted it. "I saw you come in yesterday but wasn't able to reach you. I take it you found a roommate."

"Yes." Bridgette pointed her thumb at Shirley. "Lucy Marcazy, meet Shirley... Well, I forget what her last name is." Bridgette giggled. "I do know she's from Maine."

"Davenport." Shirley held out her hand. Joan's voice in her head warned her not to crush Lucy's hand with a bear grip. Growing up in a household of brothers, Shirley was guilty of mimicking some of their rugged ways. She relaxed her fingers as Lucy slipped her hand into hers.

"Wonderful to meet you," Lucy said. "Bridgette and I were bunkmates in the WAVES." When Lucy smiled, her whole face glowed. "I warn you, Bridgette is severely strict on the room being neat as a pin."

Bridgette leaned toward Shirley. "In my defense, we failed an inspection and were made examples from there on out."

Lucy shrugged. "True. But in my defense, I didn't have the energy to tidy up after sneaking you out to dance with Lieutenant Whitley."

"Oh, hush up. That's supposed to remain our secret." Bridgette's cheeks flamed as red as her hair.

Shirley pressed her lips together to keep from laughing. She had a feeling if she stuck around with these two, she'd hear a great many similar stories.

Lucy wiggled her eyebrows. "He's here, you know."

"Who?" asked Bridgette.

"Lieutenant Whitley."

Bridgette scanned the room, neck stretched, then stilled as her gaze landed on a handsome officer with sandy brown hair peeking out from his hat. The officer, chin pointed high and body stiff as a statue, grinned and gave Bridgette an almost imperceptible nod.

"Oh boy," Bridgette whispered, visibly melting. Lucy winked at Shirley.

Something akin to jealousy stirred in Shirley. She caught herself searching the room for Captain Webber, which was ridiculous. The man had to be at least eight to ten years older than her and had experienced enough life to want a woman of grace and substance, not a tomboy who was just now leaving home for the first time.

The fact that the captain's age didn't bother her the way it did when she thought about Ernst made the gears in her brain churn.

Commander Stratton entered from the back of the room, clapping a staccato rhythm to quiet the room as she approached the podium. Lucy touched Bridgette's arm. "I'll see you later."

Within seconds, the room was still and silent. The commander explained the difference between the blue and the white uniforms they'd been issued—seabags, she called them—and demonstrated how the covers should be worn. Once again she went over the rules of decorum. They would all start out as seaman apprentices, earning fifty dollars a month, except for a few women who'd followed Commander Stratton from the WAVES who'd be trained as officers. The seaman apprentices would have the opportunity to work their way up to petty officers, which would raise them to $126 a month.

Shirley almost fell out of her chair. Earning $126 would be triple what she made in a month fishing. All food, housing, medical, and dental would be paid for by the federal government during their duration as a SPAR.

The job couldn't possibly get any better.

Then Captain Webber entered the room, and Shirley's blood heated. He joined the commander at the front and introduced his men, explaining which officers were responsible for which kinds of training. His deep voice slid over Shirley and did funny things to her head. The harder she tried not to be smitten with the man, the more smitten she became.

So smitten, in fact, she missed the dismissal for breakfast until Bridgette tapped her arm.

The cafeteria reminded Shirley of the one she'd had in high school but on a much larger scale. Like high school, the women segregated themselves into groups that would likely remain together throughout training. She was grateful to have an outgoing roommate who introduced Shirley at every opportunity.

After a fine meal, they were herded into another room where a photographer took their picture for an ID card to be delivered later. The photographer held up a finger for Shirley to stay put. He leaned over his table and wrote on a small note card. "Thank you, Shirley Davenport, number 10257."

Stars swam in her vision from the bright flash. Shirley took the card and blinked at the handwritten digits. Her number of independence.

Bridgette rushed up and linked her arm through Shirley's. "Ready to march?"

"Ready." Shirley followed her new friend to the gymnasium filled with women from all over the country. Together, they would help win this war.

≣ CHAPTER II ≣

Leo pointed to a mark on the campus map splayed across his small desk. "There."

Lieutenant Billings remained silent.

Leo regarded the man. "Did you hear me, Billings?"

"Yes, sir." Billings swallowed. Surely the California native wasn't intimidated by a few inches of snow. Or twelve.

Leo placed his elbows on his desk. "Do the outside elements concern you, Lieutenant?"

"No, sir." The skin around his eyes twitched.

The man was greener than an Irish pasture. "I think if a dorm full of women can handle it, Billings, you can too."

Lieutenants Whitley and Greenwich snickered. Leo reached for the edge of the map and began rolling it. "The gymnasium is already in use with training drills, and this field gives us plenty of room to teach the recruits their way around a ship."

Greenwich moved forward and examined the part of the map Leo hadn't rolled. The nod of the man's head was too exaggerated.

"I agree, the gymnasium is definitely the better choice for drills, Captain. You know what else the gymnasium would be good for? Dancing. I'd bet these ladies would appreciate a bit of fun after a week of vigorous training."

"No."

"But sir, we used to hold dances after hours with the WAVES. It provides relief and boosts morale. Besides, if we never interact with the ladies outside of training, how's Whitley supposed to spark his girl?"

Leo turned to Lieutenant Whitley, whose cheeks had turned a

mottled purple. His mouth opened and closed like a suffocating fish.

"Whitley isn't here to spark anything except a desire to defend his country."

"Sir, yes, sir." Whitley's voice cracked.

"Did I hear something about a dance?" Commander Stratton squeezed into the crowded room and draped her coat along the back of her chair. Leo replied with a resounding no at the same time Greenwich said yes. Leo scowled at the lieutenant.

Stratton chuckled. "Which is it?" She removed her scarf and brushed snow from her hair. It nearly fell onto the map, the room was so tiny. With five people stuffed inside, it was more cramped than the cargo hold of a cutter.

Leo gripped the curled map in his fist. "No."

Billings stepped forward. "Sir, I—"

"You're dismissed." Leo secured the band on the map, eyeing every man in the room. Disappointment clogged the air as the officers filed out. Leo walked to the corner bookcase and propped the map against it.

"I'm no expert in body language, Captain, but I do believe your men don't agree with you."

"Of course they don't. We're training for war, and all they're worried about is sparking girls."

Stratton smiled the same irritating way his mother did when giving advice with barely restrained patience. "These ladies are hardly girls, Captain."

She sat on the edge of her desk, her black shoes contrasting against the new blue rug she put down. "Flirting is a perfectly natural thing for young men to be worried about, *in spite* of war. Healthy relationships give hope. They give a sense of normalcy that is most craved during these ugly times."

She stared ahead, focused on nothing, and Leo watched her thoughts drift elsewhere. "What better spirit-lifter than love?"

Leo sighed, and he scolded himself for sounding annoyed versus just plain exhausted.

"I realize you're probably too driven, too practical for love in such turbulent waters, but the truth is, Captain, life goes on, even during war. In the deepest trenches with guns firing all around, on a sinking ship, on an open battlefield, it's a comfort to know there's someone awaiting your safe return. In fact, there's no stronger motivator to live than love."

The breakfast sitting in Leo's stomach turned rancid. He was certain the images of two beautiful females had been the last thing his brother Donald had thought of before his last gulp of air was stolen from the *Arizona*.

He pretended to browse the collection of books in the case while he gave himself time to put thoughts of his brothers' last moments from his mind. Thoughts of future decades of life they'd never live.

Once he could trust his voice, he said, "There are several classrooms that surround the library. The officers have marked them according to subject. The class schedules and list of SPARs are grouped and recorded. I put a copy on your desk."

The leather on Stratton's shoes made quiet noise as she approached him from behind. At least fifteen years his senior, her thin frame and average height didn't stand out in a crowd, but her intelligence certainly did.

"I know about your brothers, Captain."

Though his back was to her, he closed his eyes, hoping to shut out the truth.

"When are you going to stop punishing yourself?"

Shirley had only been training for four days, and she was already bushed. It wasn't the early rising that got her. She was used to that from working as sternman with her father. It was the hours of study and drills on top of surprise inspections and marching ten miles a day. The SPARs motto was *Semper Paratus, Always Ready*, and they were truly expected to be ready for anything, anytime.

She yawned and exited the serving line, glancing around the mess hall for a vacant seat. Bridgette stood a few tables away and motioned Shirley over. The woman had twice the spunk of Joan and a handful more gumption. As wonderful as it was to have found a kindred spirit from the start, at times Shirley pretended to be asleep just for some peace and quiet to process all that had happened during the day.

Shirley settled in beside Bridgette and sipped her chilled orange juice, willing the burst of flavor to energize her brain cells. She had a quiz on military insignia today, and she couldn't let last night's cramming be for naught.

Lucy, fork in hand, leaned across the narrow table and said, "I heard she's from Oklahoma. Joined in order to escape some kind of trouble or something."

"Who's she bunking with?" Bridgette asked.

Shirley cut into her biscuits and gravy and took a bite.

"No one." Lucy peeled her banana. "Her train was delayed, so everyone had already chosen their rooms when she arrived. She tried to fill the vacant bed in Roxie's room but was asked to leave. You know how Roxie is."

Shirley had no idea who they were talking about and she'd never met Roxie, but Shirley already disliked the woman. They were a team working toward the same goal. There wasn't room for pompous attitudes.

The conversation moved on to Bridgette's promotion and her training as officer. Shirley concentrated on finishing her meal. Thirty minutes wasn't long when close to half of it was spent in the serving line, and it took three and a half minutes to walk from the cafeteria to the gymnasium, where they started every day with calisthenics. Two days in a row, she had claimed her spot on the gym floor as the whistle was blowing. She would not cut it that close again.

Bridgette and Lucy followed behind Shirley to where they deposited their spent trays, still chatting about some handsome officer and a trip to town they were planning to catch a movie on their next night off.

"There she is," Lucy said, pointing to a black woman in a back corner, eating at a table by herself.

Bridgette prodded them to keep moving. "What did you say her name was?"

Lucy shrugged. "Alma something."

Shirley knew she should follow behind her friends, but her feet refused to move. So this was the woman they'd been gossiping about. She stared at Alma's bent head and watched her eat without company.

A quick glance around the room had Shirley's emotions in a knot. She knew about segregation and had read horror stories in the newspaper of places where blacks were attacked and even murdered for the color of their skin. Never venturing far from home, however, Shirley had never witnessed such things.

Alma looked up and locked gazes with Shirley. Embarrassed to be caught staring, she offered the woman a small smile. Expressionless, Alma continued chewing her bite, and Shirley got the impression the woman could read her very soul.

"Shirley, let's go." Bridgette waited in the hallway, eyebrows raised.

Torn, Shirley turned back to the woman, who'd gone back to eating her breakfast. It wasn't right that this Roxie had refused to bunk with Alma, and it wasn't right for Alma to eat alone.

"Shirley." Bridgette started walking and motioned for Shirley to follow. She did.

With each step her heart grew heavier. By walking away and following her peers, Shirley was just as guilty of ignoring Alma as the rest.

⚊ CHAPTER 12 ⚊

"If there's ever a real fire, don't put these ladies in charge." Cold air snapped at Leo's cheeks. Through puffs of foggy breath, he counted the ladies filing into the night wrapped in unbuttoned coats and robes, some attempting to trudge through a foot of snow in slippers.

"I won't argue improvement is needed." Stratton adjusted her scarf around her chin. "But they weren't expecting to be ripped from sleep at two in the morning to practice a fire drill." She hunkered against the wind. "Neither was I."

Despite teaching proper formation and speed, their lines were sloppy, and half the group would already be dead if the scenario were real.

Tension tightened Leo's jaw. "Emergencies don't follow sleep schedules."

The twenty-four hundred Americans ripped from sleep on what was supposed to be a leisurely Sunday morning in Oahu were the perfect example. He almost said as much but refrained. Stratton already knew his secrets—how, he wasn't sure—but he wasn't about to discuss it any further.

The fire alarm blared into the night, echoing off the surrounding buildings. His officers were at their posts, counting the sector of women they'd been given responsibility over. One woman fell face-first into the icy powder, lay stiff for a moment, then recovered like a true soldier.

Once it appeared everyone was outside, he walked the perimeter of the formation and waited for the officers' nods that everyone in their sectors was present. The drill seemed to take hours, and the entire time he reminded himself to be gracious.

Stars twinkled in the black sky. For a mere instant, he was transported to his childhood where he'd sat with his father and learned the basics of astronomy. A lesson Leo would carry with him for the rest of his life. No matter where he went in the world, he always felt at home when he looked at the stars.

The memory faded as quickly as it had come, and the warmth in his chest vanished like a fog, leaving a bitter aftertaste. When had he transformed into this man full of impatience and anger and disgust? He'd always been driven, but this. . . He didn't understand what was happening inside. He was rotting at his core a little each day, and he didn't know how to stop it. He only knew he wanted to be somewhere else, living a life that should be, not the reality he was given.

He hoped he might one day break free of the darkness that had a hold on him. Though he didn't deserve to, he desperately wanted to live a happy, abundant life after this blasted war was over. Whatever the future looked like.

At the last officer's nod, he gave Stratton permission to silence the alarm, and he commanded the SPARs to march back inside. He stepped aside at the main doors and allowed each lady to enter the building before himself to avoid them suffering further exposure.

One woman in particular caught his eye, mostly due to the rags tied in her hair but also because snow crusted her crown like a halo. Snow coated the end of her nose and painted the entire front of her tattered robe. She must've been the one who'd fallen.

"Are you all right, miss?"

The woman raised her frosted eyelashes. Miss Davenport.

A violent shiver ripped through her, and he reached out to steady her. That's when he noticed she was only wearing one slipper. The exposed foot was ruby red.

"Miss." He pointed to the redhead behind Miss Davenport. "See that she gets warm immediately. A hot shower, coffee, extra blankets—whatever you need. I'll send an officer around to get you supplies."

Leo pried Miss Davenport's stiff fingers from his arm and transferred her to the redhead.

"Th. . .th. . .th. . ." Miss Davenport's teeth clacked so hard in between syllables she couldn't speak.

"You're welcome." He directed his next words to the redhead. "Hurry."

"Yes, Captain. We'll get her warm right quick."

Protectiveness flared in his bones as she guided Miss Davenport inside. He waited until the last of the SPARs entered the main hall before stepping in and closing the door.

"Whitley." Leo chased the lieutenant. When Whitley turned around, Leo pointed upstairs. "One of the seaman apprentices, Davenport, is in need of assistance. Exposure."

He informed the lieutenant of what had happened and told him to fetch whatever the women thought they'd need. When Whitley headed toward the stairs, Leo let out a breath. The scant amount of sleep remaining would be slow in coming.

On the way to his room, a panicked voice shrieked from the top of the stairs. "Captain! We need a medic right away."

———≈———

The mortification of Shirley's fainting spell still clung to her the next afternoon as she transitioned from assembly hall to her rates and ranks class, hoping Captain Webber didn't notice her as she crossed his path.

As if it hadn't been bad enough that he'd seen her in rag curls, she'd had to frost herself in snow by falling, lose her slipper in a snowdrift, and then grow hypothermic during the drill. Once inside and at the top of the stairs, she'd passed out and bumped her head. The injury was minimal, but it had "bled like a stuck hog," as Bridgette had so delicately described. Add dark circles and puffy eyes from lack of sleep, and Shirley was an all-around pathetic mess.

She kept her head low and angled toward the wall. The captain passed her with nary an acknowledgment.

She sighed in relief and rubbed her burning eyes. Though she needed to study after dinner, she'd be lucky to stay awake long enough to eat. She'd pushed herself to carry on as normal, but the events of the day were about to declare victory.

It had started with Lieutenant Plumley surprising the class with a pop quiz on sailing phrases. She'd already known most of them from her fishing experience, but she needed to excel at this course to prove—if only to herself—she was good at something.

Then during afternoon assembly, Commander Stratton had introduced Lieutenant Commander Helen Schleman as her new right-hand woman. They'd been friends and colleagues at Purdue as well as in the WAVES, and they had delightful stories to tell. The two created an energy together that was impossible to ignore.

Commander Stratton folded her hands in front of her. "With the additional SPARs arriving tomorrow, I'll need you to tighten your living quarters. Even if you have to move rooms, I want every bed filled and every space occupied to make as much room for these ladies as possible."

For the rest of the afternoon, the seaman apprentices were to work on making the most of their small spaces and consolidating where needed. Inspection would take place promptly after dinner.

Shirley returned to her room in the hope of catching a quick nap only to find Lucy lounging on Bridgette's bed. Bridgette held a blue-and-white polka dot dress up to herself in the mirror. "Oh, Shirley, have you heard?"

Bridgette tossed the dress on the bed, the bulk of it landing on Lucy. "Captain Webber finally conceded to a dance in the gymnasium, since the snow won't allow us to go anywhere on our nights off. Isn't it grand?"

If Bridgette shook Shirley's arm out of its socket in her excitement, it would not be grand.

"Maybe he'll kiss you this time," Lucy said.

"Who?" Shirley looked from Lucy to Bridgette.

Lucy tossed the dress off her legs and dangled them off the side of the bed. "Lieutenant Whitley." She closed her eyes and made a kissing face into the air.

Bridgette's pale face turned rosy. "I hope he does. Kiss me, I mean."

The topic of kissing caused an unbidden image of Captain Webber to flitter through Shirley's mind. Unbidden but not undesirable.

"I'm sorry, Shirley." Bridgette grasped Shirley's elbow. "I didn't mean to embarrass you."

Shirley was not about to explain that the stain in her own cheeks had nothing to do with Bridgette kissing Lieutenant Whitley.

"Who's embarrassed and why?" A stout woman barged in, hands on her hips, one thin eyebrow raised.

Lucy explained while Shirley tucked in her sheets for inspection.

"Necking with a forbidden officer isn't the only thing you should be thinking about." The woman planted her stocky frame on the end of Shirley's bed, rumpling the sheets. Who was this brash woman?

The name tag clipped above her breast read *Roxie Brown 15752*. Ah, so this was the infamous Roxie.

"What do you mean?" Bridgette asked.

"Filling every available bed means someone has to room with Alma. So far, no one has volunteered." Roxie inspected her nails.

Lucy frowned. "Why not?"

The unspoken reason hung in the air like a bad smell. For several seconds, no one spoke.

"Isn't anyone going to tell me why?" Lucy asked.

Roxie rolled her eyes. "Because Alma is colored."

Lucy's eyes grew wide. "Oh."

"Why is that a problem?" Shirley fluffed her pillow a little too hard. "We're SPARs, for crying out loud. Sisters of mercy banding together for the same cause."

Bridgette lifted the dress from her bed and placed it back in the bureau, silent.

Roxie crossed her legs and leaned back on one arm. "Yes, and we don't hold her color against her. But where a lot of us are from, it isn't acceptable to drink from the same water fountains or eat in the same restaurants, much less share a bedroom. For others, they've not been around colored folk enough to know what to expect when living with one."

Oh the absurdity. Miss 15752 needed to find another place to gossip because they had less than an hour before inspection, and Shirley wasn't going to fail due to the ignorant convictions of her peers.

Lucy stood. "Well, I can't volunteer. I have too much stuff to move and would never get it done before. . .inspection." Her voice tapered off in guilt, Shirley presumed.

They all looked to Bridgette, who wriggled like a worm on a hook. "I'm an officer in training. I'd rather not move rooms if I don't have to since it's located conveniently to the bathroom and I'm required to report earlier than the rest of you and. . ."

The rest of Bridgette's excuses faded to white noise in Shirley's ears. She remembered all the times in school when she was left out or poked fun at because she liked to play ball with the boys and climb trees and go fishing instead of playing with dolls or dress-up or cosmetics.

It hurt.

And while Shirley wouldn't compare her discrimination to Alma's, being ostracized was painful at any level.

She scooped out her clothing from the top two drawers and piled it on her bed. "I'll do it."

Shirley retrieved her suitcase.

"Do what?" Bridgette asked.

"Room with Alma." Shirley glared at Roxie. "Unless you want to."

Roxie's mouth opened in offense, but she turned away.

"Thought so." Shirley stuffed her belongings into her suitcase, walked to the door, and tossed a disappointed look to the spineless roommate she adored.

Eyes full of regret, Bridgette nodded her approval.

With that, Shirley walked to Alma's room to bunk with a stranger she wasn't afraid to befriend.

⫸ CHAPTER 13 ⫷

Leo's shoes tapped the marble steps as he descended to his room. He reached the bottom and had almost turned the corner when a voice behind him said, "Captain, sir. Admiral Grant is on the telephone for you, sir."

Leo turned to where Lieutenant Whitley stood at attention beside the railing, ignoring the burning sensation in his eyes that could be cured with a soft pillow and shut-eye. He'd dreamed of his brothers again last night, at the beach when they'd been children, alive and vivacious and happy. He'd awoken to a bugle call in a dark room with an empty heart.

"Thank you, Whitley. At ease."

Leo climbed the stairs and walked past the young man to the office, recalling the grin Whitley had tried to hide after Leo had given his permission for them to hold a dance in the gymnasium. The officer was clearly smitten.

Stratton had been right. Despite war, men were men and women were women who had dreams and needs and desires. One day this God-forsaken war would end, and life would be waiting for them when it did.

A nudge pushed at his conscience. *Was this war really God-forsaken?*

Of course not. But it felt that way. It seemed as if evil gained more territory every day.

Leo studied his Bible as faithfully as he studied military tactics and knew God was in war. At times He demanded war. Sometimes it was to secure the freedom of His people, and other times it was the consequence of His children's rebellion.

God was in the midst of this chaos, even if Leo didn't feel Him.

"In the world ye shall have tribulation: but be of good cheer; I have

overcome the world." The verse in John whispered across his heart.

No matter how this war ended, Leo knew who would ultimately win. Until then, being of good cheer was something he'd have to work on.

Leo stepped inside the office and picked up the receiver lying on the desk. "Admiral Grant, sir. Captain Webber."

"Webber, it's about time."

"I came as soon as I heard, sir."

"The LORAN station. Admiral Hendricks of the Coast Guard needs eleven of the best SPARs to take over after training. He's sending his men out."

Leo blinked. The Coast Guard's "long-range aid to navigation" in Massachusetts was a secret monitoring station that used low-frequency radio waves to accurately locate Allied ships. Only those higher in rank knew the station existed, but even they were kept in the dark about what went on there.

"Sir, these women have only been training for a week."

"I'm well aware of that, Captain. They'll finish their training, and upon graduation you'll send a list of your best from Iowa to Admiral Hendricks. Commanders Stratton and Schleman will work on a list from Palm Beach. Admiral Hendricks will take it from there."

"Yes, sir. I'll send you nothing but the finest, sir."

"Very good. Not a word about this to anyone except Stratton and Schleman."

"Of course."

"Oh, and Captain?" The admiral's voice started faint and grew louder, as if he'd started to hang up but changed his mind.

"Yes, sir?"

"The Soviets were able to cut off German supplies. They surrendered. The Allies won Stalingrad. Sleep well, Captain."

The phone clicked in Leo's ear. He stood in stunned silence, attempting to comprehend what he'd just heard. The Germans surrendered in Stalingrad.

Hope burst like a firecracker in Leo's chest. It might be a small victory, but it was victory all the same. He would sleep well.

———— ≈ ————

By the time Shirley transferred her things to Alma's room and tidied up for inspection, Commander Stratton called them into the hallway to stand while she made the rounds. After inspection they were dismissed for dinner, which was awkward after Shirley's outburst. Needing solace in a quiet place, Shirley retreated to the campus library to study for her customs and courtesies test.

Close to nine and the lights-out curfew, she opened the door to her new room quietly, so as not to wake Alma should she be asleep. Shirley was exhausted, and she prayed they didn't choose tonight to surprise them with another fire drill. After the first one she'd learned to sleep with a pair of trousers, boots, and coat beside the bed. That way she could dress quickly before leaving the building. She would not march toward her death again.

Alma turned from the mirror when Shirley walked in. "Sorry, it's late." Shirley placed her stack of books on her bedside table.

"No matter to me." Alma tucked her hairbrush beneath her chin while she pinned back her hair.

"We didn't really have a chance to meet earlier. I'm Shirley Davenport."

Hands still occupied, Alma stared at Shirley's outstretched hand, then at her face.

"Sorry, I guess you're busy." Shirley chuckled with nervous energy. "I've heard your first name is Alma, but I don't remember your surname."

Alma removed the hairbrush and set it aside. "I'm sure you've heard a great many things about me. If you ever want to know the truth, just ask." She uncapped a jar of facial moisturizer and dipped in a finger. "I'm Alma Evans."

Shirley felt scolded even though Alma's tone was cordial and her words kind. Though Shirley avoided gossip when she could, she was as susceptible to listening to it and believing it as others, she supposed. The fact that Alma noticed she'd been the cause of talk made their small space uncomfortable.

"Nice to meet you." Shirley retrieved her nightgown and slippers and sat on the edge of her bed. She'd noticed right away this mattress had a few lumps, but she hoped she'd be tired enough every night it wouldn't bother her much.

"I'm sorry you drew the short straw," Alma said, capping her jar.

Shirley's hands stilled on the buttons of her uniform coat. To Shirley's knowledge, no one had mistreated Alma, but she'd obviously heard the gossip and felt the tension.

Swallowing to control her voice, Shirley looked at Alma and smiled.

"I didn't. I volunteered."

Expressionless, Alma looked at her, reading her for truth. Shirley continued her nightly regimen as casually as she had when she'd bunked with Bridgette. A rustle of sheets and blankets told her when Alma slipped into bed. As Shirley went to turn off the light, she noticed Alma had turned to face the wall.

No getting acquainted tonight.

Shirley switched off the light and went back to bed. She stubbed her big toe on the metal frame. She groaned, remembering the nonsensical words Daddy said whenever he hurt himself. The memory made her laugh and caused her earlier unshed tears to leak from the corners of her eyes.

"You're the only person I know who laughs when they stub their toe."

Alma's words made Shirley laugh harder. Oh, how she missed her parents. Home. Alma probably felt the same way, as did most of the SPARs at times. Truth was, no matter the color of their skin, they were all women with emotions and fears and courage, and they were all fighting for the same cause.

Shirley crawled into bed. Her bones sighed in relief beneath the blankets. "Good night, Alma."

A few moments passed. "Good night, Miss Shirley" sounded into the dark.

⧮ CHAPTER 14 ⧮

The gymnasium that normally echoed with the marching of feet, the shouts of drill commands, and the noise of calisthenics now echoed with the strains of the Glenn Miller Band through a microphone Leo's officers had placed in front of a radio. It was the most rustic dance Leo had ever attended, but officers and apprentices alike were having fun.

Since everyone was off duty, they were all dressed in street clothes, giving a sense of normalcy to the affair. Everyone except him anyway. As chaperone, he needed to command leadership, and the uniform alone went a long way in accomplishing that end.

Lieutenant Rollins went by, spinning his dance partner until her flowy skirt twirled above her knees. Then he locked his arms around her, and they performed perfectly synchronized foot moves to the other side of the gymnasium. Rollins was a klutz in many ways, but the man sure could dance.

The redhead in Lieutenant Whitley's arms must be the intended spark Leo had heard about. The newly appointed officer who'd helped Miss Davenport that night in the snow. Neither officer had attempted to dance with anyone else, and the moony expressions on their faces left no doubt as to their affections.

Commander Helen Schleman sidled up beside Leo. "No fun tonight, Captain?"

"Not tonight, sir." The title felt sacrilegious on his tongue, but she and Commander Stratton had decided it was best to address everyone as sir, even the women, to keep it easy.

Helen wiggled in front of him, mocking the movements of the younger in attendance but doing a terrible job. "All work and no play makes a navy captain a grumpy boy."

His lips twitched. Twice his age, Helen possessed the heart and spirit of a teenage girl, full of life and laughter. She'd also be the first to whip someone's hide with her intellect.

She continued her awkward jerking motions, eyebrows raised for his reply. He laughed. "With all due respect, you realize you look ridiculous, don't you?"

She grinned wide. "Of course I do, boy." She pointed her finger in the air. "But I'm having fun!"

She turned away and bounced from foot to foot, wagging her finger in the air. Leo scrubbed a hand down his face and hoped she didn't hurt herself. He really should loosen up and join in, but something inside him just couldn't cut loose. He could, however, use some punch.

He walked over to the small table in the corner that held nothing but cups and a punch bowl. Premixed in the mess hall, there was barely enough left for one dipper full. He took a sip and stepped to the side when someone yelled, "Watch out, Captain!"

A woman crashed into him, sending cold punch over his hand and onto his uniform. On instinct, his hand reached around the person to steady them both. A very soft person.

His hip bumped the bowl and it tipped off the corner and pinged against the gym floor. He looked down into the warm brown eyes of Miss Davenport, the barefoot marcher. It took a few seconds for her eyes to focus on his, but when they did, mortification bubbled from their depths.

Her cheeks grew red. "Oh, Captain Webber, I'm very sorry. He was spinning me, and I got dizzy and...oh...."

Her feminine curves pressed against him had him a little dizzy also. She wiped at the red stain on his shirt. "Oh no. . ."

"It's quite all right."

And he meant every word.

"Am I going to receive a demerit?"

Huh?

He looked up. Almost every eye in the gymnasium was staring at them. Music played but no one danced. Apparently, he and Miss Davenport were the entertainment.

That's when he remembered his rank, her rate, and that he shouldn't still be holding her against him like this.

He let her go like he would a hot coal and stepped back. "Of course not. Accidents happen." Like the sticky punch that now coated his front.

"Enjoy the rest of your evening. I'm going to clean up."

He walked out of the gym doors, his last image of her standing with her mouth agape. Oh, what a pretty mouth it was too, coated in a fetching shade of pink lipstick. A mouth that, for a few glorious moments, caused the responsibilities he carried to dissipate and made him feel like. . .

A man.

―――――≈―――――

Shirley's brain hurt. She'd been tested on customs and courtesies, then had crammed for tomorrow's test on insignia and naval time. She'd tried to sit with Alma at lunch and dinner, but both times Alma was finishing her meal by the time Shirley was ready to sit down.

Alma was polite, kind. She would speak when Shirley engaged her, but even then her answers were short, vague. Shirley hoped Alma wasn't disappointed that she'd gotten stuck with her. Shirley thought it horrible that Alma had been left to herself most of the time, but now believed Alma preferred it that way.

Shirley readied for bed and slipped beneath the covers, shivering. The high winds paired with another round of snow created blizzard-like conditions that whipped around the campus buildings and made every inch of marble and stone feel like ice.

"You cold too, Miss Shirley?" Alma tied the belt on her robe and walked to the radiator.

"Yes." Saying it without clicking her teeth was a challenge.

Alma adjusted the heat to warm up the room. "That's as high as it goes, Miss Shirley. We'll either wake up as popsicles in the morning or swim in our sweat all night."

"Thank you, Alma."

"You're welcome, Miss Shirley."

Shirley propped her pillow against the headboard, then reached to the end of her bed and dragged her textbook onto her lap. "My brain is on overload, but I'll never be able to sleep tonight if I don't feel confident that I know the material inside and out."

"Mmm-hmm."

"Would you like for me to quiz you? We could take turns. Then tomorrow we can both celebrate our As."

Alma adjusted her pillows. "Miss Shirley, you seem awfully

determined to befriend me. May I ask you a question?"

"Of course."

"Why aren't you bothered by my skin color the way the rest of those ladies seem to be?"

Shirley's heart broke. She would answer honestly but knew she'd have to use the right words if she was going to convince Alma of her authenticity.

She turned to Alma, her left arm propped against the short metal headboard. "Have you ever had a dream? One you thought every detail through so clearly, one you wanted so badly you could taste it?"

"Yes'm."

"Have you ever had a broken bone?"

Alma frowned. "Yes'm, but—"

"Me too. My right arm when I was ten. Have you ever had your heart broken?"

Alma's gaze flicked to the wall behind Shirley as she answered. "Yes'm."

"Have you ever been in love?"

"No."

Shirley sighed. "Me either." She shrugged. "So you see, on the inside we're practically the same. Like eggs."

Alma's eyebrows arched to her hairline.

"Stick with me. Eggs are all the same on the inside. It's the shells that vary in tone, a beautiful mix of white and tan and brown and blue. But they all have a fragile exterior and valuable center."

Alma chuckled. "In my long life, I've been compared to just about everything, Miss Shirley, but never a blue egg."

Shirley laughed. "At least it wasn't a green egg."

"Okay, now you're pulling my leg, Miss Shirley. Green eggs?"

Shirley threw her palms out. "I swear. We share a large chicken coop with our neighbors. There are hens that lay olive-green eggs. And some lay the most beautiful brownish-gold eggs that remind me of chocolate."

Alma shook her head. "Don't that beat all. I've always lived in the city, so I've never seen anything except white eggs and brown."

Shirley settled in, enjoying their rapport. "How old are you? Where are you from? I detect a southern accent. Have you always lived in the South?"

Alma's happy expression turned serious. "Thirty-one and yes. Now, we best get to studying, Miss Shirley. It's getting late."

The moment ended quickly, like a bucket of water on a small flame.

Shirley nodded, unable to speak. She'd somehow stepped on something hurtful for Alma but wasn't sure how.

They studied for close to an hour, taking turns asking each other questions, sometimes laughing at the other's response like too-tired crazy women doing their best to stay awake. When both of their heads were bobbing in sleep, they called the studying to an end.

Shirley yawned as Alma got up to turn off the light. "Tomorrow's test is oratory."

The room went black. "Then you best make sure you pronounce your *R*'s tomorrow, Miss Shirley. I guarantee Lieutenant Plumley ain't never heard 'cent-ah the anch-ah' before."

Shirley cackled until her stomach was sore. She'd been told by several SPARs that she talked funny, but she sounded normal to her own ears.

By the light of the moon glowing through the window, Shirley saw Alma wipe at her eyes as she too wound down her laughter.

"I'll do my best to enunciate my *R*'s." It came out as *ahs*, which made them both laugh again.

Alma blew out a loud breath. "Good night, Miss Shirley."

"Why do you always use *Miss* before my name?"

Alma was quiet for so long Shirley thought she wasn't going to answer. "My grandmother taught me to always address white folk that way. Said it was a sign of respect. Something they needed to hear from us awfully bad for some reason." Alma stirred and faced the wall. "It became a habit that stuck with me, I suppose. I apologize if it bothers you, Miss Shirley."

A sign of respect. The phrase bounced around Shirley's head as she closed her eyes. "Good night, Miss Alma."

Shirley swore she heard Alma smile, if such a thing were possible.

⫶ CHAPTER 15 ⫶

The wind at Leo's back pushed against him with icy fingers, rocking his firm footing as the SPARs marched in formation around him. The flag lashed above him, the ends snapping in the air in time with the pound of the marching.

Training had reached the halfway point, and he was pleased with the progress he saw in the women's individual skills and the way they worked together. They had a fine group that would be vital to protecting the home front.

Swirls of March snow drifted across the pavement and curled between the feet passing by. It reminded him of the night Miss Davenport fell into the snow and continued marching without a shoe. Thinking of her made him recall the night of the dance when she'd crashed into him in the most pleasant of ways. How he'd wished ever since that he could go back to that night, shirk his duties for a short time, offer a dance, and talk of everything but the war.

But that wasn't an option, and he, as a captain, shouldn't be distracted by a cute blond with a clumsy streak from a charming fishing village. He also shouldn't be keenly aware of her position throughout the day, like now, third row from the left flank in Lieutenant Plumley's division.

"Captain." Commander Shleman's voice was barely audible over the wind. She approached with a paper flapping in her grip. She tipped to the left with the gust but quickly righted herself. "Message from Admiral Grant, Washington."

Leo took the paper, refusing to let the wind steal it away. Snow crystals landed on the words then blew off. *Ciphers from northeast coast. ER targeted again. Prepare to move.*

New York, Connecticut, Massachusetts, New Hampshire, Maine.

All hot spots for German spy infiltration. Were these threats related to the ones Miss Dyer's team had cracked in Washington a month prior? And why Mrs. Roosevelt specifically?

These questions and dozens more rattled through Leo's brain as his officers inspected and approved their divisions, then combined formations to send them inside. Like a compass pointing north, Miss Davenport's position stayed at the forefront of his mind. Normally, he enjoyed the invigorating adrenaline rush that came with reassignment. This time, he ignored the pang in his stomach at the thought of leaving.

———— ≋ ————

Shirley's cheeks were numb and her legs cold and stiff, but her belly swirled with heat at Captain Webber's intense gaze. At first, she'd believed he was looking at their formation as a whole, scrutinizing areas of needed improvement. The closer she marched, however, she could see his gaze had zeroed in on her, and instead of holding a silent message of scolding, his eyes carried warmth. Dare she presume it to be attraction?

The other night when she'd spun into his arms, she'd gone from embarrassed to mortified. Then he'd looked down and actually smiled, fanning creases at the corners of his vivid green eyes. The shock of the moment had stolen her words. He never smiled, but he had that night. At *her*. His fingers had curled into the fabric at her back a second before he pushed away. Or had she imagined that part?

Forcing her eyes to focus on the back of Jane's head in front of her, she marched past the captain and into the blessed warmth of the college. Once they crossed the threshold, they were given permission to relax and disperse to other duties.

A shiver stole through her as she adjusted to the change in temperature. Thankfully, they'd skipped outdoor drills the last two days with the extreme weather. Today was still cold with a high of nineteen, but the sun was out, and the short bursts of stillness in between gusts of wind made the drills tolerable.

Shirley took off her coat and climbed the stairs to fetch her books, brushing away snow crystals that had fallen onto her uniform. Something caught her attention from the hallway to her right where the superiors' offices were located.

Roxie exited an office at the very end and closed it behind her, hand bracing the wood as if her goal was to close it as quietly as she could. Lieutenant Rollins's office, Shirley believed. Her first inclination was to think Roxie and the officer had a secret relationship, but then she remembered Lieutenant Rollins being outside assisting with the drills.

An internal warning flashed, and she pressed against the wall, peeking one eye around the corner. The woman tugged on the door handle to make sure it had locked behind her, then stuck the bobby pin back into her hair as she walked down the hallway.

Shirley pressed her back to the wall, trying to process what she'd seen. Was Roxie stealing answers to the tests? Rifling through the officer's belongings for something of value? Voices lifted over the balcony from the floor below and grew louder as the other women made their way to the second story.

Shirley took a step away, deciding to ponder Roxie's actions before she confronted the woman. Roxie came out of the hallway at the same time and the women collided.

"Sorry." Roxie looked Shirley up and down, then viewed the large group cresting the top of the stairs. Roxie peered down the dark hallway she'd vacated then narrowed her eyes at Shirley. Joan had always warned Shirley that her thoughts showed plainly on her face.

"Wicked cold out there, wasn't it?" Shirley dusted the last of the snow from her lapels.

"Terrible," Roxie replied. She went through the motions of brushing nonexistent snow from her uniform as well, knocking her name tag askew. Roxie 15752. Her last name had been blacked out.

"I need to go so I'm not late for class." Shirley backed away, feeling Roxie's scowl on her back as she followed the others to the third floor and to their rooms.

A sick sensation filled Shirley, and she perched on the edge of her bed. Roxie hadn't been outside with the rest of them during drills but had broken into Lieutenant Rollins's office for. . .what?

Should Shirley tell? Who should she tell? What would she say? She had no proof.

Alma entered and removed her hat and gloves. She did a double take at Shirley on the bed with her hand against her stomach. "You feeling okay, Miss Shirley?"

"I'm fine, Alma. Something at breakfast isn't agreeing with me, I guess."

Alma frowned. "Can I help you?"

Shirley shook her head. "It's starting to pass. I'll be right behind you."

Alma grabbed her stack of books and left the room, eyeing Shirley one last time. Shirley stood, collected her own things, and headed to her naval signals class, where she'd sit next to a lying thief.

⊱ CHAPTER 16 ⊰

Three days later, Shirley lay abed, drifting in and out of sleep. Her brain refused to let go of the image of Roxie breaking into Lieutenant Rollins's office and knocking her name tag off kilter when she'd collided with Shirley. *Roxie 15752.*

Her eyes popped open and met with the dark. Roxie's badge number had been different the first day they'd met than it had been today. It stuck out in Shirley's mind so well because her home address was 752.

Shirley sat next to Roxie in their naval signals class, which Roxie excelled at due to her time in the WAVES, and she'd been so torn by Roxie's actions and motives that she hadn't been able to look at the woman. She'd stared at the smug picture on Roxie's ID instead, trying to determine if and how she should confront Roxie.

Today, her badge read *Roxie 15732.* The inconsistency had taken Shirley by such surprise, all thoughts of a confrontation fled. She needed time to ponder it all before she made a move. Accusing a fellow service member of deception was a serious offense. She needed to make sure she had a solid case before she took such a bold step.

Alma rustled in the bed beside her. It seemed she too was restless tonight. They'd gone to bed over two hours ago, and anytime Shirley had been coherent enough to think about Roxie, she'd heard Alma thrash in her sleep for a few moments before settling back against the pillow.

Frustrated and determined to get some sleep, Shirley forced herself to concentrate on something positive. Something that relaxed her. Something that made her feel good inside.

Captain Webber's crooked smile looking down at her at the dance filled her conscience. Knowing such imaginings were wasted and dangerous, she gave his image a voice anyway, and that voice asked her to dance.

The music, the people, the lights were all a blur as they moved around the gymnasium, his eyes pinned on hers. She noticed a scar on his right eyebrow and asked him how it came about. He boldly pressed her closer and told her she looked beautiful. They talked, they laughed, the distance between them lessening as his head bent toward hers, eyelids closing and—

A whimper made her pull away from him. She studied his face. A torture-filled sob yanked her fully from her dream. She groped in the darkness, clearing the romance fog.

Alma.

Lights after ten and before five were prohibited, so she swiped her flashlight from her bedside table and shined it across the room as she untangled her legs from the blankets. "Alma," she whispered.

Alma's legs and arms fought some unseen force, and her moans became more desperate. "Please, don't take my mama." Eyes closed, tears soaked Alma's cheeks, more spilling out from the sides of her twitching eyelids.

"Alma." Shirley sat beside her friend and shook her shoulders with a firm grip. Her goal was to wake the woman without getting hurt in the process.

"Alma."

With fistfuls of blankets, Alma's eyes opened so wide the whites were fully visible. "Alma, it's Shirley. You're having a nightmare."

Alma inhaled, her entire body shaking with the effort. She sat upright and leaned her back against the headboard, wiping the tears from her cheeks with the back of her hand. Shirley clasped Alma's other hand. "Are you okay? How can I help you?"

Alma's head pivoted as she took in the room, drooping and bobbing like an intoxicated sailor. "Th–there's nothing you can do for me, M–Miss Shirley." Alma swiped at more tears.

Shirley retrieved a handkerchief from her top drawer and dabbed at Alma's cheeks. Alma took over but gripped Shirley's other hand like a lifeline. "That was some nightmare," Shirley said. "Need to talk about it?"

"That wasn't a nightmare, Miss Shirley." Alma let go and pressed the wet handkerchief into Shirley's hand. "That was just old demons coming back for another chase. Now you go on back to bed and don't concern yourself with me. I'll be fine."

The pat on her arm made Shirley feel less scolded. She wanted to press further, but Alma turned toward the wall, pushing Shirley off the end of the bed in the process. Shirley returned to her side of the room, got into bed, and turned off the flashlight. She kept it beside her in case she needed it again. Sleep was slow in coming and was quickly interrupted by the peal of a bugle.

———— ≋ ————

A train whistled down the platform, blasting through the din of disembarking passengers, banging luggage, hissing steam, and, most of all, Leo's thoughts. He'd received the admiral's telegram two days prior and made immediate arrangements to return to DC. Whether he was staying or going, he knew not, but what he did know was that he'd left the SPARs in the most capable hands possible. Stratton had been promoted to Captain, along with her formidable ally, Helen Schleman. The two women had been practically running things anyway, so his constant presence was no longer needed.

That made him proud.

And left him feeling... He couldn't describe the feeling. Wasn't sure how to put a label on it. He only knew he felt as tumultuous as the storm clouds building in the west.

Union Station was a hub for traveling workers, most outfitted in military uniforms. Leo walked east through the concourse, then around to the main hall. Admiral Grant sat on a bench, head bowed in a nap. His mustache had grown longer since Leo had last seen him, a situation Mrs. Grant no doubt worked daily to rectify. Leo had known the admiral for years, as the man and his father had grown up together. Mrs. Grant's thoughts on his mustache had been discussed at length many times. She'd claim that it tickled, in answer to which the admiral would lean over and kiss her cheek to make her squeal.

He wasn't sure why such a memory stuck with him or why it chose to resurface now, other than the idea of sharing such familiarity with a woman was becoming more welcome with every passing day.

Leo rested his small suitcase at his feet. "Admiral Grant, sir."

The admiral startled with a snort and looked around. "Webber." His eyes narrowed when they landed on Leo. "At ease, Captain." Annoyance dripped from his tone.

Admiral Grant pointed at Leo's suitcase as he pushed to a stand. "You'll stay with us tonight."

"I don't wish to intrude, sir."

"Roselynn insists and has been preparing a feast, so if you don't intrude, she'll see to it I don't enjoy my cigar and brandy after dinner. After the week I've had, I desperately need that cigar and brandy. Grab your bag. You're intruding."

Leo half smiled and obeyed orders, though they fell out of the admiral's jurisdiction. He followed his friend into the drizzly evening, grateful to escape the next round of snow predicted to hit Iowa.

The admiral's car was luxurious and reeked of expensive cigars. Another situation Mrs. Grant was vocal about. They made small talk as the car wove through the streets and parked in front of a two-story colonial brick home in the heart of Georgetown. The streets and sidewalks were wet, but the sky was clear. Streetlamps were beginning to glow as the day descended.

Mrs. Grant opened the front door. "Leonard Webber, I'm so glad you could join us."

He chuckled at her mock surprise over his acceptance of the invitation. She knew good and well he wouldn't turn her down. She and Leo's mother had been friends for over a few decades now, and she was the only one besides his mother he'd allow to call him Leonard.

He nodded as he approached. "Mrs. Grant, thank you for the invitation."

"Oh, stop that." She swatted his arm. "Like I tell you every time, you may call me Roselynn like everyone else. Or Aunt Rosie, like you used to when you were little."

She winked.

He had no wish to return to adolescence, so he replied with, "Forgive me, Roselynn."

She smiled her approval, enhancing her age with a mere lift of her cheeks. She made him miss his own mother fiercely. He would call her tonight.

Roselynn showed him to his room and gave him time to settle in before announcing supper. He dressed for the occasion in a pair of brown Oxfords, a white-collared shirt, and twill pants.

"My goodness, Leonard," Roselynn said when he stepped into the dining room. "Don't you look handsome." She tapped her husband's arm. "I told you I should've invited Miss Hamilton."

"Who?" The admiral lowered his newspaper.

"Margaret Hamilton's niece."

Admiral Grant folded the newspaper. "Run while you can, Leo."

Leo smiled. "I'm quite glad you didn't, to be honest. I've been surrounded by beautiful women every day for weeks now. I'm looking forward to the respite."

Roselynn assessed him as if he were one of her children. "Hogwash, and you know it."

Leo laughed.

She pulled out her chair, and Leo sat once she was settled. "What a gentleman." She raised a brow at her husband. "I guess after forty years of marriage, I don't need a standing ovation any longer, hmm?"

Admiral Grant stretched his open palm across the table to his wife. "I give you a standing ovation every day, my dear. Beneath a flag that symbolizes freedom, I stand for your liberty and independence."

"Very true." Roselynn smiled, a mist shimmering in her eyes. "I don't thank you near enough, darling."

"Nor I, you. Just look at this spread." He stretched his other hand to Leo. "Let's say grace."

After prayer, Leo sliced into the roast beef. Tender and juicy. Each time he sat down to a good meal, he couldn't help but think of his fellow soldiers overseas, battling in harsh conditions, some going hungry. It certainly put things into perspective.

"Speaking of surrounded by beautiful women"—Roselynn patted the corners of her mouth with a napkin—"how are things with the SPARs? I was thrilled when I heard they'd opened a Coast Guard reserve for women. And after meeting Dorothy Stratton, I was ready to sign up myself."

Leo sipped his water. "Good thing you didn't, or I'd have missed out on this fine meal. Best roast beef I've had in years."

"Thank you." She smiled. "It's your mother's recipe."

"How is Mother?"

"She's well. In fact, when I talked to her on Saturday, she sounded in better spirits than she's sounded in a long time."

"Good to hear." Shame, his old companion, rose inside to taunt him. If he'd chosen Pearl Harbor, his brothers would still be alive, and his mother wouldn't have suffered agonizing grief the past two years.

Roselynn passed Admiral Grant the saltshaker. "She's hoping that one of those Coast Guard women will catch your fancy."

"Roselynn, let the boy eat."

She sent a scolding look in the admiral's direction. "I know fraternizing isn't allowed between ranks, but you are a naval captain and won't always be working with the Coast Guard. Then you'd be free to pursue a fine young SPAR officer. It would do your mother a world of good to see you married, happy, settled. To hold a grandbaby and—"

"My mother has Gracie." Leo's words came out harsher than intended. He softened his tone. "Things haven't been the same since. . . I haven't been the same since. I'll get around to marriage. Someday."

The admiral sent a silent message to his wife that told her to drop the subject. She nodded and squeezed Leo's arm. "Just don't punish yourself too long."

The conversation turned to other matters, frivolous things that took every ounce of Leo's energy to pretend he cared after his downturn of spirit. About the time he thought he couldn't handle another minute was the same time he finished his last bite of cake.

Roselynn collected his bare dishes and left the men in blessed silence. He adored Roselynn like a second mother, but talk of his brothers always left him in a foul mood he had trouble retreating from.

The admiral pushed from his chair, a hand pressed into his lower back. "Intrude into the study, my boy. It's time for my cigar and brandy."

Leo followed him, and the admiral made quick work of sparking a fire in the fireplace before collapsing into his leather wingback chair with a lit cigar in one hand and a glass of amber liquid in the other. "Help yourself, Captain."

Leo lowered onto the small couch. The ping of raindrops tinkled against the window. "No, thank you."

He enjoyed breathing too much to smoke, and he'd never been one for drinking. Alcohol dulled the senses, and Leo craved control too much to partake. Though there'd been times since his brothers' deaths that he'd longed to sink into the temporary solace of a bottle.

But it wouldn't change reality. The pain would be waiting for him again once he sobered.

"The threats are aimed directly at Mrs. Roosevelt." Admiral Grant took a long drag on his cigar. "We're not exactly sure why, but reading between the lines of the ciphers, we suspect it has something to do with her determination to bring refugees into the country."

Leo sat forward, elbows braced on his knees.

The admiral took another long drag before continuing. "One of the ciphers includes digits we believe are coordinates. We matched them up with a map of the United States and it landed on a bridge at the easternmost tip of Maine that connects the United States to Canada. By boat, the Roosevelts' home at Campobello Island is only a dozen nautical miles away. The little town of Lubec would be a quiet place for spies to come ashore without notice."

"It also borders the Grand Maran Channel." Where spies had already been witnessed coming ashore. Leo's heart raced. "What are my orders?"

"Go there. Learn all you can. Admiral Hendricks is aware of your role in the raid on Marshall Island. He'll put together a team of his men—and women—at the Coast Guard station in Eastport that you'll spearhead."

The admiral sipped his brandy. "Captain Stratton will be compiling a list of women to transfer to the Coast Guard station upon graduation. Several SPARs were recruited from that area, two specifically from Lubec. If we haven't found the source of the threats by then, I want you to train these young ladies to go undercover."

≋ CHAPTER 17 ≋

The clank of fifteen typewriters firing letters at rapid speed pounded through the room. Shirley was a much slower typist than those around her. Knowing that made her type even slower. She could bait a hook and cast faster than most men, steer a boat through shallow waters without damaging the hull, and extract the meat from a lobster in three quick breaks. Typing wasn't, and would never be, her forte.

They'd begun typing their second week of training. First, they'd been required to type their personal information for practice—full name, age, height, weight, and other statistics using the provided format. Next, they'd been given pamphlets to copy, typing all the information, including punctuation, to be inspected by the instructor for accuracy. A week later, several rolling chalkboards lined the front of the room with information written in cursive, and they were required to type accurately. Now they were listening to a radio report about the war and were required to type as much information as they could as fast as possible.

The report had been playing for at least ten minutes and she was still working on the president's opening speech. Shirley's heart raced as Captain Stratton walked the aisle between desks, glancing at their progress, making comments when needed. She normally wasn't part of the class but checked in on training at times. This assignment wasn't graded, but typing in front of the captain made Shirley's stomach knot.

Captain Stratton paused in the aisle and stood behind Shirley to observe. This was a disaster.

A hint of rose water hit Shirley's senses a moment before the captain whispered in her ear. "Don't try and type from the beginning; just type what you hear as you go along. You're going to miss things, but the goal is to get down as much as you can as fast as you can. Hopefully you'll have recorded enough information that the holes can be filled in later, either by filling in the blanks with common sense, or by comparing your information against the information from someone else's typing. This is one method code-breaking teams use to crack ciphers."

Shirley nodded and picked up with the latest reports on casualty numbers. After the president had addressed the nation, a reporter took over the station and reported the latest news from Britain, Italy, and Russia. At his mention that thousands of Jews had been diverted to German camps, Captain Stratton stilled and leaned an ear toward the radio. Little was said, but with the way Adolf Hitler waged his war, it was doubtful the camps were for the Jews' protection.

Alma rocked in the chair next to Shirley, eyes closed, hand pressed to her chest. "Dear Jesus. Please, Jesus," she whispered. Lieutenant Plumley noticed the lull in sound and instructed them to continue typing.

Once the report ended and music took over the station, the class was dismissed. They were instructed to stack their papers on the desk before leaving.

Chairs scraped the floor. Bodies shifted all around her. Shirley stood and worked the knots from her shoulders. She overheard several women voice disappointment at their progress. At least Shirley wasn't the only one. Lieutenant Plumley reminded them typing was a practiced skill that got better and easier with time.

The paper didn't want to release from the platen as smoothly as Shirley wished. After a few tugs and a little finagling, it came out, wrinkled and smeared. Shirley sighed, causing a puff of hair to move with the action.

Two rows in front of her, Roxie released her paper, folded it into a neat square, and slipped it into her pocket. Cheating? They weren't required to bring anything to this class with them. All materials were provided anew each day. What was it that Roxie had, and why the need to secret it away in her pocket?

She didn't trust the woman. Ever since the day she'd spied Roxie leaving Lieutenant Rollins's office, her every move raised suspicion. She was positive the woman was involved in some kind of deception, and Shirley needed to pinpoint what it was and turn her in. The SPARs had no place for liars and cheats.

Roxie laid another paper on Lieutenant Plumley's desk. Shirley intended to follow Roxie, but Bridgette blocked her path. "A group of us are meeting in the library tonight directly after dinner to study. You're welcome to join us. Bring Alma too, if you'd like."

"Thanks. I'll ask her. See you there."

Shirley walked up to the desk and handed Lieutenant Plumley her paper. Captain Stratton stood nearby and frowned at its wrinkled state.

"I had a little trouble releasing the lever." Heat crept up Shirley's neck.

"I see that." Lieutenant Plumley tried to smooth the paper. "Thank you, Miss Davenport. I'll look this over and pass it to the captain for inspection right away."

"Captain Webber?" More heat rushed in at the squeak in Shirley's voice. How embarrassing for him to see her incompetence.

Captain Stratton lifted one side of her mouth. "Captain Schleman. Captain Webber has been reassigned."

"Oh." Shirley's heart took a dive. Spotting him throughout the day had become one of her favorite activities. Especially the times he also noticed her and smiled. "Thank you, Captain."

She turned away from Captain Stratton's knowing smirk and went to her room to gather her books for the next course. She should've suspected a reassignment after both Stratton and Schleman had been promoted to captains. That was the whole point of the SPARs—for women to fill positions so the men could go and fight.

Stopping at a large window to look over the dull winter landscape, she sent a prayer heavenward that her path would cross with Captain Webber's again someday and that God would protect him, wherever he might be.

She tucked away her disappointment and headed to her next class.

———— ≈ ————

Leo walked the harbor of Lubec, Maine, for what had to be the hundredth time in a week. If there was a threat, he was missing it. All the action this town seemed to get was fishing boats leaving at dawn and returning late afternoon, chimneys belching black smoke round the clock, and children being transported to and from school, bundled like little Eskimos.

He'd come up with a story to explain his presence and how he was looking for a relative who was supposed to meet him here. Everyone he'd spoken to said there'd not been any newcomers. It appeared everyone was a long-standing citizen.

He peered at the landscape again, trying it from a different mental angle. What was he missing?

A fisherman tying off watched Leo from the dock. Though Leo wore civilian clothes, in a small harbor town during winter, outside of tourist season, he was starting to raise suspicions with all his questions. That would do nothing to help his cause. He raised a hand to be friendly, turned, and ducked his head into the wind as he headed for his car.

He had no choice but to train the SPARs who called this area home to go undercover and weed out the source of the threats. He'd hoped to avoid sending women into danger, but at this point he had no choice. Shirley Davenport and Joan Fischer graduated in less than a week, and Admiral Grant was putting pressure on Leo to get the training rolling as soon as possible.

Of all the SPARs to send into the lions' den of espionage, it had to be Miss Davenport. She was smart and she was tough, but was she spy material?

He scratched at a dry patch on his cheek. The hair he'd allowed to grow there took him by surprise every time he touched his face or looked in the mirror. He'd only grown a beard one other time, in between terms, and he never could get used to it. But short of doing something crazy, it altered his appearance enough to remain incognito should his presence be required later in uniform and clean shaven.

Leo crested the hill to the parking lot and pulled the keys from his pocket. The end of his nose burned from cold. He opened the door and started to get in but noticed the tilted roof. He backed away and examined the car from the top down, stopping at the driver's side wheel. The flat rubber molded to the pavement.

He groaned. The tire had been just fine when he'd parked an hour ago. Upon examination, he noticed a puncture in the sidewall, the width and thickness of a knife. He examined the back driver's side tire and found it punctured as well, this time in the tread.

Leo assessed his surroundings. Though everything appeared normal, like it had the past week, he couldn't shake the feeling someone was watching him.

Angry, he slammed the car door and began walking to the small gas station two blocks over. If they couldn't patch his tires, they'd at least let him use the phone.

He'd be lucky to make it back to the Coast Guard station by nightfall.

Something was going on in this town. It irked him that he couldn't pinpoint what.

≣ CHAPTER 18 ≣

The library was blessedly quiet. Groups of SPARs had met after dinner all week to study or browse the tomes and read until curfew. Alma always turned down Shirley's offer to join her study group, claiming she studied better in the quiet of their room. Shirley didn't press, but she had a feeling Alma's reasons went deeper than that.

A copy of *Gone with the Wind* tempted her from a nearby shelf, but Roxie was browsing the titles and Shirley didn't have patience for the woman tonight. Oh, but how she wished to push aside nautical terms, the parts of a ship, customs, and insignia and grip her aching, overtyped fingers around a story she could escape into for a little while.

A letter home was long overdue, and she needed to stop making excuses as to why she was too busy. One, she wasn't sure what to say, as they'd taken an oath not to reveal anything related to assignments or military workings. Two, she was sure her father's disappointment over her joining hadn't dissipated over the last five weeks, especially now that he was short a sternman. She took out a clean sheet of paper and a sharpened pencil from her study supplies.

> *Dear Mom and Dad,*
>   *I apologize for the delay in writing, but I've been*
> *busy from sunup to sundown with classes, training, and*
> *inspections. I'm doing well. Better than I expected, I must*
> *say. I miss you both dearly and*

A body sank into the opposite seat, startling her. Her heart took a minute to recover as she stared at the glorious male in front of her, clothed in full uniform and sporting a thick dark beard.

A male she'd never expected to see again.

She started to stand at attention, but he mumbled a quiet "At ease," so she sat back onto her chair.

Good thing. Her legs felt a bit like jelly, and her brain was so busy trying to compute he was here, sitting in front of her, that she couldn't speak.

He leaned forward, sending a waft of his soap her way. He rested his elbows on the table and clasped his hands. "I need to speak with you. Can you spare the time?" He pointed at her letter.

She looked down at it and blinked. Could she spare the time? Of course she could! The letter was already five weeks overdue. What would another day matter?

"Um, yes. I was just. . .writing home." She folded the paper in half and tucked it inside her book. Roxie stared at them from the stacks, a book open in her hand.

"That's what I need to speak with you about."

"Oh. Am I not allowed to write home?"

"You may."

Fear gripped her. A captain taking time out of his evening to speak with her privately about home. . . "Has something happened? Are my brothers all right? My parents, are they—"

He held up a hand. "To my knowledge, your family is fine." He glanced around. "Can we speak somewhere else?"

Shirley had seemed to garner the attention of every library patron, few as they were. Roxie returned the book to the shelf and slipped a piece of paper in between two titles.

Whatever the captain had to say, she didn't want Roxie hearing it. "That would be wise."

Maybe this private conversation with Captain Webber would provide a good opportunity to mention Roxie and her suspicious actions.

Shirley stood and stacked her things, but before she finished pushing in her chair, Captain Webber scooped up her belongings and led the way out of the library. Silly as it was, she couldn't help but feel like a schoolgirl, her beau carrying her books. To her chagrin, his fast, long-legged stride revealed he was only carrying them in an urgency to find privacy and speak his mind. She struggled to keep up.

The captain looked back, noticed how far behind she'd fallen, and waited for her. "Sorry. Would you be comfortable taking a walk with me outside? It's a tad warmer than it has been. No breeze. It's a pleasant evening."

Her mouth hung open. She wanted to scream, "Yes!" but knew that would be inappropriate, so she nodded instead.

"I know this seems odd, but I need to speak with you right away about a matter of great importance. Lieutenant Whitley will chaperone. I'll wait here while you retrieve your coat."

He handed her the stack of books and papers, brushing his fingers on the back of her hand in the transfer. A delightful blend of goose bumps and desire skittered across every inch of her skin. She hurried up the stairs, reminding herself this outing was anything but a courtship.

Oh, but a woman could dream, couldn't she?

She burst through the door to their room and rushed to the bureau for her coat. Alma, who'd been studying on her bed, jumped up. "What's wrong, Miss Shirley? You runnin' from a fire?"

"I'm sorry, Alma, it's just that Captain Webber is back and he—" The hood of her coat slapped her in the face. She shook her head and thrust her arms in the sleeves, whispering, "He wants to speak privately about an important matter."

"Oh." Alma retrieved Shirley's gloves from the dresser and handed them to her. "That could mean either a world o' good or a world o' bad. How typical of a man to be vague with his intentions."

"You think there's intentions?"

"Now, calm down, Miss Shirley. I have no idea what he wants to speak with you about, and furthermore, intentions of the romantic kind are forbidden among us. My guess is he wants to speak with you about something else entirely."

Relief and dismay cloaked her at the same time. It had to be that something bad had happened back home. "Yes, of course, you're right. That makes the most sense. Thank you, Alma."

Shirley embraced her friend, who stiffened like a piece of driftwood. She hadn't realized how much she'd missed the comfort and support a simple hug induced until now. Especially in such a moment of uncertainty.

Shirley let go. "I'll be back."

She left Alma stuttering and went to meet Captain Webber.

⟩ CHAPTER 19 ⟨

The light of the full moon poured over everything beneath it, casting a silvery sheen on the landscape and the delicate features of Miss Davenport. The air was crisp but tolerable. It would be a lovely night for a walk, if circumstances were different.

Leo opened his mouth to speak and a cloud of breath escaped. "I've just returned from Lubec. Your hometown is very charming."

"Captain, is everything all right? Did something happen to my parents? To one of my brothers? I promised myself I'd be patient and let you tell me in your time, but I can't bear it any longer."

Lieutenant Whitley walked a few hundred feet behind them, as he'd been instructed. Close enough to chaperone but far enough away not to overhear. The sound of Whitley's footsteps clicked off beat with theirs.

Leo flexed his fingers. "What I'm about to tell you is classified information that must remain classified under penalty of federal law. Do you understand?"

Her innocent brown eyes widened. "Yes, sir."

He stopped and faced her. "No matter how much this information may involve you or your loved ones personally, you are bound by your country to maintain secrecy under penalty of federal law."

Her face took on a greenish tinge, and she swallowed. "I understand, Captain. What is it?"

She grabbed his arm. Out of fear or a need to steady herself he wasn't sure, but he enjoyed her touch more than he should, which made his next words more difficult.

He continued strolling to break the contact. "I don't mean to upset you, Miss Davenport. To my knowledge every member of your family is well. What I'm about to tell you, however, may or may not involve them in some way, and I want you to be aware of the seriousness of the matter."

"Yes, Captain." Her voice was fragile.

"The United States Navy and a code-breaking team have cracked a cipher stating a direct threat to the First Lady."

"Mrs. Roosevelt? Why on earth?"

"We believe it involves her work in aiding refugees."

Miss Davenport took a few steps ahead of him before turning back. "What does this have to do with my family?"

Her features were taut, the skin around her eyes and mouth especially so. She was in torment, and he needed to curtail the conversation for her sake, and not raise anyone's suspicions as to why they were taking a nightly stroll together. He'd love, however, to stand here beneath the moon and take in her beauty a little longer.

"The threats are most assuredly coming from the eastern tip of Maine. The code-breaking team discovered coordinates that point to the bridge between Lubec and Canada. Since Lubec is a quiet community as far east in the United States as you can get—and a short boat ride to the Roosevelts' home on Campobello Island—it makes the perfect location for a radical group to form."

"Does this put my family in targeted danger? Do you suspect they are involved? What are you saying?"

"I'm trying to be as thorough with you as I can, but you have to let me speak."

"I'm sorry. Go on."

"This past week, I settled into the Coast Guard station in Eastport. I've been reassigned to work with a team under Admiral Hendricks to investigate everyone and everything in the town as deeply as we can. We discovered nothing amiss. I was starting to think that we were mistaken in believing the threats stemmed from Lubec, as it could just as easily be from a nearby town or island, until I found the sidewalls of my car tires punctured with what appeared to be a knife. Forensics at the Coast Guard station confirmed it."

"Someone was aware of your presence." She looked away, frowning. "I can't imagine anyone back home wanting to do you harm. And certainly not my family."

"No harm yet—simply a warning. And no, I don't suspect the threats are from your family, but what I need to say next will affect your family."

She gazed at him with a mix of confusion and adoration that

punched his gut. That sweet innocence was partly what drew him to her. "Do you know a Miss Joan Fischer?"

"Joan is my very best friend. We joined the SPARs together."

"Several of you will be stationed in Eastport when training is over. But Admiral Grant has asked me to specifically train any SPARs from Lubec—you and Joan—as spies, so you can aid us in weeding out the traitors."

"Spies?"

Pale, she turned away and put a hand to her forehead. A few tentative steps later she let out a wry chuckle. "That's crazy. Joan and I used to pretend such things as children, spying on my older brothers or our parents, but to actually do it?"

She sighed and continued walking, faster this time.

He raced ahead and caught up with her. "I know this is asking a lot from two women who a few short weeks ago were homespun civilians, but your country needs you. Someone wants to bring harm to Mrs. Roosevelt—possibly multiple someones. Only you and Joan can return home and investigate without raising suspicion because you're both local. People trust you. You both know the lay of the land better than anyone—coves and abandoned buildings that would make good places for spies to hide."

Unshed tears shimmered in her eyes.

"You signed up because you wanted to be an asset to your country. It's risky and dangerous. We wouldn't ask this of you unless we were sure it was the best way. Unless we were certain you could do it successfully." He stopped, and she bumped into him. He steadied her by gripping her upper arms and couldn't make himself let go. "Please, Shirley. I'll be with you every step of the way."

Her chin quivered. "You will?"

It registered to Leo that he'd used Shirley's given name as if there were no authoritative rank between them and he had a right to do so.

"I will."

Lieutenant Whitley, who'd dutifully stopped several feet behind them, sniffed, looking up into the sky as a guise. The chilly night air was causing Leo's nose to run too.

Shirley shoved her hands in her pockets and began walking again, head down. "How are we supposed to go back home and act like everything is normal? We joined the SPARs. We wouldn't just get through training and then go home."

Leo clasped his hands behind him. "Correct. Captain Stratton and I are still working out the details. Since the citizens of Lubec are sitting ducks, it would make sense to overtake the town for their safety. Especially since Eastport is so close.

"In the meantime, tell no one what we've discussed tonight. Your duties as a spy begin now. Get through this week, act normal, pass your final exams, and graduate the program. At that time, we'll have clearer orders for you."

She paused and closed her eyes, face heavenward. "Yes, sir."

They turned and began walking back to the main entrance, Lieutenant Whitley now in front of them. The warmth of the building was blessedly welcome. The hallways were empty. When they reached the bottom of the stairs, Shirley gave a quiet laugh. "Won't my brothers be jealous. . ."

Leo smiled. He supposed his would too.

The best way to honor their memory would be to win this blasted war, and victory hinged on brave individuals like Shirley Davenport.

"Good night, Miss Davenport. I'll be in contact." He gave a slight bow.

"Good night, Captain Webber."

He turned and went to his chamber. He rather liked the way she'd said *captain*, all soft-spoken and feminine with the emphasis on the *A*. She spoke it with conviction and trust, which made him want to be worthy of the title even more.

⫶ CHAPTER 20 ⫶

Shirley took her time walking back to her room, every step weighted with the information Captain Webber had thrust upon her. Her life would never be the same. For their safety, she wouldn't be able to tell her family about the assignment. Perhaps Nazi spies had come ashore and set up headquarters there, or someone she knew and loved in her small town wanted to hurt Mrs. Roosevelt.

If that were the case, she didn't think she'd ever get over knowing that someone she trusted had been leading a double life. The idea made the balance of living so fragile, and the discovery would be laid in her incapable hands.

She wasn't a spy. The few times she'd tried to get away with lying as a child, she'd been caught every time. Her facial expressions always revealed her thoughts. She doubted Captain Webber's training could teach her otherwise.

"I'll be with you every step of the way."

Words she'd daydreamed about hearing from him but never in this capacity. Was he going to Lubec with her? How would she explain her sudden presence back home? How would Joan? Everyone knew SPARs were trained to take over jobs so the men could go abroad and fight. There were no jobs to take over in Lubec.

Her thoughts swirled so fast they made her dizzy. She knocked and then opened the door to her room. Alma knelt beside the bed, shoulders heaving in silent sobs.

Shirley closed the door. Alma leaned back on her haunches, cheeks wet.

Shirley rushed to her side and knelt beside her. "What's wrong? Did something happen?"

Alma wiped her tears. "Not to me, Shirley. Not today."

"What is it, then?"

"I's just talking to my Lord. Sending pleas to the Almighty for the poor Jews in those camps."

Shirley sat on the floor. "It's okay, Alma. The reporter didn't say much on that account, so we don't know for sure they're suffering."

"Oh, Miss Shirley. You got a lot to learn." Alma pulled up and perched on the edge of her bed and patted Shirley's hand. "One group of folks don't herd another group of folks into one area unless they mean to do them harm. Trust me, I know."

The intensity of Alma's gaze, the despair in her words, made the little hairs on the back of Shirley's neck tingle.

"What are you saying?"

"I'm not saying anything, Miss Shirley. I don't go back to that night for anything and for no one." Alma retrieved her nightgown from the drawer. "What I am saying is that you need to pray for those Jews every chance you get. Ain't nobody deserve to be mistreated because they're different."

Shirley nodded. Alma's words collided with Captain Webber's and shook like an earthquake in her stomach. Queasy, Shirley readied for bed also.

Alma turned off the lights. She insisted upon it every night when they dressed for modesty's sake. "How did things go with your Captain Webber?"

Her Captain Webber. If only it were true.

Shirley peeled back her blankets, thinking he looked more distinguished with a beard. Though without one, he appeared younger. "He's been reassigned to an office near my hometown. He had some questions about the area."

To her surprise, the half-truth slipped off her tongue without any prior thought. Alma didn't question her further, and Shirley didn't offer any more information.

The sheets were cold against Shirley's skin. She wished she'd left her long socks on. Within a few minutes, Alma's soft snores rumbled from the other side of the room.

Shirley went back over the night's events, starting with the letter to her parents she needed to finish.

> *Dear Mom and Dad,*
>   *I'm writing to inform you that someone in our*
> *hometown has made threats against Eleanor Roosevelt,*
> *and I've been chosen to spy on everyone to find out who's*
> *causing the trouble.*

It was a good thing she wasn't allowed to tell anyone about the assignment. Who would believe her anyway?

Shirley sat up. In the moments between writing her letter and Captain Webber's glorious appearance, Roxie had slipped a paper in between two books in the stacks. Shirley closed her eyes and imagined her exact position in the library to determine where Roxie had been standing.

She shouldn't.

She should close her eyes and pretend Captain Webber had made any other request than the one he had. Yes, that was the best and most practical option. Not sneaking into the library to see what Roxie had left behind.

Biting her lip, she swung her legs out of bed. The woman was up to no good, and if Shirley noticed it, then it was her duty to bring it to light. That's what she'd be doing as a spy anyway.

As silently as she could manage, Shirley pulled on her long socks, grabbed her flashlight, tiptoed to the door, and slipped into the dark hallway. The marble was like ice, even through her wool socks. In the blackness of night, she padded through the maze of hallways to the library and paused in front of the closed wooden doors.

The handle rotated fully in her grip. The wood groaned with the force of her push. She cringed, waited several seconds, and then stepped inside.

The cold space sent a shiver through her. It was eerie to be alone among the books in the dark, but Shirley reminded herself of her mission, gathered her courage, and followed the beam of her flashlight to the shelf where Roxie had stood.

Cupping one hand around the end of the flashlight to dim the beam, she started at the top of the shelf and worked her way down, fingering spaces in between books. Halfway down, her spirits plummeted. Had the person Roxie left the note for already found it? She kept skimming until she reached the bottom and tried again.

A cough sounded from the hallway. She turned out the flashlight and snuck behind the shelf, heart pounding in her ears. It was probably one of the captains checking the lights-out curfew or a custodian walking past. After several minutes, she chanced turning the light on again. Third shelf down, her finger grazed the corner of a paper wedged between two books. She pulled it out. It was too risky to stay here and read it. She needed to get back to her room before anyone noticed anything amiss.

She retraced her steps as fast and as silently as she could. Once she was back in her room, door closed, and settled under her blankets, she turned on the flashlight. Her heartbeat pounded a deafening rhythm in her ears. Nerves buzzing, she took deep breaths to calm herself and unfolded the paper.

Random letters that formed no apparent language filled the first half of the paper.

Code.

Shirley tucked the paper under her pillow, stunned. It appeared Lubec wasn't the only place where things weren't as they seemed.

⧓ CHAPTER 21 ⧓

Leo sat in the chair behind his old desk, now Captain Schleman's, and fought the urge to doze. His train left in three hours, and until then he unofficially oversaw the captains' official orders to each SPAR. They had assigned each seaman a role to fill, decided where best to station them, and made their travel arrangements.

As the admiral had requested, five SPARs who'd trained at the teachers college would be assigned to run the LORAN station in Massachusetts, and six from the Florida training center would join them. One of the women chosen from the Florida center had been Joan Fischer, leaving Shirley to return home alone.

While the admiral had tried to persuade the Coast Guard into letting Joan advance her rate and train as a spy, Joan's skills were unmatched, and her assistance at the LORAN station was vital. After much debate, Admiral Hendricks and the captains had decided to advance another SPAR to assist Shirley and send several others to Eastport.

Leo would remain at the Coast Guard station, since it was closer to Lubec than the naval base. The arrangement wasn't typical, but training and communication would be easier, and he'd be closer to assist Shirley when needed. They were still deciding on which lady should assist Shirley in Lubec, and they hadn't yet told Shirley that the weight of this task would fall temporarily on her shoulders after tomorrow's graduation.

Like a synchronized dance, Captain Schleman signed the orders, then handed them to Stratton, who added her signature and then stamped the official certification. The rhythm of the thumping stamp every few seconds and the suffocating temperature in the room beckoned him to nap.

His heavy eyelids had begun to droop when a knock joined the beat. He stood and blinked, looking to Stratton for approval to answer the door. At her nod, he complied.

"Shir—Miss Davenport."

Her somber expression turned to surprise, then instant alert. She snapped to attention. "Captain."

"At ease. Please, come in."

She stepped inside, and he closed the door behind her. "I'm sorry to interrupt. There's something of utmost importance I need to speak to the captains about."

"Come in, Miss Davenport." Captain Stratton motioned her closer. The women ceased with the paperwork. "How can we help you?"

"Well." Shirley clasped her hands together. Swallowed. Leo went back to his seat and watched Shirley fidget.

"If your conversation is of a delicate nature, I can ask the captain to leave." Stratton looked at Leo.

He started to stand, but Shirley protested, pressing a hand to her stomach. "I've observed some strange behavior from Roxie Brown these past weeks."

Stratton and Schleman looked at one another and then back to Shirley. "It started after one of the outdoor training drills. I was one of the first ones back inside the building. While walking to my room to retrieve my books, I saw Roxie leaving Lieutenant Rollins's office. Her manner was sneaky. She tried the doorknob to make sure it had locked behind her, and then she slipped a bobby pin back into her hair. I believe she picked the lock in order to get inside."

Stratton crossed her arms. "Go on."

Shirley clasped her hands in front of her until her knuckles turned white. "Then I noticed a change in her badge number. I know because it was close to my home address, so it always stuck out in my mind."

Stratton's eyebrows drew together. "Anything else, Miss Davenport?"

"I've witnessed her writing and typing notes in class and secreting them away in her pocket. Then a few nights ago, I saw her wedge a piece of paper in between two books in the library."

With a shaky hand, she reached into her pocket and withdrew a paper she handed to Stratton.

"Why haven't you brought this matter to our attention before now?" Captain Schleman rested against the back of her chair.

"I didn't want to accuse anyone unless I had proof of wrongdoing."

Shirley stared at her toes. "I should've brought you this note sooner, but I was trying to make sense of the code first in case it was nothing. Again, as not to accuse anyone without proof."

Captain Schleman scanned the paper and grinned. "Did you crack the code?"

"No, sir, but my conscience would not allow me to keep quiet any longer."

No matter how many times he heard it, Leo couldn't get used to women being called sirs.

Stratton smiled. "Astute observations, Miss Davenport. You have the makings of a fine spy. Fortunately, for Mrs. Roxie Rollins, you weren't able to crack the code. I'm sure she would've been mortified, as these are secret love notes to her husband. . .Lieutenant Rollins."

Shirley's mouth gaped. "But"—her face and neck turned red—"I thought. . ."

"It was illegal to marry within the same division?" Stratton folded the note and set it aside. "It is. That's why when Roxie found out Lieutenant Rollins was being assigned here, she transferred from the Navy WAVES to the Coast Guard SPARs. Once they were in separate divisions, they could legally marry. They had a hasty ceremony the day before they arrived on campus."

Captain Schleman wiggled her eyebrows. "We've been delightfully teasing Lieutenant Rollins about it from the first day. Though we've tried to keep it quiet. They technically haven't broken any rules, but with Lieutenant Rollins helping to oversee training, we decided it was best to keep their relationship looking as platonic as possible."

Shirley shrank lower into her shoulders until she resembled a turtle. Poor thing. Here she'd thought she was on a mission of honor, only to discover a secret love affair.

Stratton smiled. "That also explains the change in her badge number. A copy of their marriage certificate came in a week after badge day, so the last two digits changed to mark her record as married. A new ID was issued with the new badge number, but they forgot to change the last name, so we blacked it out."

Shirley winced. "I'm so embarrassed."

"Don't be." Stratton picked up her stamp. "It took great courage to do what you just did."

Miss Davenport backed toward the door. "I'm glad the situation wasn't what I thought it was. Good day." She turned and placed a hand on the doorknob, lip trapped between her teeth, nose scrunched.

Leo schooled his amusement. He didn't want to add to her shame, but the debacle was humorous, and she looked mighty cute when she was embarrassed. Like the night he'd found her in rag curls.

She left the room, no doubt punishing herself the entire way out. The captains chuckled and returned to their assembly line. Leo remained standing, debating going for a walk to jolt his sluggish senses.

The stamp clattered to the desk. "That's perfect." Stratton looked at Leo. "That's how Miss Davenport can go back home and spy without anyone being the wiser."

How? Leo waited while she finished calculating her thoughts. Helen signed the paper before her and leaned back in her chair, waiting also.

"A false dishonorable discharge for a relationship within ranks."

Leo let out a breath. Captain Schleman considered it and nodded.

The shock of it sent Leo back to his chair. "There's got to be an easier way. Think of what it will do to her reputation back home."

"Which makes it a perfect alibi for spying." Stratton folded her arms across her desk. "Admiral Hendricks said that your team investigated every documented citizen in the area and all of them claimed to have not seen any strangers. That leads the admirals to believe the threats are coming from a local. No one is going to trust Shirley if she's working for the same government they're trying to overthrow. We need an underdog and an alibi for her being back home when there aren't any Coast Guard jobs for her to take over outside of Eastport."

Leo considered it.

Schleman did too, nodding as she worked the details aloud. "A dishonorable discharge means no threat to the culprits because even if she did discover a traitor, no authority or military personnel would listen to her. And it explains perfectly why she's suddenly been sent home after weeks of training, while she's supposed to be holding a job anywhere else in the country. She'll live at home under the protection of her parents, which would make it look all the more real. I like it."

"I don't." Leo rubbed his forehead. If he knew Shirley at all, and he really didn't, he'd bet she wouldn't like the idea either.

"Yes." Captain Schleman smiled wide. "It's perfect. And it explains your sudden presence in Lubec as well."

Leo shot up. "Me? What do I have to do with any of this?"

Stratton continued with her stamp, prompting Helen to finish signing the last few documents. "Your presence has already been noticed and will continue to be as you lend assistance. Now you have an alibi."

Had he dozed off, fell out of his chair, and cracked his head? This was insane. "It won't work."

Schleman handed over the last paper. "I agree with Dorothy. It works better than any other angle we've tried."

Anger shot through him. As if they weren't asking enough of Shirley, destroying her reputation was definitely going too far. She'd be ostracized. Even once the war was over and it became public knowledge that she'd been undercover, the damage would be done. "Admiral Grant and Admiral Hendricks won't approve."

Stratton studied him like a mother reading her child's thoughts. "Maybe not, but I'm going to suggest it anyway."

⟩ CHAPTER 22 ⟨

In the space of an hour, Shirley was given her graduation certificate and advancement in rate to petty officer third class, followed by dishonorable discharge papers. They were falsified, of course, and documented with the federal government as being her cover for spying. Still, the gravity of what she was about to do weighed heavily.

Shirley packed the rest of her belongings in her suitcase and closed the lid. The clasp protested but finally clicked into place around the burden inside, the sound sealing her coming days like bars closing on a jail cell.

She'd been ordered to return home and tell her family she'd been dishonorably discharged for having an inappropriate relationship with a superior officer. Word would spread around town and reach the ears of any perpetrators, explaining Captain Webber's presence over the past several days. Discharged together, it was plausible he'd meet with her parents for permission to marry and then look for suitable housing.

They were to work together, though she'd be under the authority of Admiral Hendricks. She and Leo were to be seen in public together, and when seen, they were to imply an actual relationship without overstepping the bounds of propriety.

The government could guarantee her continued paychecks, now $126 a month. They could guarantee that her records would be declassified after the war and would celebrate her role as a SPAR. They could even guarantee communication and full cooperation of the US Coast Guard and Navy as extra safety measures.

They couldn't guarantee that her brokenhearted parents would open their hearts and home to her again. They couldn't guarantee that her reputation would indeed recover someday. They couldn't guarantee that her sacrifice would save the life of Mrs. Roosevelt.

But after much prayer, Shirley felt God resolve some of the turmoil in her heart.

He was the One who'd given her this mission, not the federal government or the admirals. He had already gone before her to pave the way. When He gave His children a job to do, He also gave them everything they needed to accomplish the task.

He already knew the outcome.

Though the unknowns ahead filled her with trepidation—she wouldn't be human if they didn't—she was at peace with the job. What she didn't have peace about was the way the job had to be done.

Alma touched her sleeve.

"Miss Shirley, I sense a torment inside you. Have ever since that night you met with Captain Webber. Are you okay?"

Alma's eyes, so warm and filled with compassion, made Shirley's throat clog with emotion. "I'm all right. I sure am going to miss you though, Miss Alma."

Those dark eyes were also wise, observing good and ugly and always speaking truth. Those eyes told Shirley that Alma knew her distress went much deeper than a severed friendship.

Shirley looked around the room, so pristine, as if they'd never been there. "A telephone operator in the Capitol. What an honor, Alma. I'm proud of you."

With a roll of her eyes and a smile on her face, Alma shook her head.

"What?" Shirley asked.

"You're more gracious with your words than any white folk I've ever met."

Shirley shrugged. "No reason not to be." She grasped the suitcase handle and tugged it off the bed. Its weight caused her to bob to the side.

"You never said where you're going, Miss Shirley."

"They've found a job for me at the Coast Guard station in Eastport, Maine. Close to home. Sounds like I'll mostly be filing paperwork."

The first of many lies.

"At least it's not typing." Shirley nudged Alma with her elbow.

Alma chuckled. "Well, it may not be what you'd hoped, but I've no doubt you'll be the best paperwork filer the military has ever seen."

Shirley laughed and threw her vacant arm around Alma's neck. She closed her eyes to keep her unshed tears at bay and inhaled the familiar scent of Alma's pomade.

"You do beat all, Miss Shirley." Alma didn't seem as blindsided by the gesture this time, but she didn't hug back all the same.

Roxie stepped inside the room, tapping the open door with her knuckles. She frowned at the witnessed embrace. "Captain Stratton would like to see you, Shirley."

The women released each other.

"Uh. . .take care, Alma." Roxie offered a tentative hand, which Alma shook cordially.

Inhaling a breath for courage, Shirley followed Roxie down the hall. Along the way, she passed several women she'd come to know as friends, including Bridgette, and stopped to wish them well. Friends who were now storekeepers, accountants, yeomen, purchase agents, and telephone operators. Many of them were scheduled to board trains this very day, likely never to see each other again.

Once they were walking away from the crowd and toward the captains' offices, Roxie spoke. "What time is your train?"

"Five."

"Mine's at seven. I'll be stationed in San Francisco."

"And your husband?"

Roxie grew somber. "He's shipping out on the USS *Yorktown* come Saturday." She put her hand on Shirley's arm and ceased walking. "Captain Stratton told me you found my secret note." She giggled and flushed pink. "Sorry for the mix-up."

Shirley grinned. "It's actually funny now that I know you're not a spy."

Hopefully Shirley's family and friends would feel the same once they realized Shirley hadn't acted dishonorably, that she had been risking her reputation to save the First Lady.

Shirley continued walking. "Congratulations on your marriage. It must've been hard to be separated these past weeks."

"Has it ever. But we'll have a few days together before we have to part again. I'll live with Henry's parents while he's away."

They reached the closed door of Stratton's office. Shirley set down her heavy suitcase, arm aching. "Godspeed to you both."

"Best wishes in all future endeavors," Roxie replied, shaking Shirley's hand.

Shirley stared at the nameplate on Captain Stratton's door, waiting for the sound of Roxie's footsteps to fade before knocking.

The door swung open. Captain Webber's tall frame nearly swallowed the narrow space. His eyebrows slanted above regretful eyes, causing deep grooves in the skin above his nose. His Adam's apple dipped along his snug collar. Before she could even salute, he said, "At ease. Enter."

He picked up her suitcase and carried it inside as if it weighed no more than a leaf. Was he acting as a gentleman or already pretending to be her beau?

Shirley followed him into a room filled with captains.

Her stomach knotted like the soft pretzels Mr. Schmidt made at the bakery back home.

Captain Webber placed her suitcase along the wall and stood with his back against the wood, stiff and still and as glorious as a Renaissance statue.

Captain Stratton smiled and walked around to the front of her desk. "Please, have a seat." She gestured to a vacant chair along the wall opposite Captain Webber.

Shirley sat and tangled her fingers together. The knots in her stomach tumbled around, bringing an ill feeling into her throat. She glanced at Captain Schleman, whose lips always held a hint of amusement at the edges.

"After speaking with Captain Webber and fine-tuning details with Admirals Grant and Hendricks"—Captain Stratton leaned onto the front edge of her desk and crossed her ankles—"we've decided to have you return to fishing and lobstering, while really helping to patrol the waters, of course. Do you own your own boat?"

"I own a dory. The fishing boat is my father's. I act as his sternman. From November to May, he works at the lumber mill in Whiting. At times he allows me use of his boat unattended, but I'm not sure if he'll give me permission to haul pots by myself."

"Pots?" Captain Schleman tipped her head to the side.

"Lobster traps. It's what we call them."

Captain Stratton nodded. "Let Captain Webber know immediately if you run into any trouble using your father's boat. That will certainly make this more difficult as we'll have to provide a vessel and then figure out an explanation for it, but it can be done."

"Yes, sir." The notion that her father would be angry enough to deny her anything nearly had her fleeing the room.

"Communication with Captain Webber has to be precise and careful. We don't know who's behind these threats. They could be coming from a common housewife, a banker, a fisherman—anyone from anywhere. We can't allow any messages or correspondence into the hands of the enemy."

"I understand." Shirley rubbed her palms along her thighs and swallowed down the nausea.

Captain Stratton swiveled and retrieved a paper from behind her. "You're going to communicate in a way the military has never used before. With buoys."

Captain Webber pushed away from the wall, reached for the paper, and knelt beside Shirley. His beard was gone, and she could smell the lingering scent of his shaving soap.

The paper was filled with various-colored buoys. "It's a Morse code of sorts," he said. "Each buoy conveys a different message. A different urgency." He pointed to the writing beneath each one.

He scratched his cheek, which had a fine layer of tiny red bumps. "When you come across a piece of information I need to know, put a message in a corked bottle, slip it inside a lobster trap with the corresponding buoy attached, and drop it at these coordinates in Johnson Bay." He pointed at the numbers across the top.

"Petty Officers Alli McNeil and Mary Rogers at the Coast Guard station have been assigned to patrol those waters twice daily—morning and late afternoon. Lieutenant Bradley Dillon will patrol after dark.

"This buoy here"—Captain Webber pointed to one painted yellow with three blue stripes—"that buoy alone will tell me you're in need of assistance immediately without the need to hide any correspondence. I will come to you at these coordinates." He pointed again. "Then we can converse in person without hard evidence for anyone to find."

Sweat beaded on Shirley's skin. "All right."

"Memorize this on your journey home. Once you're there, burn it."

"What if there's an emergency and I need to speak with you but can't leave a buoy?"

Captain Webber extracted two small strips of material from his pocket. "This number will ring my personal room at the Coast Guard station." He handed her a strip that said *C. W.* and then a phone number. "This one rings the Coast Guard station. Sew them both into the inside lining of your coat, favorite sweater, whatever you choose."

She nodded.

"When you call either number, only say, 'I have the wrong number.' That way you don't alert anyone who may be listening on the line."

Shirley rubbed her forehead. Miss Earlywine, the town's telephone operator, was nosy and at times a gossip, but she couldn't imagine her wanting to harm the First Lady.

"Above all, your mission is to appear as if you're trying to pick up with life where you left off before joining the SPARs. Work, be a good neighbor, go to the grocery store and the pharmacy and church. But always have your eyes and ears open. Put what you know about everyone away and see everyone as a potential traitor."

Captain Schleman rubbed the back of her neck. "To preserve the integrity of this mission, you cannot tell anyone, even your parents, the truth. You're going to be tempted, especially when the shame of a dishonorable discharge causes tension at home. And it will. But for your family's safety and yours, this information stays only with the people in this room."

The weight of it all grew heavier, putting a strain on Shirley's very soul. Using the devil's tactics to save a life? To help her country? Tears threatened to tattle on her waning courage. "I understand."

Captain Webber placed the buoy paper in her lap. "I apologize this situation isn't ideal, Miss Davenport. I wish we could do this some other way, to guarantee your safety and your reputation."

"But there isn't another way." Shirley searched his gaze. Something passed in the silent air between them. An understanding, a connection, a bond.

"I'll be right there with you." He stood and picked up her suitcase. "I'll carry this out."

Captain Stratton looked at the wall clock. "If you'll please wait outside the door, Captain, I'd like to have a quick word with Miss Davenport."

He left the room without another look. Captain Schleman followed and closed the door behind them.

Captain Stratton walked to the window and stared out at the bleary landscape. "'The time has come,' the walrus said, 'to talk of many things: of shoes—and ships—and sealing wax—of cabbages and kings.'"

Shirley waited for an explanation to the riddle, but none came, as the captain seemed to be lost in thought. "Sir?"

The captain shook herself from wherever she'd slipped off to and turned to Shirley. "One of my dearest friends and fellow colleagues in Indiana spoke of that Lewis Carroll poem often. She's no longer with us, God rest her soul." She folded her hands in front of her. "The poem deals with the cunningness in human nature.

"What you're about to do is probably going to be one of the hardest things you'll ever do in your lifetime. You will face heartache. You will betray the ones you love, and you will be betrayed. But you will be accomplishing something very few women in history are given the opportunity to try."

Shirley's nose burned with emotion. "I'm so scared."

"It's never easy being a pioneer." The captain gestured for Shirley to join her at the window. "The world is changing. And with it, the opportunity to show the world we're good for more than birthing babies and cooking dinner and playing the piano at church. All of which are wonderful accomplishments that any woman should be proud of, but we can do so much more."

Shirley went to the window, swiping tears. "I guess our foremothers didn't have it easy either, did they?"

Captain Stratton put her arm around Shirley and pulled her into a hug. The dam holding Shirley's emotions at bay collapsed. She missed her mother desperately and would likely return home to a cold reception.

She must have voiced the thought aloud, as she tended to do, because the captain rocked her back and forth and said, "Often when one fulfills her destiny, there's collateral damage. Just ask Joan of Arc. Madame Curie. Eleanor Roosevelt."

Shirley let out a breath and stepped away to collect herself. "Until last week I didn't even know I had a destiny."

The captain smiled. "Neither did my good friend Amelia Earhart. She just loved to fly like the birds. And because of her, the world of aviation will never be the same again."

"You knew Amelia Earhart?"

"Very well. She was my sounding board and co-conspirator at the college." The captain sighed. "I miss her friendship every day. But the pride that swells inside me when I hear little girls say they want to grow up and be just like Amelia Earhart dulls the pain of losing her a little. Amelia had a purpose, and she fulfilled it." She released Shirley. "Now go. Fulfill yours."

Shirley squeezed the woman's hands. "Thank you, Captain."

"I'd like to give you something someone once gave me." She went to her desk and pulled out a worn Bible. "Carolyn Shoemaker was Dean of Women at Purdue until she passed away unexpectedly in 1933. I was asked to replace her. I found this Bible inside her desk. It was the only thing of hers left inside the office, as if it had been left just for me.

"The tearstained pages, the notes in the side margins, the underlined passages have all given me courage and direction and reminded me I'm not alone. For He is always with me."

The captain placed the Bible in Shirley's hands, the cover supple and nubby in spots. "Now I'm passing it to you. I've made a good many marks in it myself. Let it lead you, light your path, and remind you that no matter how lonely you feel, you are not alone."

Shirley hugged it to her chest. Too fragile to speak, she nodded.

A glance at the clock told Shirley she had to leave if she was going to make her train. "Thank you, Captain Stratton. It's been an honor serving with you."

"As with you, my dear."

Shirley gathered the papers Captain Webber had given her, tucked them inside the Bible, and opened the door.

As she turned her back to the captain and stepped over the threshold, the captain finished her poem. "'And why the sea is boiling hot—and whether pigs have wings.'"

⟩ CHAPTER 23 ⟨

The ride from Bangor to Lubec was long, windy, and quiet. Leo took his eyes off the vacant road long enough to glance at Shirley in the passenger seat. She stared blankly through the windshield, eyes wide, clutching her purse in a white-knuckled grip. Under any other circumstance, he'd think his driving was scaring her, but since the speedometer only registered thirty-five miles an hour and he was an excellent driver, he knew her fear was born of the mission that would begin at the end of this fifty-mile stretch of sea salt–coated road.

He shifted in his seat. "I'll bring your pay each month. Cash. Don't deposit it at your bank. We don't want anyone to notice you're receiving regular payments from somewhere. Stow it away in your bedroom or another safe place."

"Thank you. I hadn't thought of that." Her tinny voice was almost a whisper.

"If there's anything you need—anything at all—let me know. I'll make sure you get it."

"Thank you."

Leo rounded a sharp curve then straightened the wheel. "I know I said it on the train already, but I really am sorry about the dishonorable discharge. I never would've imagined them using this—using us—together. I mean, saying we're. . ." He wagged his finger between them. "That's ridiculous."

Her head swung toward him. Stricken. Her shoulders wilted. "Yeah, ridiculous."

He blew out a loud breath. "I'm sorry, Shirley. I didn't mean to imply a relationship with you is ridiculous. You're young and healthy, beautiful and smart. You have a lot to offer a man. I just. . .wish there'd been another way. I worry for your reputation. Greatly."

She swallowed. "Me too."

He was just as nervous about all this as she. It was just a different kind of nervous. His stakes were much different than hers.

They drove for several miles in silence. Leo had never been one who'd felt a need to fill the quiet, but they still had a long way to go, and his nerves were on edge. The more he learned about the town and its people, perhaps the smoother the mission would go. Besides, if he got her to concentrate on something, it might help settle her down.

"Tell me about your family. Relay as many details as possible." There'd been a million questions he'd wanted to ask on the train but felt it best to wait until they had privacy.

She flexed her fingers and wiggled in her seat. He too was getting stiff sitting for so long. "My father, Winston, is a herring and lobster fisherman. He learned the trade from his father, who learned it from his father when they immigrated from Nuremburg, Germany, after tuberculosis nearly wiped out the town's inhabitants."

"Do you speak German?"

"Very little. My parents used it more often when I was a kid. Mostly when they didn't want us to understand what they were saying, I think. I rarely hear them speak German anymore."

"Your mother is of German descent too, then?" Leo adjusted the gas heater to clear the foggy windshield.

"Partly. Her father was German, but her mother was Irish. I never got the privilege of meeting my grandparents, but I've heard tempers ran high between the two at times."

He chuckled. "I can imagine. Any siblings?" He knew the answer, of course, but sensed her relaxing the more she talked. The more she was reminded that this mission would protect the liberty of her loved ones as well.

"Four brothers. All older than me. I blame them for my being a little rough around the edges."

She smiled.

He'd meant what he'd said earlier. He was madly attracted to her. She was beautiful, especially when she smiled. Her round cherubic face seemed to glow. Like sunshine.

And those thoughts were exactly why it shouldn't be him pretending to have taken advantage of his rank.

"Walter is the oldest at almost thirty. He owns his own shipbuilding business in Bath with his wife and three kids. When we joined the war, the navy hired him to repair and enhance existing ships. His last letter before I left home said he was grateful to help his country but looked forward to when he could craft vessels for everyday use again—fishing boats, sailing ships, dories. His passion."

A day of sailing and leisure sounded heavenly. "I understand. I look forward to the day I can take my boat on the water again."

"You sail?"

"I have a Broads yacht. It's light and completely propelled by air. She's a rustic beauty."

"She? What's her name?"

"*Allegiance.* She hasn't been out for a couple of years now. Been dry-docked where my parents live in Connecticut. I'm sure she'll need some work before she can sail the open seas again. Maybe when the war is over, I'll have your brother give her a go-over."

"If he hasn't tried to kill you by then."

He blinked.

Her lips twisted in an impish grin. "I am the baby of four brothers. When word gets out you compromised my reputation, they might forsake the war and come after you instead."

"Even though my intentions are honorable?"

"They don't know that."

"Then I'll make it clear."

"What do you mean?"

"Your reputation, your relationship with family and friends, is going to take a giant blow. The least I can do to try and soften that blow is to be remorseful and make it clear I intend to do right by you."

She faced the window looking out to sea. "I appreciate that, Captain Webber."

"Leo."

"What?"

"People aren't going to believe we're in a scandalous relationship if you don't use my first name."

"Leo." She rolled it around on her tongue. "Short for Leonardo?"

"Leonard. After my grandfather."

"I'm Shirley, after my father's last words right before I came screaming into the world. 'Surely this one will be a girl.'"

He laughed.

"Do you have any siblings?"

His joviality split apart at her question. He didn't want to discuss his family. He wanted to discuss hers, but it wasn't fair if their comradery was always one-sided. "Younger twin brothers."

"Are they navy men too?"

He swallowed. "They were until Pearl Harbor."

The air in the car went still. "I'm sorry, Captain—Leo."

She stared at her hands, and he felt like a jerk for making her feel bad. "Tell me about the rest of the Davenport clan."

She adjusted so she was angled toward him. "Charles is twenty-eight. His wife inherited her family's farm in Aroostook. Mostly cattle and potatoes. They have two children, a boy and a girl. We only see them once a year around Thanksgiving. Not this past year, though, as Charles was stationed in Europe somewhere."

"Was?"

"He was injured and sent home right before Christmas. Left leg amputated."

"I'm sorry to hear that. I can't imagine."

"He's had a rough go of learning to walk with a prosthetic, but we're all grateful he's alive."

Leo nodded.

"Thomas is twenty-five. A plumber and electrician. He's married, but they've not announced any children yet. They live in Dennysville. He was in Algeria last I heard."

Leo would have to find out the name and number of Thomas's battalion to keep up with the news for Shirley. Guilt kicked Leo's gut. He should be at the front too, not escaping death because his poor choices left his parents to bury two sons.

"Lastly, there's James. He's twenty-four and single. Before he joined the armed forces, he was a park ranger in Acadia National Park. We've always been close. Home was never the same after he left."

He understood well. The family unit was perfectly established and ordained, yet bittersweet in its constant state of motion.

"Sounds like you have a wonderful family."

"I do." Her wistful voice filled the car. "I just hope. . ."

Silence cloaked the car in melancholy the last few miles of the trip.

As he drove, dusk faded into night. A mile from town, she placed a hand on his sleeve. "Drop me off at the end of this street, please."

"But your house is farther on."

"My parents will process this much better if I tell them by myself. Trust me."

"I can't—"

"Please. I know them. And I need. . .some time first. To gather my thoughts, my courage. To pray."

"But—"

"Please, Leo. I'll be fine. I need this."

Everything in him wanted to refuse. However, if this mission was going to be successful, they needed to listen to each other. Trust each other. See to each other's needs.

He pulled to the side of the quiet street and retrieved her suitcase. She closed the door behind her and reached for her belongings with a shaky hand. Leo wasn't sure what to do to comfort her, to encourage her. He placed a hand on her shoulder and gently squeezed.

"I have total faith in you, Shirley. You're a strong and intelligent woman who's doing an amazingly brave thing for her country."

"Goodbye, Leo." Her voice broke.

An elderly woman holding a cat watched them from a window across the street, frowning.

"Hey." He lifted her head and brushed her cheek with his thumb. "I'll give you twenty-four hours to tell your parents and settle in. Meet me Wednesday morning at zero six fifty. Use the coordinates to the cave."

She placed her hand over his. So soft. Then she turned and walked away. The cat lady moved behind the curtain and disappeared.

Night sounds settled around Shirley in rhythm with her footsteps crunching on gravel. She stopped where the long pathway to the house met the road and listened. A buoy bell clanged a staccato beat in the distance with the rising tide. The rumble of waves crashing the rocky shoreline was comforting in the sense it sounded like home even though ominous in its power.

How many summer nights in her lifetime had she fallen asleep to these sounds filtering through her open bedroom window? Come tomorrow her world would be entirely different. Would these sounds ever hold the same meaning again?

Light blinked in the sky from the West Quoddy Lighthouse, signaling any passing vessels to safety. God went before the Israelites in a pillar of fire to light their way at night. Was He doing the same for her as well?

She leaned her head back and gazed at the glowing galaxy above. A soft breeze whispered across her cheeks, reminding her the Lord held everything in His control, even the wind.

Even war.

Oh, how she wished her dear friend was here to do this with her. Joan had always given her courage when she had none, offered encouragement when she needed some, and brought life to dull moments.

Joan had also gotten them into a fair share of mischief, but Shirley wouldn't trade any of it for all the gold in the Black Hills of South Dakota. While Shirley had entertained the idea that they'd always be at each other's sides, she'd known there'd come a day when life would force them to part ways. Joan was highly intelligent, talented, and fun. After whatever secret circumstances caused Joan to return home after only a semester in college, Shirley was happy that her friend was getting a second chance to show the world what she could accomplish. Wherever the Coast Guard had sent her.

Halfway to the house, a creaky door sounded, putting Shirley on alert. "Who's there?" The low growl in her father's booming voice rent the air. Her legs shook. "It's me, Daddy."

The porch light blazed on. "Shirley?"

She stepped toward the house, taking in the large man swallowing the doorway. A sob escaped him. He stepped off the porch stoop, jogged to her, and swallowed her in his arms.

His body shook them both as he silently cried. Her heart broke into a thousand shards. She'd been told she'd have to explain the discharge to her parents once she arrived home, but somehow, they must've already heard.

And he still loved her anyway.

Hot tears rushed down her cheeks. *Thank You, Lord.* At least the hardest part was over with. When it came to her parents anyway.

They stayed locked around each other for a while before he pulled away and wiped a hand along his weary face. "You're probably freezing. Let's get you inside, baby girl."

Her heart did a little skip. She should have known that despite her parents' disappointment they'd still love and nurture her. After all, that's what God-fearing, loving parents did.

Why had she doubted them?

He ushered her into the house and the blessed warmth of the kitchen. "Helen, Shirley's home," he called up the stairs.

Movement stirred on the floor above. Daddy took her suitcase and set it against the wall before he lowered himself into a chair at the kitchen table. Deep lines marked his face around grief-filled eyes. She hated deceiving her parents but felt sure they'd understand once she was able to tell them the truth.

The stairs creaked as her mother descended. The house's sounds, the smells—oh, how she'd missed this place.

Mama appeared and Shirley sucked in a breath. Helen Davenport had never looked rough a day in her life. Shirley's brain didn't want to accept Mama's ratty hair, bloodshot eyes, and deeply creased clothing.

"Oh, Shirley." Mama's face twisted in agony before her arms wrapped around Shirley like a vise.

The kitchen filled with cries, soul-deep and mournful. "It's okay, Mama."

Shirley rocked her mother and patted her back.

A kettle whistled on the stove. Daddy handed her a handkerchief before seeing to the kettle.

Mama wiped her eyes and cheeks, looking fifty years older as she tucked the handkerchief into her shirt pocket. "How'd you get here so quickly? I didn't figure you'd come."

Where else would she go? "I came as soon as I got the paperwork."

Shirley pulled out a chair and sat, filled with exhaustion from the long trip and her conflicted mental state.

Mama sat across from her while her father poured hot water into mugs. "Paperwork?" A knot formed between Mama's eyebrows. "We just received the telegram this afternoon."

The government told her parents about her infidelity in a telegram? If Miss Earlywine took the message, then the whole town knew by now.

Heat swept through Shirley. "I'm sorry you had to learn about it that way instead of from me first."

Her father carried three mugs to the table, tea bag threads draped over the sides of each one. "How long have you known about this?"

"Since it happened." Why were her parents asking such odd questions? Where was the anger? The lecture? The disappointment?

"But. . ." Her father took a vacant chair. "It just happened yesterday. How were you able to get home so quickly?"

Shirley's stomach soured. "I'm home because. . . Wait. What's going on? Did something happen?"

Her parents looked at each other, confused. Daddy wrapped his giant hands around his mug. "Then you don't know? We received a telegram this afternoon that James died in Italy yesterday." Daddy's voice cracked. "You're home on bereavement leave, aren't you?"

Shirley slapped a hand over her mouth. She was going to throw up. Her breaths came in rapid succession.

Mama touched Shirley's arm, chin trembling. "You didn't know?"

Daddy scooted back his mug. "Then why are you home?"

Shirley couldn't speak.

James.

Dead.

Shirley wanted to run from the house screaming. How could they go on without him? How could she possibly add to her parents' pain by exposing her dishonorable discharge now?

⌿ CHAPTER 24 ⌿

Thirty-six hours had passed with no word from Shirley. Leo paced the shoreline outside the little cave, worried and livid. He'd waited for hours yesterday, then sailed around looking for her on an unmarked sardine boat loaned to him by the Coast Guard.

By the time he'd given up and gone back to the Coast Guard station for his car, it was almost evening. He'd driven to Lubec, parked in an inconspicuous area, and walked toward her house to assess the situation. Her parents could've handled the news badly and sent her away. Or, worst-case scenario, she could've changed her mind. Since he refused to believe the latter was a possibility, he watched her house until dark. No movement had come from inside or outside. Furthermore, her father's boat appeared to have never left the dock that day.

Leo had discovered the same scenario this morning, except today, a black wreath hung on the front door. Something had happened, and he needed to speak with Shirley. Now.

Blowing into his hands and then rubbing them together, he climbed the hill from the dock and took a shortcut down two roads to the Davenport home.

A woman not dressed nearly warm enough for the chilly spring day was passing a casserole dish to a woman who answered the door, an older version of Shirley. Her mother, he presumed. The woman nodded at whatever the visitor said and then backed inside the house, scowling at Leo as if she had trouble seeing from that distance.

He waited for the visiting woman to walk away before he approached the house. She walked through the Davenports' yard toward the neighboring house on a knoll about a half acre west. The Fischers' house.

Leo had a feeling his timing was the worst possible and he was really going to regret disturbing the household, but he had to speak with Shirley.

Hands in his pockets and sending up a short prayer for wisdom, Leo hopped onto the portico and knocked on the door. A few seconds later, it opened. Not to the woman who'd been there a moment before but to a barrel-chested man with a bushy mustache and eyebrows slanted inward, arms crossed.

Leo waited for a "Can I help you?" or "Who are you and what are you doing here?" but received nothing but a murderous glare.

Leo cleared his throat. "I'm Captain Leonard Webber. Shirley and I—"

The man stalked toward Leo, forcing him off the portico. Leo threw his hands up.

"How dare you come here at a time like this." Winston's finger stabbed the air.

"Sir, I—"

Shirley bounded out the door, coat in hand, and dashed around her father. Winston tried to grab her but wasn't quick enough. She yanked on Leo's arm and tugged him away at an impressively fast pace.

"Shirley," Winston yelled.

She broke into a jog. "Hurry. I'll deal with him later."

They slowed to a walk once they reached the end of the street. Shirley shoved an arm in her coat sleeve, and Leo held the back while she slipped her other arm inside. Neither spoke until they reached a pebbled beach at the opposite end of town.

"Is everything okay?" Leo flipped his collar up around his neck.

"Oh Leo, it's awful." Her bottom lip wobbled. She stopped walking and turned to face him. "My brother James was killed in battle in Sicily the day before we arrived. I thought my parents were grieving because they'd already heard about the discharge, and they thought I was home because I'd heard about James, and then. . ."

She wiped her cheeks, voice breaking. "And then I had to look them in the eyes and tell them that while their son was giving his life for his country, I'd been discharged for having an inappropriate relationship with a captain."

That explained why her father wanted to kill him. Leo sighed. "I'm sorry, Shirley. I would've handled that differently if I'd known."

"He won't even look at me now." She was trying to be brave and contain her emotions, but the more she tried, the more she cracked.

"Come here." Leo pulled her to him and wrapped his arms around her shoulders, tucking her head beneath his chin. He looked out to sea, hating all over again the execution of this mission.

She clung to him like a lifeline.

"I'm sorry about James." He kissed the top of her head, surprised at his actions. Something about this woman, her gumption, her fragile strength, the way she fit against him just right made holding her, kissing her, as natural as the granite cliffs surrounding them.

An invisible force in his chest cracked. Something shifted inside him, painful yet wonderful. In his quest for justice, freedom, and liberty, he'd closed himself off from life and happiness. His tunnel vision had expanded, and the light was both startling and stunning.

"What can I do?" he asked.

She held tighter. Cried harder.

They stood that way for what seemed like hours, until her grief had calmed to nothing but an occasional sniffle. Cold as he was, he was hesitant to release her, afraid he'd never get the privilege of holding her again.

She was the first to pull away. "The army isn't sending his body home. There's too many. How are we supposed to have closure, to grieve without seeing his body? A part of us will always wonder if they made a mistake."

"I know exactly how you feel. My brothers are forever entombed in the *Arizona*. I know this, yet there are times when part of me doesn't want to accept it."

"How do you get past it?"

He didn't want to speak of it, but the earnestness in her eyes begged him to share his grief so she'd know she wasn't alone. "I haven't. It's my fault they're locked inside a watery grave."

Her lips parted in shock. "What happened?"

His mind went back to that day three years ago in Admiral Grant's office. "My superior, an old family friend, offered to send me to Pearl Harbor. He teased that the tropical climate would help me relax, slow me down from the rigorous schedule I insisted upon keeping. I told him a tropical paradise was the perfect base to send my rookie brothers—they liked being lazy. I wanted to be somewhere guaranteed to see action."

"Oh, Leo."

"It should've been me."

"Don't do that to yourself. What happened isn't your fault."

If only he could believe that. "I just. . .I understand what you're going through. I'll see what I can find out regarding the whereabouts of your brother."

A rumbling sound bounced off the cliffs surrounding them. A lobster boat emerged from around a giant rock and sliced through the water, then disappeared around the other side. Shirley watched it long after it was gone. "I don't know that I'm strong enough for this. Not now. Not without James."

Acid burned at the base of Leo's esophagus. "Without a completed mission, we can't just assign it to someone else and send you back with the SPARs. You'd have to reveal the secrecy, and that would compromise the entire thing. You really would have to be discharged, ensuring your reputation would never recover."

Shirley made a noise, shaking her head. She looked around like a caged animal ready to bolt. To keep her near, he pulled her to him again and looked down into her eyes. "I don't say that to threaten or scare you. I'm telling you, as your friend, the reality of what that option holds."

She lowered her head and rested her forehead on his chest. A moment passed, and then she pushed away just enough to look up at him again. "Why? Who besides my parents would ever find out? Who would know that a relationship between the two of us ever existed?"

He bent to whisper in her ear. "The man on the cliff who's been following us ever since we left your house."

———————≈———————

Rain pinged the glass of Shirley's bedroom window. The ocean beyond was still and empty of vessels. She cocooned herself in a blanket and sat in the chair she'd placed beside the window. Her stomach growled, but the casserole Mrs. Fischer had brought that morning hadn't been appealing at dinner. Not that it wasn't good. Mrs. Fischer was a wonderful cook. Shirley just couldn't stomach the thought of food after the events of the past two days.

She closed her eyes against the bleary evening and remembered the soothing cradle of Leo's arms. The first time she met him at the recruiting station, she'd been dumbfounded by his fierce good looks. She'd nursed a schoolgirl crush throughout training, considering herself wise, and yet she'd been completely blind.

Today, Leo held her as a woman. A woman whose eyes had been opened when the First Lady's safety had been placed in her hands, when her closest brother had been declared dead half a world away, when her lies had severed the family cord. The Bible said a threefold cord was not *easily* broken, but Shirley had proved it could be broken.

That brokenness brought her eyes open again. Like her reason for coming home, Leo's affection today had been a ruse. Even if it had felt real. It was a way to make it look to the outside world as if he truly held affection for her.

Starting with the man who'd been following them. As soon as he'd realized they'd noticed him, he'd vanished. Shirley hadn't recognized him and couldn't imagine why he'd been spying on them.

A shadow moved beside the barn. She pressed her nose against the glass and squinted to get a better look. A man holding an umbrella stood talking to her father from outside the barn door. Her breath hitched. Leo?

Her breath fogged the glass, and she stood for a clearer view. Her father looked up at her bedroom window. The other man did the same. Joan's uncle Ernst offered a tentative wave, mouth turned down in serious lines.

She pushed away from the window. In her time away, she'd forgotten all about Ernst and his odd ways, his forceful actions at the lighthouse.

Dousing her bedroom light, she lay on her bed and stared at the wall, missing the life she'd lived only a short week ago. She missed her refreshing camaraderie with Alma. She missed the naivete of believing everyone she'd ever known was honest and good. She missed Joan.

Above all, she missed James.

Memories played like a reel of film. The time they'd found a seal pup asleep in their father's dory and had taken it home to keep as a pet, hiding it in the bathtub. The time they'd raced to see who could climb their pine tree the fastest, and he'd fallen and busted his head open. The time he'd drawn spots on his skin at recess and told the teacher he needed to go home because he had chicken pox. The time he'd covered for her when she'd arrived home past curfew on a date with Ted.

Ted Lawley. Another young soul taken too early because of this insufferable war.

A need to be close to James overtook her so strongly, she could no longer lay still. She arose and padded to the bedroom James had always shared with Thomas growing up, still wound in her wool cocoon. She opened the door quietly, so as not to wake her mother, who'd retired to bed long ago.

The light flickered a few times as it turned on. Clean and recently dusted, the room smelled stale from disuse. She closed the door and leaned her back against it, memories assailing her at the rate of her tears. How she possibly had any left to cry, she didn't know. Somehow, they kept coming.

After a while, she pushed away from the door and made a circle around the room, touching things James once touched, remembering the noises and laughter that used to emanate from the room.

The items in the closet smelled musty, so she went through his dresser instead. A couple of trophies, a few baseball cards, a copy of *Vogue* magazine with Muriel Maxwell on the cover, applying lipstick in a seductive manner while pretending to hike the great outdoors.

She shook her head. Mama obviously hadn't found that yet.

In the next drawer she discovered a few coins and a notebook. She opened the cover to his masculine handwriting and flipped through the pages. She perched on the edge of his stiff bed. Shirley hadn't realized that James kept a journal.

The book was marked with dates and places and seemed to be about his outdoor adventures. From the time he'd been a young boy, he'd dreamed of being like L. L. Bean and living all the life he could in nature, helping others to enjoy it as well, maybe one day opening his own outdoor recreation store.

For an hour, she read the passages, smiling at his humor, imagining herself living every one of those adventures with him. How he must be enjoying heaven right now—hiking streets of gold, lying beside the crystal sea.

On the next page, she spotted her name and skipped ahead. He was recounting the time they'd walked the eight miles to West Quoddy Lighthouse just after dawn. He'd been sixteen and she fourteen. They'd gone after hearing that, thirty years before, a pirate name Gulliver had buried treasure in a cove known as Gulliver's Hole.

Their quest for gold and jewels turned dangerous when James had slipped on a wet rock, hit his head, and fallen into the cold Atlantic. The heavy pack of tools he'd carried on his back acted like an anchor, holding him under the waves. Thankfully, the water hadn't been too deep in that spot. Shirley had helped him to safety and then they'd trekked the eight miles back home, sore, tired, and soggy.

Despite the dire situation, there were no theatrics. Shirley kept a level head, assessed what needed to be done, and took action. She isn't like other girls, and I mean that in the best way. Shirley is as good as any brother when you're in a pinch and is destined to grow up and do great things.

Great things.

She placed the book in her lap, waiting out the eerie rush of goose bumps crawling over her skin.

Destined to grow up and do great things. She heard him speak it as if he were in the room with her.

Saving Mrs. Roosevelt would fall into the category of great things, even if she risked her life. She recalled what Captain Stratton had said to her on that last day. *"Often when one fulfills her destiny, there's collateral damage."* Shirley knew if James were alive, he'd tell her to fulfill her destiny, to heck with the repercussions.

She reverently closed the book, kissed the cover, and placed it back in the drawer. "Thank you, James," she whispered. "I love you."

Turning off the light and sealing off the room in its small corner of the house, she went back to her bedroom for a good night's sleep. Tomorrow, she would rise early and fulfill her purpose.

☰ CHAPTER 25 ☰

The sound of dishes clattering in the sink echoed up the stairwell as Shirley descended to the kitchen. Her first step on the linoleum floor caused the room to go silent. Daddy stared at his cup of tea, and Mama stood at the sink, staring out the window, as if she couldn't stomach the idea of Shirley being in the same room.

"Morning," Shirley mumbled. She hated that they were heartbroken over something she hadn't really done and wished she could scream the truth. Instead, she upended the kettle and poured steaming water in a mug.

Mama continued washing dishes. Daddy went back to his newspaper.

Shirley scraped the last of the scrambled eggs from the cast-iron skillet onto her plate and added two pieces of very dark toast. She didn't feel much like eating, but she'd need all the strength she could muster in the coming days.

After taking the last bite, she announced she planned to return to fishing, since that was all she knew how to do. Mama gauged Daddy for his reaction. He grunted but stayed hidden behind his paper.

"I know we usually take a break until May, but I figured it best to earn my keep. I'll pay for the gas I use and rent for staying here, if you'll allow me to continue on."

Silence.

"May I have use of the boat, or do I need to purchase my own?"

Daddy folded the paper and set it aside. "That depends. In the future, do you plan to defy me as you did with that man yesterday?"

Mama turned. Soap and water dripped from her hands onto her clean floor. Unfounded shame flamed Shirley's face. "I figured it best to get him away from here before you tore him to pieces."

"I have the right to tear him to pieces!" His big fist slammed into the

132

table and shook it so hard Shirley's fork clattered to the floor. They hadn't discussed the matter since her first night home when she'd confessed their indiscretion. The anger and unanswered questions had obviously been swirling like a tornado inside her father in the hours since.

Pressing her lips together, Shirley picked up the fork. "It's not entirely Leo's fault. I'm half to blame."

As soon as she said the words, she wanted to snatch them back.

"Is that his name? Leo?" Mama asked.

Shirley nodded. "Navy Captain Leonard Webber."

"Some navy captain," Daddy spat. "This is war. He needs to be navigating ships, not my daughter's body."

"Winston!" Mama turned back to the sink, a wrist pressed to her forehead.

With every lie spoken, she was digging a larger hole that would be harder to climb out of. Would she wake up one day and find she'd dug her own grave?

"It wasn't like that," Shirley whispered. "The way we feel for one another isn't sleazy at all."

Another grunt. "That man is not welcome to step one toe on this property unless he's prepared to face me like a man and give me a detailed account of how he plans to rectify this situation."

"Yes, sir."

"I mean it, Shirley Jean. Not one toenail. If the man isn't willing to marry you, then he'd better run fast. 'Cause if I catch him, I'll kill him."

He shot up from his chair, bumping the table with his paunch. He blew past her and out of the room without a second glance.

Mama sniffled. Shirley took her plate to the sink and washed it, expecting her mother to walk away from such close proximity, but she didn't.

"Should I. . ." Mama let out a shaky breath. "Be expecting any more grandchildren soon?"

Shirley nearly choked. "Not unless Thomas or Charles are adding to their families."

Mama nodded in relief and fixed her gaze out the window.

Shirley rinsed off the plate and placed it on the drying rack. "I never meant to hurt you and Daddy."

Shirley took her coat off the peg by the front door and laced up her boots. Her outfit wasn't as prestigious or fashionable as her SPAR uniform, but it would keep her warm on the open sea.

She removed the boat keys from the hook and twisted the knob on the door. Daddy never had answered her about using the boat, but she needed to get a message to Leo.

"Do you love him?"

Shirley squeezed the keys in the palm of her hand. "I do."

Peace blossomed in her chest. She hadn't known the captain long enough to fall in love with him, yet her admission felt as natural as the salt to the ocean.

Mama sighed. "Then I'll start planning a wedding."

———※———

A yellow buoy with three blue stripes.

Leo watched it dance atop the water. This particular pattern signaled him to find her immediately. She hadn't been home long enough to find the perpetrators. Yesterday, she'd mentioned a fear of not being able to carry out her orders. He was afraid what she had to tell him today was just that.

The coastline was too jagged to anchor by the cave, so he moored at a little dock in North Lubec and drove to the cave in a car on loan from the government, one much different than the sedan the criminals expected he'd be driving.

He walked the half mile to the edge of a cliff where the cave lay underneath, open during low tide, and made the short climb down. Shirley appeared from around a stack of ropes and busted lobster traps by the entrance. Her petite nose was red from the cold.

Leo slipped on a wet rock but caught himself. "Have you been waiting long?"

"No." Her teeth chattered. She buried her neck farther into her coat.

Leo tugged her inside the cave, then pulled off his scarf. "Here." Without her permission, he wrapped it around her in a way that should help ward off the wind.

"But..."

"I'll be fine." Dread pooled low in his gut and simmered. "Why the urgency?"

"Can we go for a drive?" Her teeth wouldn't stop chattering. "My father will be home from the mill in a couple of hours, and I need to be home before then. A drive would be good to help clear my head."

Leo looked to the water. "Lead me down the back roads where we're less likely to be seen?"

She nodded and pulled the scarf closer around her face. Her fingers were red and chapped.

"Where are your gloves?"

"I left in a hurry this morning and forgot them. Things were. . .tense at home. I went out to set the buoy so I could have the boat back before my dad noticed it missing."

Oh, Shirley. He reached for her hands and pressed them between his. Friction was sometimes the best heat, so he rubbed his palms over the backs of her hands and then each individual finger. As he worked on thawing her out, she studied him like a curious kitten.

"What?"

A knot formed between her brows.

He smiled. "I'm not all growls and commands. I have a nurturing side too."

"I get the impression not many get the privilege of seeing that side. I'm glad I get to be one of them."

Heat filled his hands too, and not just from the friction. "A short-coming I need to work on."

After a few minutes of warming, they climbed the rocks to his car and drove in the opposite direction. His hands tingled on the steering wheel, still buzzing from her touch.

She guided him onto a side road that led away from the water and dropped her hands to her lap. "I'm going to see this through."

Leo released a breath he hadn't realized he'd been holding. "I was hoping you'd say that." Minus the danger it might put her in. "Is that the urgent message?"

"Yes. And a good test to see if our system works."

He smiled. "We wouldn't have set it up if we'd thought it wouldn't work."

"It was still good for my peace of mind."

She told him about her brother's journal and the day he'd almost drowned at the lighthouse. "He said I wasn't like other girls. That I was destined to grow up and do great things. Protecting the life of the president and his wife is certainly a great thing."

"I agree." The car wound past houses that sat back off the road and around patches of woods that gave glimpses of the water in between. "I also agree that you're a remarkable woman."

He couldn't tell if her cheeks were still pink from the cold or from his compliment. The remark bordered on flirtation, but he found that the more time he spent with Shirley Davenport, the more natural his flirtatious behavior came.

"Remarkable enough to marry me?"

His foot mashed the brake, sending them both forward. "Come again?"

She laughed. "I'm sorry. I should've worded that differently. The connection from my brain to my mouth is still frozen."

He worked on slowing his heart rate and continued driving. She tugged off her knit hat and fluffed the curls that had gone flat. "My father has hardly looked at me the past two days, much less spoken to me, but this morning he made it clear that he's expecting a proposal, and my mother is ready to distract herself from her grief with a wedding. I never expected this to get so complicated, and I don't wish to hurt anyone."

"I don't either. Believe me, I tried to talk the admirals into some other way."

She sighed. "So what do we do now?"

He lifted and dropped his shoulders. "Break up."

She looked at him like he was crazy.

"I can't look your father in the eye and ask for your hand knowing I have no intention of going through with it. And your poor mother."

"It would be cruel to let her plan a wedding for nothing."

Leo thought for a moment. "I'll send you a letter saying I'm shipping out and that it would be best for you to go on with your life."

"If you don't come around, how am I supposed to keep you up to date with what I find?"

"We'll have to meet only in secret. Not make the production of a real relationship like we'd originally planned. My job was to bring you back home, train you to spy, and make sure you have everything you need at your disposal. You're technically under the authority of Admiral Hendricks, so my being reassigned at some point in the future is a real possibility."

"I could lose you?"

"I've always been told I'm hard to get rid of."

"That's good."

He refused to let those two little words bolster his ego. "Besides, the first time we met, you said you knew the best places to catch a seafood dinner. I'd like to see if you were telling the truth."

"A clambake it is then."

"It's a date." He let the comment hang in the air, kicking himself for throwing it out there but enjoying it all the same. "May I request lobster over clams?"

"Absolutely. I'll use only the best bugs from the haul."

He curled one corner of his upper lip.

She laughed. "*Bugs* is our nickname for lobster."

"I guess they do look like giant bugs, now that I think about it."

"It's a date." She angled toward her window, smiling.

He let a few seconds pass before he changed the subject. "We may have to give you a different direct contact now. I'll talk to Admiral Hendricks and let you know. And I'll also let you know who will be giving you your pay each month."

"Where do I start? Are there any leads at all?"

"Not yet. Whoever is involved is very good at covering their tracks. Telegrams are sent and received in the telephone operator's office in a small room at the back of the post office. Do you know where that is?"

"I've never been behind the counter, but yes, I know it's there."

He pulled a paper from his pocket and handed it to her. "Here's a list of all the communication devices in Lubec and North Lubec. Stratton has handpicked two SPARs to take over the telephone and telegraph office—one for each shift—until we find our traitor. They can connect you with whoever you need to contact or send any message you'll need. Keep in mind, though, the lines are public. If there's an emergency and you need to call the Coast Guard station directly, Ensign Edward Geddy runs the West Quoddy Lighthouse. He has a direct line to the station."

"I know Mr. Geddy. He scolded James and me most of the way home for attempting to find the pirate treasure."

Leo chuckled. "Best not to remind him of that."

"Agreed. What about Miss Earlywine?"

"The telephone company is assigning her elsewhere for now. She'll be fine."

"What else?"

"Everyone is a suspect until proven innocent. Use your words carefully so you don't tip anyone off. And don't trust *anyone*."

"Especially charming captains who coax me into giving them my heart just to abandon me and ruin any future chances at love?"

"Especially charming captains."

They'd looped back around to the pull-off above the cave. Shirley placed her hand on his arm. "Goodbye, Leo. Until our paths cross again."

She got out of the car and began walking toward home. He watched her until she was only a speck in the distance. He hoped their paths crossed again soon.

⌘ CHAPTER 26 ⌘

Shirley tied off the boat and walked up the knoll away from the harbor and into town. A week had passed since she came home, and she hadn't come across anything odd or out of place. Business went on as usual in their sleepy town, the citizens the same as always. Though not as friendly to her as they'd once been. Word of her indiscretion had leaked into every crevice of every home, and she had definitely been marked a Jezebel.

The pebbled parking lot by the dock was empty, much like her heart. A few days after they'd planned their breakup, she'd received the promised breakup letter in the mail. She'd always accused Joan of being too dramatic, but it turned out Shirley was just as talented. She found, however, that the idea of losing Leo forever really did break her heart. The emotions she was processing after losing James were still fresh, allowing her to make a convincing case.

She'd not seen Leo in the flesh in several days. When he was near, his firm determination gave her courage, and his smile and touch gave her hope. Having neither to bolster her stability and no leads in the investigation made her restless.

She still grieved for James every moment something else didn't steal her thoughts. It killed her to add to her parents' grief, and their love for her was chipping away in the silence and with every harsh word. Hopefully, they'd forgive her deception someday.

Her stomach let out a mighty growl. Mama's cooking had waned, and Shirley's kitchen skills were limited, so she'd been no help. None of them had much of an appetite this past week, but Shirley's body had reached its limit. Her limbs quaked. She needed food. Now.

Heidelberg Bakery was one block over. Her mouth watered at the thought of Mr. Schmidt's moist stollen. The dense German bread baked with candied fruit and dusted with powdered sugar was her favorite. With the sugar ration, Mr. Schmidt hadn't made it in quite a while. He was a master at sweetening his desserts using other methods, and she was certain he'd have something of value to satisfy her appetite.

She crossed the street and rounded the corner of the pharmacy. Mrs. Downy and her daughter, Betty, emerged with shopping bags dangling on their arms.

"Shirley! How are you?" Betty smiled, revealing crooked teeth. "How's military life?"

Mrs. Downy steered Betty away. "Move along, Betty, we're needed at home."

"But..."

Mrs. Downy continued tugging her daughter toward their car while whispering in her ear. Betty looked over her shoulder, mouth gaping, then went on with her mother without another word.

Embarrassment pummeled Shirley and filled her entire being. She'd noticed the blunted greetings, the way some people looked away when she passed, the way no one went out of their way to talk to her. But she'd never experienced such blatant rudeness. Such open judgment.

She felt small and insignificant. Rejected.

Branded.

If she felt this utterly wretched having done nothing wrong, how much worse would it be if she had?

She continued on to the bakery, passing a boat gliding on the water and two ospreys arguing over scraps of food in an open waste bin. Upon her approach, they flew away, like everyone in the rest of the town.

She wanted to find something to report to Admiral Hendricks. Something to focus on. Something to assure the Coast Guard they hadn't made a mistake in choosing her. To assure Leo he could rely on her. To give James something to be proud of when he looked down from heaven.

The air smelled of brine and yesterday's rain, not the usual warm, yeasty scent that filled this side of town. She climbed the three concrete steps to the bakery door and pulled. Locked. A paper hung from a window to her right. *Closed on Wednesdays at noon.*

Shirley sighed. The rations must have affected the business harder in the short time she'd been away. Her hungry stomach would have to wait.

Shoving her hands deep into her coat pockets, she bowed her head to the northern breeze and turned on the sidewalk toward home.

"Hello, Shirley."

She spun around. "Uncle Ernst."

"Please, just Ernst." The man stood before her, towering. He ducked his head, jittery and awkward. She started to go around him, but he moved in front of her.

"Please." He looked chagrined. "I am regret for my doings at the light tower."

She processed his odd use of words. "You're apologizing for your behavior at the lighthouse?"

"*Jah*. My English not strong. Miss Nelson still learning."

Teaching, but Shirley didn't have the energy to correct him on it or how his teacher's name was Neilson and not Nelson. "I accept your apology."

"*Bruder*. I regret your loss." He rubbed his chest in the area of his heart.

Her eyes stung. His action described it perfectly. "Thank you."

"You go home?"

"Yes."

"I walk you."

Part of her wanted to protest, but she couldn't help wondering if she'd misjudged him. She'd never really given him a chance. Now that he knew some English and could communicate with words more so than looks and gestures, he wasn't as scary. Besides, he was the only person willing to be seen with her right now. That had to speak for his character in some way, right?

She nodded, and they walked down Main Street. He slowed his strides to remain in pace with hers. "What you go to bakery?" he asked.

She guessed he was asking her what she purchased at the bakery and replied with, "Nothing. They were closed."

"*Jah*. No Weddays."

She bit her bottom lip to keep from giggling at his attempt to say *Wednesdays*. "What has you in town today?"

"Letter and gypsy lady."

Gypsy lady? She wasn't sure how to decipher that phrase. He had come from the direction of the post office, so that at least answered part of her question.

"Have you heard from Joan?" Shirley's gaze roamed the area around them, searching for signs of anything amiss.

"*Jah*. She finished learning—"

"Training."

"Training." Ernst said the word slowly, as if chewing to see if he liked the taste.

"Now she's secret job. No talk."

"Ah." Well, that made two of them. How she wished her friend were here to help now. Maybe the Coast Guard had Joan spying in another part of the country. "Does she sound happy?"

Ernst frowned, thinking. "I say, yes?"

Shirley smiled, not completely feeling the emotion. "I'm glad."

She was glad. She just wished she could find some joy in her own life too.

"I regret your home." He stopped at the fork in the gravel path that adjoined both of their properties.

"I don't understand."

He shook his head in frustration. Clearly, he felt stuck between two worlds. "The man. The high man." He gestured above his head to mark height. "He love you, then leave."

Leo.

"I regret it for you."

Ernst was sorry that Leo had used her and left. If only he knew what an honorable man Leo really was.

"Thank you."

"You very pretty. And nice. His leave no scare me."

Ernst had made it clear before she left that he found her attractive and wanted more than a neighborly friendship. He was handsome and kind and just declared that her situation wouldn't scare him off. No other man would probably ever feel that way. Their families were close and had much in common. Under normal circumstances she should give Ernst a chance, even if he was close to twenty years her senior.

But he wasn't Leo.

No man was Leo.

"I appreciate you saying so." She patted her chest where her heart lay beneath, the way he did when speaking of her brother.

He grinned. "Good day, Shirley."

"Good day."

He walked east on the forked path toward the Fischers' home, and she went west. A few feet from the barn, the clouds parted and a ray of sunlight burst forth. Shirley stopped walking and turned her face to the sky, reveling in the magic and warmth. Though she knew it wasn't, she chose to think it was James's way of telling her he was pleased with her decisions and encouraging her to continue forward.

The clouds once again swallowed the sky, plunging the earth in gray. Disappointed, she opened her eyes and strode to the house. She went to close the front door and spotted a sleek black car parked in the trees at the bottom of the steep hill.

She stepped back outside and shielded her eyes for a better view. It was hard to see through the windshield at this angle, but the driver appeared to be a heavyset man. Not recognizing the vehicle, she took a few steps forward, but before she could gauge what make and model the car was, it pulled out and drove away.

The month of April was waning with above average temperatures in the lower forties, a heat wave compared to when Shirley first arrived back home. The breeze blowing off the Atlantic was still cold, but her work wasn't as miserable as before.

Ripples reflected the sunlight, making the ocean a blanket of sparkling diamonds. The air was salty and fishy but fresh. She reeled in the rope until her arms burned and the lobster pot breached the surface with a splash. The long-handled hook was easily guided into the pot, and she hoisted it into the boat.

There were no bugs inside, which she expected since she hadn't placed any bait to attract them. The glass bottle she used to hold messages rolled from side to side as she placed the pot on the coaming. Though she was the only person in a mile of open sea, she still looked around before uncorking the bottle and reading the message in Leo's familiar handwriting.

Local authorities have been notified of suspicious car with your description. Be careful. Waters dangerous. American ship narrowly missed a torpedo off Halifax harbor.

Today was Friday. Leo must've placed this in the bottle after she'd left her message yesterday morning. She didn't have anything to report other than the car watching her from the trees.

Water splashed the deck as she lowered the pot. She went inside the small cabin to retrieve a paper and pencil and scribbled the only change she'd noticed since arriving home—the bakery now closing at noon on Wednesdays.

She folded the paper and tucked it inside the bottle, pressed the cork in firmly, and returned to the deck to put it inside the trap. The same buoy would be sufficient, since there was nothing urgent to report.

She wished she could see Leo in person so he could tease her about calling lobster traps *pots* and lobsters *bugs*. She could still hear the deep rumble in his laugh when she'd explained her vocabulary in the cave the day he'd met her to explain that in future she was to report directly to Admiral Hendricks and Captain Cook. Leo would be phasing out of the mission at some point in the future, and the thought made her melancholy. She enjoyed his company more than she had any man's, and she counted it a privilege to glimpse the softer man that lay beneath his tough outer shell.

Daydreaming about her favorite captain, however, and woolgathering about a life that would never be wouldn't help put food on the table, so she lowered the pot and watched it sink beneath the water. Once the rope was taut and the buoy was once again floating on the waves, she spent the rest of her morning hauling pots and collecting bugs, setting the pots in new areas when needed.

By the time the sun was high in the west, she approached the northeastern tip of Johnson Bay. Popes Folly was the last island before crossing into Canadian waters. For decades, the two countries debated who owned the little island, causing trap wars and cut lines. Even now, some fishermen made trouble for the other side. Lubec fishermen were strategic in their trap placement around the land mass, but the trap wars had never stopped any of them from using the area altogether.

She skirted the cove on the southern tip, driving carefully through the buoys. A rope in her rudder wouldn't do her or the fisherman who owned it any good. She slowed to a near crawl to avoid scraping bottom in the shallow water.

A flash of yellow snagged her attention from the rocks surrounding the shore. She retrieved her binoculars and set the color within her sight. It looked flimsy yet weighty, and something thrashed within its grasp. She let the motor idle as she watched the material move, splashing water at its base, and then still. Something was trapped, and she prayed it wasn't a person.

No other boats were around. Whatever the yellow mass was in the rocks hadn't been there two days ago when she'd set the traps. Whatever was captured may not live much longer if she didn't intervene.

She set the anchor and lowered the small dinghy that was tied to the washboard. The water was calm, which would make getting ashore easier. She pushed off the side of the boat, rowed to a sandbar, and climbed out. The dinghy slid through the mucky sand as she heaved it far enough inland it couldn't escape. She backtracked to the yellow material, her boots unsteady on the slippery, mucky shore.

Approaching carefully, she knelt beside the rubbery material to assess the moving object inside. "Hello? I'm here to help."

More thrashing but no one answered. After determining it was best to unfold and peel back the material, she worked the heavy thing farther inland. Ropes and straps revealed themselves with each pull.

An inflatable raft. Well, inflated at one time anyway.

The thrashing grew stronger. A fin flopped back and forth, and she dropped the raft to find a small seal captured within the ropes. "Hey, there. It's okay."

The seal's eyes grew larger, revealing the whites. Blood marked nearby rocks where they'd beat the poor animal as it tried to escape. She reached inside her jacket for the knife she carried when hauling pots in case she needed to cut a tangled rope.

She spoke to the harbor seal in soothing tones. As if it knew she was there to help, it calmed enough to allow her to slip her hand between its body and the rope while she sawed. She hoped it would live. It was pretty battered but still had plenty of strength.

With one last slice through the rope, it released its hold on the seal, who blinked twice before rolling over and flopping the few feet it needed to fully submerge into the water. It slipped beneath the waves like the majestic creature it was.

About the raft. . .

Shirley assessed her surroundings. She knew for certain it hadn't been here two days ago because she'd traveled the entire west side to the island. How had it gotten here? Who was crazy enough to travel these testy waters in an inflatable device among so many jagged rocks? Was the person stranded on the island, or had they been rescued?

The end of the raft bore a giant hole. A clean slash, as if it had been pierced and ripped by a knife. The raft had also been bundled and shoved between the rocks, but with yesterday's high winds and the tide last night, the raft had probably unfolded just enough to be a hazard to the seal, who'd let his curiosity over the bright yellow material cause him harm.

If someone was stranded on the island, now was their chance to leave with her or they might never leave.

For the next hour, she walked the perimeter of the island, calling out to whoever may be there, looking for signs of another human. Nothing.

Her foot sank and she almost fell over. A perfect boot print molded to the dirt that had recently been stirred. The soil was darker in this spot than anywhere else around it.

Someone had dug here.

The island was mostly rock, making digging nearly impossible. Why here? What had they buried?

A stick snapped behind her, and she jumped. A bird looked down at her, then flew away. The back of her neck prickled, and her inner voice told her it was time to leave. Something about this whole scenario wasn't right. She needed to leave a message for Leo, but if she went back to their contact point in Johnson's Bay, she wouldn't make it home before dark.

Acting as if she hadn't noticed anything amiss, in case she was being watched, she shrugged, returned to her dinghy, and rowed back to the boat. Once aboard, she inspected the boat for any intruders, then retied the dinghy to the washboard. It wasn't until she was a few nautical miles from home that she released her breath and thanked God for His protection.

☰ CHAPTER 27 ☰

Shirley pulled away from the lobster pound, moored the boat, then hopped over the side onto the dock. Her boots made a squishy noise as they hit the wood. She assessed her appearance. Fishy-smelling overalls, mucky rubber boots that went up to her knees, an oversized coat that had seen better days, and she was certain her curls had grown wild in the windy, salty air.

She should go home and change before she contacted Leo. The postmistress and anyone else Shirley would encounter would appreciate it, she was sure. If she took the time to do that, however, it was likely the post office would close before she got a chance to get her message to the undercover SPAR switchboard-and-telegraph operator.

At least needing to do something about how she smelled, she shed the coat and left it in the cabin and exchanged her rubber boots for her lace-up ankle boots. The cold walk to the post office would do her good anyway and hopefully aerate her overalls.

The town hummed with action. Cars traveled on the streets, women and children bustled along the sidewalks, and the bell buoys clanged in the distance. Some acquaintances were polite enough to nod at her; others offered dirty looks or ignored her altogether. She'd once heard Eleanor Roosevelt say that often during times of disaster, people showed their true colors. At the time, Shirley hadn't really thought through what that had meant. Now she understood.

Now she felt it.

The kaleidoscope of colors her world once held wasn't as bright and lovely as before.

She opened the door to the post office at the same time Mr. Applegate was stepping out. She stepped aside and held the door for him, bracing herself for a rejection. The man looked up from the letters in his hand, right into her eyes, and smiled.

The kind and simple gesture made her want to cry.

"Hello, Shirley."

"Good afternoon, Mr. Applegate."

"I sure am thankful to your dad for letting my boy ride with him to the mill every day."

A woman Shirley didn't recognize wanted to enter, so Mr. Applegate shuffled out of her way, apologizing to the woman as he did so.

"He's happy to do so," Shirley said. At least she figured her father was. He still wasn't speaking more than a handful of words to her.

He pointed the letters in front of them, clueing her to walk with him. "My deepest condolences for the loss of your brother."

Air left Shirley's lungs like a punch to her stomach. The grief never fully left her, but it dulled at times. Then in times like these, it came back to rob her again.

Before she could offer her thanks, he continued. "Losing a child is never easy."

Staring out to sea, she recalled that his son, Mark, had drowned during a dare to see which boy in his class was brave enough to walk to the end of the breakwater during a storm. A swell had taken him by surprise, and he'd washed ashore a few hours later.

Mark had been in her brother Charles's class, barely fifteen years old, and the entire town had mourned the loss of one so young.

"I never had a daughter." He scratched the white scruff on his cheek. "So maybe I'm out of line to say this."

Her stomach cramped. "It's okay to speak your mind, Mr. Applegate. Everyone else has." Her last words came out at a near whisper.

Wind stirred his thin puff of hair. "Your father was telling me the other day how he was grieving for two children. One who'd never live under his roof again but whose legacy would live on, and one who lived under his roof whose legacy would anchor her for the rest of her life."

She turned away, tears pricking her eyes.

Mr. Applegate threaded his arm through hers, catching the attention of old Widow Sutherland and earning them a bulldog scowl.

They stepped off the sidewalk, and he tipped to the side. She yanked on his arm to right him. He patted her hand and continued shuffling to his car. "I told your father he was a fool."

Stunned, Shirley stopped in the middle of the road and faced him. He cleared his throat. "I've known you since you were the size of a sardine. Now I know people make mistakes, but you're a smart girl, Shirley Davenport. I told your father you weren't foolish enough to get kicked out of the military on account of some smooth-talking captain. I told him to look a little harder before he put you and your future out to pasture."

She swallowed. Was she so poor a spy she was that obvious? Or was he part of the threat and onto her game? Leo had said to trust no one.

A horn honked, and she jumped. Mr. Applegate waved an apology, and they walked the remaining short distance to his car. Shirley opened his door. His gray eyes assessed her beneath thin, droopy eyelids. "Am I right, Shirley girl, or am I an optimistic old fool?"

Mr. Applegate was too genuine to be a threat. Still, she couldn't reveal anything for the sake of the mission and for his safety.

She placed her hand over his thin, wrinkled one. "Thank you for your faith in me."

He winked, as if knowing she couldn't say more. She waited to close the door while he eased behind the steering wheel, and waved as he backed out of the parking space and drove away.

His words stuck with her as she walked back to the post office and waited at the counter for Miss Middleton to assist her. The movement of bins and wheels echoed from the room behind the counter. A post office box clanked closed. Ernst rounded the corner, a stack of letters in his hand.

His smile was warm. "The day is good, Shirley."

She chuckled. "Yes, it is a good day."

Surprisingly, she meant every word. Ever since she'd arrived home, her days had been filled with challenges to overcome and sadness to carry. Today was the first actual good day she'd had since stepping off the train.

Minus the discovery of the raft and the feeling someone had been watching her.

Ernst shifted his weight from one foot to the other. "Will you eat tomorrow night?"

"I'm sure I will."

"I know you must miss your lover, but I wonder if you will eat tomorrow night. With me."

Her lover? Heat scorched her face.

Of course, Miss Middleton would pick that moment to walk to the counter. Scowling. "May I help you?"

Shirley looked at her feet and closed her eyes in mortification.

"A letter to mail, please."

Shirley opened her eyes to see the letter Ernst pulled from the stack in his hands addressed to Germany. Probably a letter to a relative back home. But. . .was that Joan's handwriting?

She stood on her toes for a better look, which earned her another scowl from Miss Middleton. The woman whisked it away to a bin of outgoing letters before Shirley could blink.

The spinster returned and stood at the counter, staring at Shirley with eyebrows arched. The woman didn't like Shirley before she joined the SPARs, but now she seemed thoroughly disgusted with her.

For kicks, Shirley gave Mrs. Middleton her sweetest smile. "I'd like to send a telegraph, please."

"The operator is currently out. You'll have to come back tomorrow."

Tomorrow?

Shirley opened her mouth to protest, but the woman cut her off. "We close in two minutes. Is there anything else you need?"

"No, ma'am." Shirley bit back her frustration. She needed to tell the captain about the raft on Popes Folly, but she couldn't call him from her home phone without the neighbors listening in. She'd have to use the phone at the West Quoddy Lighthouse instead.

Shirley left the building frustrated and mortified. Miss Middleton was the champion of town gossip. By dinnertime, everyone in a three-mile radius would hear that poor Shirley Davenport had been abandoned by one lover just to take up with the next.

"Shirley, wait."

She slowed her steps so as not to be rude. Miss Middleton's treatment was a slap in the face to the integrity Mr. Applegate believed she had. How finicky the human race could be.

"I regret my talk," Ernst said. "I still learning."

In some ways he was like a giant, helpless child, and as always with children, Shirley couldn't stay mad. "It's not your fault, Ernst. The people in this town have made up their minds about me, and it wouldn't matter what anyone said. People like Miss Middleton don't change their minds."

"I am im–imbecile."

"No, you're not. I am."

"I know you are broken. I broken as well."

She wished she'd brought her coat after all. The air was getting colder now that the sun was beginning to descend. "Is that why you came to America?"

He nodded. "Wife die in '39. Murdered by Gestapo for helping Jewish family feed their children."

And here Shirley was foolish enough to think she had problems. "Oh, I'm so sorry."

"Some hate for good reason." He pointed to himself. "Some hate for bad reason." He pointed to her. "No government treat everyone fair. Someone always loses."

Shirley was taught there was never a good reason to hate, but she supposed hating the Gestapo and corrupt government was good reason if there was one.

"You young and pretty. I know I much older, but I provide good. I like to provide dinner tomorrow."

Shirley's stomach clenched. She didn't want to hurt Ernst after the horror he'd been through or offend the Fischers by turning him down. She couldn't start a relationship with anyone right now, and when she did, she wanted it to be with Captain Webber. Which would never happen.

"I—" A female voice called out Shirley's name. She peeked around Ernst and squealed as Alma jogged toward them. Why wasn't she in Washington?

Shirley jogged to close the distance. "Alma!"

Alma threw up her palms. "I'm sorry, ma'am. I'm not sure who Alma is. I'm Gypsy Rose, one of the new telephone operators. I overheard you tell Miss Middleton you was needin' my help."

Shirley truly was the imbecile. Leo had told her that they were sending a SPAR as an operator to screen telephone calls and telegraph messages. It made sense that was the only reason Alma was in Lubec, and that she'd go by an alias. Here she'd thought Ernst had been talking about an actual gypsy the last time they'd spoken. Alma had been here the whole time.

"I apologize, Gypsy. Yes, I needed to send a telegram." Ernst stood waiting with his hands in his pockets. "I'm trying to find information on my deceased brother's whereabouts."

She hated using James as an excuse, but it was the only thing she could come up with on such short notice.

Alma—Gypsy frowned. "My condolences, ma'am." She handed Shirley a small pad of paper to write on and a pencil. "Write down the receiver's information and what you'd like to say, and I'll bring a bill round tomorrow morning. I's getting ready to shut down for the day, but I can send this before I leave."

"I'm grateful." And amazed at how Alma had altered her speech to play the part.

Shirley scratched out her message about the raft and its location in as few words as possible. Below, she wrote down her address and handed the pad back to Alma.

"Thank you, ma'am. I'll see you tomorrow."

Thankfully, Ernst had started home without Shirley. Several feet ahead, he walked with his hands in his pockets, shoulders hunched.

A broken man.

In a world full of brokenness, Shirley had an opportunity to make something right. She just had to figure out who in this town was playing her for the fool.

⚡ CHAPTER 28 ⚡

A German spy.

Leo fingered the yellow rubber raft, beaten and shredded into several pieces by the recent storm. Frost dusted the island of Popes Folly. It had been close to twenty-four hours since Shirley'd seen the raft. By the time Leo had gotten her message from Petty Officer Alma Evans and he'd rounded up his team, it had been dark. Admiral Hendricks had ordered them to wait until dawn. By that time, if the spy had still been on the island, they'd fled.

"What do you think?" Lieutenant Clanton snapped a picture with his Speed Graphic. The photo would later be developed and logged as evidence.

"I think we're about four days too late." A splash of water soaked Leo's shoe. "The spy must've come ashore the same night the U-boat attempted fire on the *Neal*."

"We've searched the entire island, and no one is here. Where do you think he went?"

Leo stood and gazed out at the swells. Popes Folly wasn't far from Lubec, but it was closer to New Brunswick, where the Roosevelts owned a retreat home on Campobello Island. Either place was too far to swim. With a disabled raft, how would the spy have traveled?

"I don't know. Alert the authorities in Lubec. Also, alert Edward Geddy. Tell him to be extra vigilant at night and to notify us immediately if he sees anything suspicious."

Leo had met Edward on his first trip to Lubec. The man was not only a steadfast lightkeeper but also a Coast Guard officer, inducted before the war when the Lighthouse Service dissolved. It was either continue to serve as lightkeeper as a civilian or join the Coast Guard.

Edward joined the Coast Guard.

The lieutenant nodded.

Leo pressed his chapped lips together to quell the burning. "Alert the Canadian Coast Guard as well. The spy could be anywhere."

With a cold, soggy shoe, Leo walked to the other side of the island, Lieutenant Clanton close behind. Thank God Shirley had noticed the raft when she had. The knowledge that a German spy could be on US soil and anywhere near his Shirley made his blood boil.

His Shirley? The notion hit him so hard his feet stopped moving. Lieutenant Clanton almost plowed into him. "Sorry, Captain."

When had Leo come to think of her as *his*?

The idea was ludicrous. Yet it unlocked something inside him. Something raw and as natural as God's creation.

"You okay, Captain?"

"Yeah, just thinking."

Leo continued the journey to the Coast Guard officers who were examining the hole Shirley had found. Shovels lay around the three-foot hole and a pile of disturbed earth. "Any luck, Captain?"

Leo knelt beside Captain Baldwin.

Captain Baldwin handed Leo a handheld radio and pointed to a charred German naval uniform. Leo bit back a curse. The faded yellow embroidered eagle with outstretched wings above a swastika sealed their suspicions.

Where was the dirty spy?

Breakfast roiled in Leo's gut. He needed to tell Shirley and offer her extra protection.

Now.

———————≈———————

Shirley buttoned her dress and slipped into her cardigan sweater. The rayon dress fit against her just right, its cream-colored fabric splashed with lavender, yellow, and olive flowers. The print was pure spring, perfect for the sunny, if chilly, Easter morning.

She hadn't been able to resist purchasing the dress she'd seen in the window of Freese's Fashions when she'd gone with Mama to Ellsworth to volunteer to sort and pack Armed Services Editions paperbacks for the soldiers overseas. The print was small but would allow them to carry the books in their pockets.

She shouldn't have left town for two days, but her parents hadn't given her any choice. Shirley had provided Alma the phone number to where they were staying. Truthfully, with everything that had transpired since she'd arrived home, she needed a short getaway.

Mama had questioned Shirley's wisdom in buying such an expensive outfit with no real means of supporting herself, especially when such a pretty dress would only draw attention to herself. Shirley's ability to support herself had never been an issue before Shirley had joined the SPARs. After making a "mistake" that left her husbandless, it was suddenly a subject that came up daily.

Daddy yelled her name up the stairs. She shoved her feet into her new nude-colored heels and descended to the first floor. Alma stood in the kitchen, her mouth twisted in frustration.

Daddy put his hands on his hips. "This lady has a telegram for you. Claims she can't drop it off, that she has to hand it to you personally. Official military business."

He spat the last sentence, no doubt believing it was either in regard to her dishonorable discharge or Captain Webber contacting her for another tryst. Shirley held out her hand. "Thank you, Gypsy."

It was scary how easily the lies rolled off her tongue these days. She opened the envelope and pulled out the paper.

WQL today—stop.

It must be urgent if Leo was summoning her on Easter morning. "May I use the car, please?"

"Absolutely not." Daddy gripped the back of a chair, his tie askew.

Having delivered the telegram, Alma let herself out.

"Please, Daddy. It's urgent."

Mama came into the kitchen, her slippers shuffling on the floor. "What's going on?"

"Your daughter wants to use the car to meet up with her deadbeat captain."

Mama's mouth fell open.

"The telegram isn't from Leo," Shirley snapped, then blushed at the casual use of his name. "Banished or not, I still have a few friends in the Coast Guard. I asked them to help us find any information they could on James. I'm trying to bring him home."

"Shirley," Mama breathed, a hand pressed to her stomach. "They said they'd buried him overseas. Do you think there's a chance they'll send my boy home?"

Shirley folded the telegram and tucked it into her pocket, hating herself for the lie. "I'll walk to the dock for a ferry to Eastport if I have to, though I'd prefer to drive."

Mama grabbed Daddy's arm with her other hand and looked at him with desperate eyes. "Winston, please."

Daddy remained silent, studying Shirley with an icy expression. Guessing she wasn't going to get a response, Shirley walked to the front door and pulled her dressy trench coat off the hook and put it on.

"Take the keys." Daddy's defeated voice sounded behind her. "We'll walk to church."

She met Daddy's gaze. A broken man. "Thank you."

"What are you about, Shirley?"

"What do you mean?"

"Someone said something to me the other day that I can't get out of my mind. The more I think about it, the more none of this makes sense. The more it makes perfect sense. I don't know what to think anymore."

He ran a giant hand down his face and neck, knocking his tie loose.

Shirley approached and straightened it for him, holding the tip to keep some connection to her family that was quickly slipping away. "Eleanor Roosevelt once said, 'Do one thing every day that scares you.' Sometimes that entails coming to reality with the bad, and sometimes it's choosing to believe in the good, even when it doesn't make sense."

She stood on tiptoe and kissed his rough cheek, then took the keys off the hook and closed the door behind her.

⧉ CHAPTER 29 ⧉

"Captain Webber, would you like to join me for coffee?"

Leo stopped pacing long enough to acknowledge Mrs. Geddy, the light-keeper's wife. He must've looked as helpless as he felt because she smiled as if she'd just read all his secrets and found them amusing. "No, thank you."

"Are you sure?" She held out a mug. "The ration has finally ended, and if you don't stop marching back and forth in front of those windows, you're going to wear holes in my new rug."

Smothering a growl, he reached for the mug.

"She'll be here, Captain."

"It's been hours."

She looked at her pocket watch. "Not quite two."

Defeated, he blew out a breath. "I'm sorry."

"Don't be." She smiled, deepening the lines aging her face. "You should never be sorry for love."

"Love? Who said anything about love?" He sipped the coffee and winced as it burned his tongue.

"Your reputation precedes you. Captain Webber is known for being direct, hard, and getting the job done. A man who keeps cool under pressure."

He drank more, knowing it would hurt. If anything, just to punish himself for being such an obvious idiot.

"Seeing as your expected guest is a young lady, and you're—forgive me, but you're a mess—I wager it's because your heart is involved."

He turned back to the breathtaking view of the Grand Maran Channel. "It's about much more than my heart."

She chuckled. "With military men, it always is."

She patted his arm the way a sister would and left him in peace. He needed to see Shirley for himself, see that she was whole and unharmed. Admiral Hendricks had refused to offer Shirley personalized undercover protection, and Leo had been beside himself knowing there was a German spy running free.

Ten minutes later, a tan car pulled into the driveway and parked beside the keeper's quarters. He placed his mug on a nearby table and stalked to the door. Mrs. Geddy beat him to it, and he had to remind himself it was her house. Edward was sleeping, as he'd tended the light through the night, being extra vigilant for German U-boats.

Shirley met his gaze over Mrs. Geddy's head. Something in her eyes danced, and her creamy cheeks pinked in a way that made him want to hold them in his palms.

"Come in, dear." Mrs. Geddy gestured her in, nudging Leo back. He was nearly standing on top of them, so he cleared the space.

Mrs. Geddy closed the door. "There's plenty of coffee in the kitchen, my dear. Have as much as you want and make yourself at home. Here, I'll take your coat."

Shirley slipped out of it, and Leo's breath hitched. She was so beautiful it hurt. He was used to seeing her in uniform or in fishing gear, and though he'd found her appealing then, her styled hair and lipstick and dress as colorful as a store-bought bouquet was...

"Are you all right?" She stared at him, a knot forming between her brows.

He caught himself rubbing his sternum and clasped his hands in the small of his back. "Quite fine."

Mrs. Geddy turned and winked at him. "I'll leave you two to talk. Feel free to use the parlor, or you may use the tower if you'd like."

She left, inviting an awkward silence to the room. He swallowed. "Sorry to keep you from church on Easter."

"I'll be sure to say an extra-long prayer before bed."

Bed. Years of denying his flesh helped him direct his thoughts elsewhere, though with her lips looking like that, it wasn't easy.

The air crackled between them. He had to move, or he was going to burst through his skin.

He took her hand and guided her through the door that led to the tower. Entwining his fingers in hers, he climbed the spiral stairs, mindful of her fancy shoes, and paused at the landing that led to another set of steps. There were only about ten or so, but they were much steeper.

He stopped and she bumped into him. He took a deep breath. "Are you well?"

"I am," she said, a little breathless. "Though the stairs are difficult to maneuver in heels."

"I'm sorry." He took the next few slower. "The raft on Popes Folly is German. We dug up a radio and a charred German naval uniform. We have no idea where he's gone. It's likely he's in New Brunswick, but he could also be here. When I couldn't contact you yesterday, I almost went out of my mind."

"You? I don't believe it."

"Like George Washington, I cannot tell a lie."

She raised a brow and smirked.

"Unless it's for an important military operation." The sun spilled down through the opening that led to the lens, wrapping her in a halo of light. He tightened his hold on her hand. "I was worried."

"About me? Why?" Her big eyes blinked with false innocence.

Someone had turned saucy since he'd seen her last. Or maybe she felt the freedom to be bold due to his boldness. He wanted to be much bolder but didn't have the right.

Yet.

"Come on." He climbed the final steps to the lens and reached down to help her up the last step. Keeping her hand in his, he walked to the front of the lens and the view beyond, the heat from the sunlight warming the enclosure like a greenhouse.

"Oh, Leo." Shirley craned to see the tops of the pine trees lining the jagged cliffs, exposing a perfect view of her slender neck. He tore his gaze from the delicate spot where her pulse thrummed to the blue water that went on forever. The distant line of New Brunswick stood on the horizon where osprey scouted for food.

Her company. This moment. The view. For the first time since his brothers died, he believed he had a future waiting after this war ended. Not only believed it but looked forward to exploring it.

Without thinking, he let go of her hand and wrapped his arm around her back, resting his fingers on her hip. She tucked herself against him. A perfect fit.

"I'm failing, Leo," she whispered.

He turned her to him, placing both hands on her waist, holding her closer than he should. "Why would you say that?"

"Other than a seal caught in a raft, I can't find anything. Everyone and everything in town is the same as it's always been. Only more judgmental."

His jaw flexed. "I'm sorry if you're being treated poorly."

Her shoulders lifted, then dropped. "If we're able to save Mrs. Roosevelt it'll all be worth it, but I'm failing."

"Stop." He pressed a finger to her mouth.

She stilled. Desire pooled in her eyes, buoying his instincts.

"Have you noticed anything at all this week?"

"Not really," she said against his finger. He moved it and brushed her cheek with his thumb. So soft.

"Only discovering that Gypsy is really Alma, my roommate from Iowa, and that my neighbor is mailing a letter to family members in Germany."

"Ernst." He hadn't meant to say the name like a curse word. "Be leery of him."

"You know him?"

"I know of him. I've watched him fall smitten with you since I first brought you home."

"You've been watching me?"

"I promised to protect you."

She laid her head against his chest, facing the ocean. "You're a good man."

"Good would require that I not be holding you while training you for a mission." But he couldn't help himself.

She started to pull away, but he pulled her closer, one hand in her hair. Right now, he just wanted to be a man with no titles. He bent to whisper in her ear. "I'm tired of being good."

Her heart beat so hard he could feel it against his chest. He'd made the mistake of failing to protect those he loved in the past. He wouldn't make that mistake again.

His brain told him it wasn't practical to love someone after so short an acquaintance. His heart said it couldn't be anything else when she filled every fiber of his being whether they were together or miles apart.

"Does me being with Ernst make you jealous?"

She was fishing, and he was more than willing to take the bait. "Are you saying you're with Ernst?"

"No."

"Why?"

"He's much older than me."

"So am I."

She pulled away enough to look up at him. "With you it's...different."

With his thumb, he traced her jaw, her chin, her lips. Her chest rose and fell.

"With you," she whispered, her eyelids fluttering closed, "the whole world is different."

That was all he needed to hear. He lowered his head to hers, stopping shy of her lips. "Permission to come aboard."

"Permission granted."

He dove in, cautious, testing the waters. Her lips were softer than a summer breeze and every bit as warm. Like a dip on a hot summer's eve, he played, explored. Relished the experience and swam deeper.

She gave him full access, kissing him back with equal fervor. He backed her against the lens and braced his hands against the glass to keep them from exploring too.

To heck with war. All he wanted to do was hide away with this woman and love her until the whole thing was over.

She said his name over and over, which didn't make sense because her lips were captured by his. She shoved his chest and inclined her ear toward the door in the floor leading down the tower. It wasn't Shirley who had been calling his name. It was Mrs. Geddy.

He cleared his throat and watched Shirley lick her swollen lips. "Yes, ma'am," he said loud enough for Mrs. Geddy to hear.

"Edward's awake. He'd like to speak with you. I have a cinnamon crumble cake fresh out of the oven if you're in the mood for something sweet."

He rolled his eyes. Shirley groaned and thumped her forehead on his chest.

"Thank you, Mrs. Geddy. We'll be right down."

Leo palmed the back of her head and kissed her temple. "I apologize for my enthusiasm," he mumbled. "I'm used to taking charge."

"And I'm used to following." She laughed wryly and leaned back against the lens. "I didn't smell any cinnamon when I arrived. Have we been up here long enough for her to bake a cake?"

He laughed and pulled her steady on her feet. She straightened her dress, fluffed her hair, and hunted for the earring that had fallen on the floor somewhere.

He cracked his neck from side to side, taking pleasure in the pop. It was a good thing Mrs. Geddy interfered when she did before they had a chance to prove the rumors true. He'd like to think he was more honorable than that, but captain or not, he was a red-blooded male.

He wiped a hand over his mouth. Not to erase the feel of her kiss but to eradicate the waxiness of her lipstick.

"Found it." She held up the sparkly stud, then worked on clipping it back on her earlobe.

"Um. . ." He moved his fingers in a circle in front of his mouth.

"Oh." She wiped the pads of her fingers around her lips.

Before she could descend the steps, he tugged her close and laid his forehead against hers. "We're getting close, Shirley. Keep looking."

"And then what?"

"And then I'm going to clear your name and court you properly."

"Can we do that? It's not against the rules?"

"Technically, what we just did is, even though we're in separate branches, but it won't be once I move on to another assignment. I vow not to kiss you again until then, no matter how hard keeping that promise might be." He released her. "What do you say? May I court you?"

She wiggled her eyebrows. "Aye, aye, Captain."

She started down the steps, but he stopped her again. "I don't want to do this in front of the Geddys. First, here's your pay."

He pulled an envelope from his pocket and handed it to her. Wariness crept into her face as she studied him and tucked the envelope in the pocket of her sweater. "Second?"

He blew out a breath. "Alma mentioned you using the excuse of finding your brother's whereabouts as a means for her to send me that telegram. I hope you don't mind, but I inquired about James's body."

"And?" Shirley moved closer, the hopefulness beaming from her nearly breaking him. He wrapped his arm around her waist and pulled a note from his pocket with the other.

"I'm sorry to report they won't be sending him home. He's buried with the rest of the casualties from his division outside of Florence, Italy."

He reached into his pocket and pulled out a chain with a thin metal tag. "I was able to procure this for you before they sent it to be delivered by a stranger. I'm sorry I can't do more."

Shirley curled her fingers around James's dog tag and wept against him.

At least she had a token to hold, something to offer a sense of closure. He'd had nothing to offer his mother when he'd delivered the news that her youngest sons wouldn't be coming home. Nothing to offer Meredith when she told Gracie stories about her brave daddy one day.

Leo rubbed his hand up and down Shirley's back, relishing the feel of her as their pain mingled.

He would not fail someone he loved again.

≣ CHAPTER 30 ≣

That afternoon when Shirley arrived home, the house was empty. No feast or celebration for Easter this year. Their hearts were too heavy. Taking comfort in the dim, quiet kitchen, she pulled out a chair and sat. She needed time to process the events of the morning—the evidence of a spy, that earth-shattering kiss, Leo's promise of courtship, and the reality that James would never rest on his beloved rocky shore again.

She pulled the dog tag from her pocket and arranged it neatly in the middle of the table. Shot in the back after being commanded to retreat.

She wouldn't tell her parents the truth of James's death. Daddy had decided James was killed carrying out orders in the valiant way he did everything he set his mind to, and Shirley would let her father hold on to that.

She unfolded the paper the army commander had sent to Leo with the exact location of James's body, then took out the envelope with her pay and laid ten dollars on the table as well. It seemed cold not to give her parents these items in person, but she knew that their disappointment in her mingled with their grief in such a way, they'd need to process it all in private. She needed to rid herself of the telegram Alma had delivered so it couldn't come back to haunt her.

Rejuvenated in heart but weary in mind, she got back into her coat and walked the grassy patch past the barn to where their property ended at the high, jagged cliff. She took out the telegram and folded it the way James had taught her when she was a child. Holding it between her thumb and forefinger, she sailed the paper airplane into the air.

It swirled and dipped several times before landing in a frothy wave churning around a small boulder. The water was a lovely cerulean that lightened to a teal green at the shoreline. Her heart ached for her brother and how he'd never sit with her in this spot again to enjoy such a beautiful scene.

She whispered a goodbye to James and imagined her words, audible and not, being carried to him through the tiny plane.

A noise distracted her musings and she turned toward the house, expecting to see her parents in the driveway, but then movement at the Fischers' caught her attention. Mrs. Fischer stepped outside with a basket on her hip and began hanging wet garments on the line.

Being the Sabbath and a day of rest, Shirley found it odd that Mrs. Fischer chose Easter Sunday to do laundry, but most people didn't have children as rambunctious as Maxwell, Ike, and Ina.

Shirley hadn't visited the neighbors who were like her second family since she'd returned home. She hadn't meant to ignore them, but with the scandal of the discharge, James's death, and avoiding Ernst, she hadn't been very neighborly.

She walked the lengthy stretch to their house, waving as she neared. Mrs. Fischer raised from her bent position over the basket, a hand pressed against her back as she winced. "Good morning, Shirley. It sure is good to see ya."

"I'm sorry I haven't been over before now."

"You've had a lot going on, girl. My, don't you look pretty. If Joan were here, she'd be mighty jealous of that dress."

"Thank you." A breeze blew a strand of hair into her face, and she tucked it behind her ear.

Mrs. Fischer bent and pulled up a beautiful red, brushed-velvet coat with brown fur trim. The coat was Joan's most prized possession; she'd ordered it from a Parisian fashion catalog on her twenty-first birthday. "How is Joan? I miss her terribly."

"*Ach*, you know that crazy girl." Mrs. Fischer stuck a hand inside her apron pocket and pulled out a clothespin. "Taking the world by storm with that top-secret mission of hers. Knowing that girl, she's puffed it up to give her boring day job a little spice."

The line sagged with the weight of the coat. Shirley held it while Mrs. Fischer finished pinning it to the line. "Thank you, dear. Either way, she sure is enjoying herself."

Shirley ran her fingers over the fur collar. "She's so proud of this coat. I'm surprised she didn't take it with her."

Mrs. Fischer chuckled. "Me too. If she knew Ina had sneaked it from her bureau to wear it during her dolly tea party and dribbled jam down the front, she'd burst a blood vessel."

"That she would."

Shirley bent and handed the woman a worn shirt. "Thank you, dear." Mrs. Fischer reached for another clothespin. "She's met a nice young man." Her face paled. "Oh, I'm sorry. I shouldn't have mentioned that to you."

"It's okay." Shirley smiled. The fact that Mrs. Fischer was willing to stand and talk to her at all was a testament to their relationship. "I'm happy for Joan."

Mrs. Fischer looked at the house then back to Shirley. "Just between us"—she lowered her voice—"I know how you feel."

Shirley waited for an explanation.

The woman's mouth pinched. "I too was in love with a soldier once. Before Olaf. Before moving to America. His name was Heinry, a soldier in the German military, like my father. Father didn't approve, of course, so he used his influence to have Heinry shipped to Austria. His assignment was basically a life sentence, so we parted with the most grieved of hearts."

"I'm so sorry."

Mrs. Fischer waved her off. "*Ach,* 'twas many years ago. I was so young." She stared across the sea as if seeking the man out wherever he was. "I hate how the government, no matter where one lives, can dictate whom you may love."

"It is a travesty."

Mrs. Fischer shook her head and continued pinning clothes to the line. "Don't get me wrong, I love Olaf very much. He's a good man. But I admit, at times I wonder what my life would have been like had I been free to marry Heinry."

Shirley picked up the empty basket.

"At least I started over in a new world. You have been branded here. You'll be hard-pressed to find a man willing to marry you now."

Not if Leo's kisses that morning held any indication of her future. "I suppose you're right."

"Of course I'm right. I've heard the talk around town." Mrs. Fischer started toward the house and Shirley followed.

"Ernst would make you a good match. He cares not that you're no longer pure."

As if someone held a match to her skin, Shirley heated. Her mouth dangled open.

"I know you are not yet ready to marry. A broken heart takes time to heal. But Ernst will not wait forever. At one time we thought he would make a good match with Joan, but it wasn't to be."

Shirley halted. "What? I thought Ernst was her uncle."

"Heavens, no. Ernst is an old family friend. Joan began calling him uncle after she turned down his advances. A little reminder to him to keep his thoughts in a familial way."

Shirley couldn't have been more shocked had she stuck her finger in an electrical socket. That was a different story than what Joan had told her. She needed to turn down Ernst as well so he'd stop pining for her too. "Is Ernst home at the moment?"

Mrs. Fischer stepped on the porch and reached for the basket. "He is not. Do you wish for me to give him a message?"

"No, it's fine. I would like Joan's address though. To write."

"Of course, dear. I will be right back."

Joan was going to hear about Shirley's feelings over omitting the fact that Ernst wasn't really her uncle. How dare she try to foist the man on Shirley just to avoid him herself?

Across the way, a car pulled up to Shirley's house and dropped her parents off. She loved them so much and didn't want to lie anymore.

Mrs. Fischer returned. "Here you are, my dear. This is to her apartment she shares with two other young women in Massachusetts."

"Thank you."

"Would you like to come in for tea? Ernst should be home soon."

"No, thank you. My parents just arrived home from church. They'll be wondering where I've taken off to."

Mrs. Fischer assessed Shirley's clothing. "You didn't join them for services?"

"Not today."

An odd gleam flickered in the woman's eyes.

"Good day." Shirley stepped onto the grass.

"Would you like for me to send Ernst over when I see him?"

"No, ma'am. I'm sure I'll see him later."

Shirley left Mrs. Fischer standing on the porch, disappointed. As she passed Joan's red coat, she eyed it for any jelly stains, but the fabric was as pristine as always. Just like Joan.

≣ CHAPTER 31 ≣

A week had passed since Leo kissed Shirley, and it was all he could think about. Even now as he stood in the New Brunswick police station with Coast Guard officers, two navy admirals, and four navy captains of both the United States and Canada.

A grizzly bear of a man, twenty-four if he was telling the truth, sat in a chair behind a desk surrounded by men, reeking of booze and old vomit. Hans Muller had confessed to exiting a German U-boat via inflatable raft onto Popes Folly in the middle of the night almost two weeks ago. He'd been picked up by his informant in a boat and taken to Campobello Island.

From there, he spied on the Roosevelts' home and discovered the weakest places to infiltrate. Then, while awaiting orders, he'd gotten bored, broken into the Roosevelt home for valuables, and decided to spend some time at the Seaport Tavern in Welshpool. After nearly a week of no orders and running up a bill of drink and women so high he couldn't pay, the proprietor tied up his incoherent patron and called the authorities.

Hans Muller was now a prisoner of war.

After hours of interrogation, the man was still refusing to reveal the name of his superior and their location, the name of his informant, and the purpose behind harming Mrs. Roosevelt.

The man did, however, take much pleasure in telling the Coast Guard that his informant lived locally and patrolled their waters. It was meant as an intimidation tactic, but the ignorant Nazi had obviously never dealt with the United States military before. He'd issued the challenge, and the armed forces wouldn't sleep until they sniffed out every dirty German this side of Newfoundland.

He needed to warn Shirley and inform Admiral Grant. The few sailors who were stationed in Eastport hadn't found a thing, which made Lubec still the most likely place for a spy.

> Be careful, Shirley. Spy keeps mentioning a place called Flagg's Point. Our maps are coming up empty. Can you inquire? I'm watching from afar.
>
> Yours,
> CLW

The closing paragraph of Leo's note filled her heart to bursting. He was hers. Hers!

In the middle of a world war raging with hatred and evil, while death pervaded and swelled to unimaginable proportions, Captain Leonard Webber was staking his claim.

On her.

Reassuring her heart that despite how badly she might've ruined her reputation, she had a future.

Wouldn't her eighth-grade teacher Mr. Lasley be proud? She'd finally developed an appreciation for pronouns.

She laughed and plopped down onto the washboard. Water lapped against the transom, and the sun was warm on her back, though clouds were rolling in and the breeze was chilly. How she wanted to savor his letter like an expensive cut of meat, read it over and over again until every word was seared into her memory.

Only she couldn't. All correspondence once read had to be destroyed. Captain's orders. And she would do anything asked of her to help end this war. She couldn't begin her future with Leo fast enough.

After reading his words one more time, she dipped the note into the ocean and watched the water soak into the paper and smear the ink.

Watching from afar. She gazed around, seeing nothing but herself and colorful buoys floating on the surface. The notion he was always nearby comforted her.

She'd better finish up and get back to shore. The clouds were tinting darker. Storms had a timing all their own and were impossible to predict. She'd known too many fishermen who hadn't practiced caution and regretted it later.

She returned the empty bottle to the pot and attached the purple buoy with one vertical white stripe to signal to the Coast Guard there was no message inside. Steering carefully around the buoys, she headed north out of Johnson Bay.

Close to home, she got out her binoculars to see if her father was home. He wasn't. She lowered the binoculars but raised them again when she spotted a flash of red. There. Using her left hand, she slowed the throttle.

A flash of red slipped into her view, and it took her a moment to refocus. Joan's red coat hung from the clothesline at the Fischer home. Good grief. If Ina didn't stop playing in it, the soft velvet would be ground to sandpaper when Joan returned home. Shirley had been witness to Mrs. Fischer's scrubbing on laundry day and—

Tingles ran up Shirley's spine. She hadn't thought a thing of it the other day, but her memory now recalled just how soft and velvety the coat was when she'd touched it. The fur dry. Nothing like the texture if recently laundered.

Now the coat was hanging again. Four days later.

Shirley opened the throttle. It was nothing. A coat, for crying out loud. There was a perfectly good explanation for why the coat wasn't wet. Maybe Mrs. Fischer had only spot-cleaned it that day. Maybe she let the bulk of it dry by the fireplace before taking it out with the rest of the clothes.

And there was a perfectly good explanation for why it was hanging out again. When and how the Fischers handled their laundry was none of her business. Though Leo encouraged her to always follow her gut, that didn't mean her gut was always right. The Fischers were like extended family, a second home she knew as well as her own. Joan was the sister she'd never had—even if Shirley did want to throttle her for not revealing that Ernst wasn't really her uncle.

Burying her wayward thoughts, she continued to the harbor, moored the boat, and changed into her less smelly boots and coat. On the turn toward home, Ernst stepped onto the sidewalk by the pharmacy and disappeared around the corner. She dreaded having to turn him down after all the heartache he'd endured with his wife and then coming to America in hopes of making a match with Joan. But Shirley couldn't continue to drag Ernst along, make him believe there was hope of a future together when there wasn't.

She was going to take the proverbial bull by the horns—and use Joan's hanging red coat to do it. If she could catch him on his way home, they could talk without an audience.

She followed him from a distance, passing Mrs. Emberly from church, who ignored her in passing. Overlooking the silent barb, she skirted around the bookstore owner locking his store for the day. The wind had kicked up, though the dark clouds hadn't yet made it to shore.

Ernst went into the post office, and a minute later, Shirley did too. The room smelled of paper and lemon polish. She heard a metal post office box clink, and then Ernst rounded the corner, a surprised yet pleased smile on his lips.

"Good day to you, Shirley."

His broken English was improving, despite his thick accent. His lessons with Miss Neilson were paying off. "Good day."

She hadn't thought ahead to what she would say to him, which made this moment even more awkward. He stared at her, waiting. She shuffled one foot over the tiled floor.

"Is everything well?" He clutched a stack of letters in his hand.

"Yes. Sorry to keep you." She pointed to the clerk's desk.

He moved to go around her then paused. "May I and you walk together, home?"

This was her opportunity. She opened her mouth to answer when a little boy burst through the doors and ran straight into Ernst's legs. He stumbled backward but caught himself. Letters scattered across the floor.

Joan's little brother Ike cackled, revealing a missing bottom tooth. "Sorry, Uncle Ernst. We were racing and I won!"

Maxwell entered the building, acting, for once, like a civilized child. In no hurry, he'd clearly allowed Ike to win.

Ernst muttered something in German Shirley assumed wasn't appropriate for little ears. She knelt and helped him retrieve the letters.

Her hand stilled on one addressed to somewhere in Germany. Mrs. Fischer's handwriting jumped off the page. Shirley would recognize those odd loops and swirls anywhere. Kurrent, the woman had called it, encouraging Joan to use the same penmanship throughout grade school. Joan had always refused, claiming she didn't want to write differently than other children and didn't have the time to write such complex letters.

Only the return address was marked with Joan's name, not Mrs. Fischer's.

The letter was snatched from her hand. She looked up, expecting the abruptness to have come from one of the boys, but it was Ernst who held the letter, the skin around his eyes tight as if he was straining to hold back a scowl.

Face heating, Shirley continued helping with the letters and handed them to Ernst straightaway.

Maxwell tugged on his hat. "*Mutter* sent us for you. Storm's coming."

Distress wrapped around Shirley like a deadly snake. There certainly was, and not just the atmospheric kind.

Ernst frowned. "Go ahead. I will walk with Shirley."

"It's okay. We can talk another time." Shirley backed toward the door as Miss Middleton approached the counter, her neck extended to see what all the commotion in the lobby was about.

"It's not good timing for a stroll anyway," Shirley said. "Take care, boys."

Before Ernst could protest, she was out the door and into the lashing wind. The storm clouds were closer, and even if she ran, she'd be lucky to make it home before the downpour.

On the edge of town, fat, cold raindrops pelted her head and back. Someone called her name, and she looked back to find her father approaching in the car. She waited while he slowed to a stop, then got inside.

"Perfect timing. Thank you."

Her father grunted and drove them home.

Inside, she toed off her boots, hung up her wet coat, and climbed the stairs to her room to change. Needing to feel a connection to someone, she went into James's room and pulled a flannel shirt from his closet. Peeling off her clothes, she wrapped herself in his oversized shirt, the fabric still smelling of him—earth and sunshine.

She glanced out his window that faced the Fischer household and gasped.

The red coat flapped in the wind.

On the clothesline alone.

In the pouring rain.

⊒ CHAPTER 32 ⊒

Leo squeezed the telephone cord in his hand until he thought it might snap. "I know, sir, but we could really use some backup. The Coast Guard is busy patrolling for U-boats and making sure the trade routes remain active at the same time. The Grand Maran Channel is the main water highway to carry supplies from the US to New Brunswick and Nova Scotia, and ships full of needed supplies haven't been coming to port."

"I'm aware of that, Captain." Admiral Grant's voice wavered, his tone full of exhaustion and downright frustration.

"Thing is, Webber, my hands are tied. Hundreds of our men are dying overseas every day. The ones that are alive and able-bodied are being used in every capacity. I can't spare any of them for the protection of *one* woman."

He wondered if the admiral would feel the same if that one woman was his woman.

"I've done everything I can." Something rattled on the admiral's end of the line, like paper being crumpled into a ball. "The Roosevelts have more Secret Service surrounding them than ever before, with triple the men when Mrs. Roosevelt goes out alone. You've two SPAR agents dividing shifts with telephone and telegraph operations, and the civil defense is patrolling the area as well."

Leo remained silent.

"You're the most proficient man for the job, Captain, which is why I put you in charge. Put your emotions aside and trust in your abilities. Get the job done."

Leo wanted to yell. Instead he mumbled a "yes, sir" and held back a sigh.

"Webber, I trust your instincts. If any of those women's lives come into imminent danger, you have my permission to take action. I'll clean up the mess later."

"Thank you, sir."

"And what of the prisoner?"

Leo's temper was still running high from seeing the smug-faced Nazi spit on the floor after another refusal to reveal his informant. The man had taken great pleasure in telling them it was a woman though, one so smart, and a German so American, they'd never find her.

He relayed the details to the admiral, who balked. "A woman?"

"Yes, sir."

"Maybe it's a ploy to throw you off the trail."

"Perhaps."

"I'm sorry, Captain. I wish I could do more."

The admiral hung up, leaving a maddening silence in Leo's ear. He was sorry too.

He slammed the phone in its cradle a little too hard and stalked from the room. If Shirley's safety rested solely on him, then so be it. He'd make sure nobody harmed a hair on her head.

Nothing and no one involved in this war was going to take away someone he loved again.

———— ≈ ————

A woman.

Tears welled in Shirley's eyes as Leo's warning blurred in her vision. She shivered. Bundled in warm gear against the damp in the air, she shouldn't be cold. Her emotions had run high ever since she'd spotted the red coat last evening. The canned peaches she'd added to her pancakes that morning hadn't helped, as they added an odd queasiness to her stomach. Mama had received them in a care basket left on the porch and had offered them to Shirley, as Mama and Daddy didn't care for the fruit.

With half-numb fingers she crumpled Leo's note into a ball and tossed it in the gray water. The storm two days prior had ushered in rain that seemed as if it would never leave. Mud season was bad enough without the extra rain.

In the boat's cabin, she fumbled for her pencil and paper and sent a prayer heavenward she'd be proven wrong.

Ingrid Fischer suspect. Red coat hanging on clothesline that faces water at odd times as if a secret signal. Will tell Alma to watch as well.

Breakfast churned in her stomach and threatened to return. She had to be wrong. Had to be. But the red coat was the only thing out of place in this town, and that along with Ingrid being a woman and of German descent made her a suspect.

She folded the note and tucked it inside the bottle. She stared at it, not wanting to release it from her grip, as if the facts would change as long as she didn't send it.

But that was absurd, and she reminded herself that as long as Mrs. Fischer wasn't at fault, everything would turn out all right.

The bottle rolled to the back of the trap, knocking it off balance. She secured the latch and let it go, watching it sink until it was gone.

She pressed her wrist to her forehead and inhaled a deep breath for courage. It was done. Now she needed to finish checking her pots and go home. Her body ached, and her skin felt flushed with fever.

She opened the throttle to finish her route. With every passing minute, illness claimed more of her body until she was unsure if she'd be able to make it home. She passed an unfamiliar boat and started to flag it down for help, but with her next blink it was gone.

Hallucinating. She was prone to that when enduring a high fever. Shirley willed her mind to stay alert and follow the way home. If she could just get home.

From there it was all a blur. One second she was on the boat and the next she was lying on the slick, cold dock. She wasn't sure how long she'd lain there until strong arms hoisted her up. She opened her eyes to focus on Leo's strong profile but was met with Ernst's large, slightly crooked nose.

She tried to wriggle free of his strong hold, but he whispered, "Hush now, Shirley. I'll get you home."

His blessedly cold hands pressed against her forehead. "You're burning up."

His accent sounded different. The whole world sounded different. It was spinning off its axis like a ride at the county fair. He yelled for someone to moor the boat and take the lobsters to the pound. Then he ordered someone to send the doctor to the Davenport home.

Time passed, how much she wasn't sure. Something bumped her

head and pain exploded in her temple. She groaned.

"My apologies, Shirley." Fear snaked up her spine at Ernst's voice, and she opened her eyes to see why he'd hit her.

They were in a stairwell. He was carrying her. He must've bumped her head trying to squeeze up the narrow space. Mama climbed the steps in front of them, her backside swaying her skirt at her knees.

Home.

She was home.

Her aching body was laid out on her bed, followed by Mama's gratitude and shooing hands. Ernst's face screwed up in worried lines before he fled the room.

Mama fussed over her, touching her face and removing her clothes. Shirley's shivers were more like convulsions now. Warm cotton glided over her skin. Mama tugged the blankets from under Shirley and yanked them over her body.

She tried to speak. To tell her mother not to let Ernst or any of the Fischers into this house, but her tongue wouldn't cooperate.

"Shh, sweet girl. The doctor will be here soon."

"B–boat."

"Rest, Shirley. I'll have your daddy double-check the mooring."

Her mother sat on the edge of the bed and then lay beside her for extra warmth, the way she had when Shirley'd been young, humming soothing sounds of comfort.

All Shirley could think about was Leo and the note and Ingrid and the red coat, and then everything faded to black.

≡ CHAPTER 33 ≡

Leo rubbed sleepy eyes. When Alma had called his direct line, he'd braced himself for bad news. It was, but to his relief it wasn't that Shirley had been harmed; it was that she was sick. He hated to hear it, of course, but she was safe and at home, being cared for.

"What does the doctor think is wrong?" He stifled a yawn. Sleep usually came in starts and fits for him, but tonight of all nights, he'd been sleeping like a baby.

"Don't know for sure." Tension buzzed in her voice. "There's talk of possible tuberculosis. Or polio."

"What?" He was wide awake now.

"Or poison."

Leo shoved his fingers into his hair and pulled. "Poison?"

"That's what folks are saying. I heard the doc report her fever is higher than what he normally sees with a common illness, and she's expelling to the point of concern. He says there's something in her body that it don't like."

He blew out a breath. "Go to her house. Find out all you can. Make up whatever story you have to."

"Yes, sir."

"Call me anytime. If I'm not here, leave a message. Continue your vigilance with the Fischers. We're opening our investigation in"—he glanced at the clock—"six hours."

"I did overhear one thing, Captain. Ingrid Fischer talking to a Mrs. Hedger in Pembroke 4145. Said that Ernst fellow planned to propose to Miss Shirley before she got herself sick. I expect he still will once she's feeling better."

Ludicrous. The man was twice her age and not a legalized citizen. He hadn't been around long enough to woo Shirley, which told Leo the man merely wanted a marriage of convenience to become a citizen. Leo intended to promise her *much* more than that.

"Thank you, Alma. If the investigation proves the Fischers' guilt, Shirley will be spared the inconvenience of having to turn him down."

They ended the call, and Leo walked back to his room and sank onto his bed. As if he'd sleep the rest of the night now.

He punched his pillow and lay on his side, staring into the darkness. His mother had taught him that if he couldn't sleep, he should pray. So he prayed for Shirley, for her safety and for her illness to be minor. He prayed it wasn't poison. He prayed for the mission and that the Lord would reveal whatever they'd been missing.

Before it was too late.

———————≈———————

Shirley sat up in bed and pushed greasy hair out of her face. Her limbs were weak, and a cloak of exhaustion clung to her like the damp nightgown she wore, but at least her fever had broken in the night. The doctor had come immediately. Her lungs were clear with no coughing, and her bloodwork looked normal, so he'd ruled out tuberculosis. She could, however, have polio, but since she wasn't experiencing any numbness or tingling in her body and she had a full range of movement, the doctor believed she'd contracted some kind of virus or food poisoning that simply had to run its course.

And now that it had, she needed a shower and clean sheets. The scent of coffee and bacon wafted up the stairs and into her open doorway. Her stomach growled.

Food. She needed food.

Moving slowly, she stood, fending off a wave of dizziness. She wrapped her robe around her, tucked her feet into slippers, and started for the kitchen. Daddy's voice, rarely raised, echoed up the staircase.

Her parents were arguing? She sat on the top step and eavesdropped the way she had as a child. It was wrong, but she'd been sick for four days. She needed to know what she'd missed.

"I think you're reading more into this than needs be, Winston. She's your daughter, not a lunatic."

Dishes clanked together and a cabinet door closed hard. Shirley swallowed. They were talking about her.

"Am I? Then how do you explain her crazy talk? How do you explain this?"

Something rattled like a newspaper being folded or unfolded in haste. Had something been printed in the paper? Had she done something to expose the mission?

Despite her weak knees, Shirley hurried down the stairs. Daddy sat at the kitchen table in his usual chair, dressed in work clothes, and enraged. Mama turned from the stove and looked at Shirley, a ladle in hand. Gravy dripped onto the floor.

"What's going on?" Shirley wrapped her arms around her waist.

Mama plastered on a fake smile. "Nothing. We're so glad you're feeling better. Would you like breakfast?"

"Please. Thank you, Mama." Too tired to continue standing, Shirley pulled out a chair across from Daddy and sat. "I'd also like to know why you're both arguing over whether or not I'm in charge of all my faculties."

Her back to Shirley, Mama released a strangled sound.

"Very well. You're a grown, *independent* woman who wants to make her way in the world." Daddy downed the last of his coffee and slammed the mug on top of his haphazardly folded newspaper.

"Explain this." He pulled a small notebook from his pocket and tossed it on the table. The notebook she'd been using in his boat to write messages to Leo to put in the bottle. She fought hard to school her features the way Leo had taught her. "It looks like a notebook to me."

"Don't play coy with me, Shirley Jean. Open it."

He was furious. Pretending nonchalance, she opened it, and her mouth fell open.

"Care to explain why you believe our neighbor and oldest friend is a suspect? And a suspect in what, I ask."

Shirley blinked, stunned. Scratches from a charcoal pencil covered a page that should've been blank. The one directly beneath the one she'd written her last note on to Leo. White letters appeared between the charcoal smudges.

Ingrid Fischer suspect. Red coat hanging on clothesline that faces water at odd times as if a secret signal. Will tell Alma to watch as well.

Her mind swam and scrambled for a reasonable explanation. Maybe she should claim insanity.

Her father leaned back in his chair until the back creaked. "Suspect. A red coat. Secret signal. What's this about, Shirley Jean? Who are you writing to, who's Alma, and why was this in my boat?"

Tears sprang to her downcast eyes. She'd compromised the mission. Ill or not, she'd been careless. She'd failed Leo, failed her country, and put her parents in danger. "It's nothing, Daddy."

"Nothing? Nothing!" Her father stood so fast his chair almost toppled backward.

"Winston, please." Mama rushed to him and rubbed his arm, attempting to calm him as if he were a growling cat.

He shrugged her off.

"I want an explanation, Shirley. Now."

"I. . ." *Oh, God, what do I say?* "I was raging with fever, Daddy. I was hallucinating. Who knows what all I did that day?"

"That's true, Winston. She wouldn't have even made it home if not for Ernst."

Shirley thought back to that day and vaguely recalled Ernst scooping her up off the dock and carrying her home.

Fear struck her to the core. Had Ernst seen the note as well?

"I'm not buying it. Until you confess, you're denied further use of my boat." Daddy inhaled a deep breath and released it slowly.

Bile bubbled in Shirley's stomach. "Who else has seen that?"

Daddy looked to her mother, then back to Shirley. "Does it matter?"

"It does." Daddy had used the oldest trick in the book and had so easily discovered her secret. She needed to know now how bad the damage was.

"No one except your mother and me. Now, out with it. What was this notebook doing on my boat? What does this babble mean? What are you involved in, and who is this Alma?"

If only her parents knew of this, maybe all hope wasn't lost. "It's just a notebook I sometimes take with me to help pass the time. To write down my thoughts. Poetry. Lists. I was out of my head that day, and the words on this paper mean nothing."

"Nothing? Is that why the authorities showed up at the Fischers' yesterday and interrogated poor Ingrid over her laundry?"

"Winston, stop it!" Mama stamped her foot in a rare display of insubordination. "This family has been through hell the last two months. We lost a son and could've easily lost our daughter. She was out of her mind with fever, and if she says that note is nothing, then it's nothing."

Mama's voice crumbled at the last, taking Shirley's heart with it.

Daddy's hard features softened, and regret played on his face. "I'm sorry, Helen. But part of the hell we've endured is because of that girl." He pointed and stared at Shirley.

Shirley's heart broke.

"Something is going on, and we have to face the facts."

He stalked through the kitchen, opened the door, and turned to face them, mouth grim. "Either Shirley has completely lost her mind, or she's returned home a spy."

The door slammed shut.

⊰ CHAPTER 34 ⊱

Leo panted as he ran down the basketball court. His skin was drenched with sweat, and his left ankle throbbed. Shoes squeaked on the wooden floor. Lieutenant Dirks passed the ball to Emblidge, who passed it to Leo.

Ball cradled in his palm, Leo thrust his arm and watched the ball arc toward the net. It hit the rim and danced along its circumference, then dropped to the floor. Leo dove for it as the whistle sounded.

Guffaws and victory claps resounded from the other team. His ankle wasn't the only thing hurting now.

A hand waved in Leo's face, Emblidge offering to help him up. Leo accepted and rose onto his feet. Dirks slapped Leo on the back. "Not bad, old man."

Leo wiped his face with a towel. "You're lucky we're off duty or you'd be eating that ball for such disrespect."

Dirks laughed and chugged his water.

They'd made a habit of playing in the local high school gymnasium after school hours when their schedules aligned. The lieutenants were at least ten years his junior, but Leo kept up with them fairly well. This would be their last game, as they were shipping out tomorrow.

They gathered their belongings and followed each other out the door. The fresh sea air was most welcome.

Leo stretched the muscles in his neck as he walked, listening to the men tease each other and issue dares. The Coast Guard boys were more rambunctious than he was used to, but they kept him from being bored. And my, how he'd missed being on the water.

He inhaled a breath of salt-laden air and took off at a jog toward the station. He was still frustrated over the fact that Ingrid Fischer was a dead end. He agreed with Shirley. Something was definitely going on, but what? They were missing something, and he feared it was so close to their faces they couldn't see it. Now that Shirley was on the mend, according to Alma, they'd have to work harder to get to the bottom of it all.

Leo entered the base and jogged toward his room. A note was attached to the door. *Admiral Grant to see you. Admiral Hendricks's office.*

Admiral Grant was here? Concern stole away the frustration in Leo's body. It was an awfully long way for the admiral to travel, and everything the man did had purpose.

After taking a quick shower and dressing in a clean uniform, he went to Admiral Hendricks's office and knocked on the door.

The door swung open, and Leo snapped to attention. Admiral Hendricks ordered him at ease and then invited Leo inside. "Admiral Grant, sir."

"At ease." His old friend smiled. "Captain Webber, good to see you. I've just returned from visiting our prisoner of war. He says the Royal Navy is treating him right fine in captivity."

"Best for him he was arrested on the Canadian side then."

Admiral Grant chuckled. "He's since divulged his guilt in breaking into the Roosevelts'. He claims he sold the valuables intending to pay his brothel bill with the proceeds, but he rather enjoyed spoiling the ladies."

"Do we know what he took?"

"A few silver spoons and a coral necklace of Mrs. Roosevelt's. Her butler confirmed the items missing. The First Lady was furious when I told her. Said it was a gift from their daughter, Anna. Thought she'd bust my eardrum through the phone she was complaining so loudly. I asked her to describe the necklace to me so the authorities could search the local shops. Sounds to me like the loss of it was a blessing—a big gaudy thing with two strands of coral beads and a double brooch at the bottom."

Admiral Grant always did find feminine things a nuisance. Unless it involved his wife, of course.

Leo took a nearby chair. "We thought we had a lead in Lubec, but the trail ran cold. He keeps mentioning a Flagg's Point, but we've yet to discover the location."

"Blast it. Well, who's to say the informant is even still in Lubec at present. The signals have gone silent lately. Hendricks is shipping out with his men tomorrow. Since the SPARs are already here, they can continue the investigation under Captain Cook. You're needed in Washington."

Leo coughed. "Washington, sir?"

The admiral frowned. "Admiral Gregory Wiseman has suffered a terrible case of appendicitis. Almost died on the operating table. Lost a lot of blood. He'll be out of commission for a while. You're the only one I trust to take his place."

"Sir?"

"You're being promoted to rear admiral for the duration of this war. I know it's what you've always wanted, Webber. I'm proud to see it happen." Admiral Grant patted Leo's shoulder. "We'll return to Washington on the four o'clock train."

"Tonight, sir?" Leo detested the adolescent tone in his voice.

Admiral Grant frowned. "Is that a problem, Captain?"

Cook, who'd been observing from the corner, looked at Leo as if he'd lost his mind. No man questioned or complained about a promotion. Especially when being promoted to admiral.

Admiral.

It was a title he used to dream about and thought he'd never obtain. He'd achieved everything he'd ever wanted now.

Except Shirley. He couldn't leave her now that things were heating up.

Leo scratched his cheek. "Sir, I believe the informant is in Lubec right under our noses. Those SPARs could end up in grave danger."

Admiral Grant stood. "Which is why Captain Cook and his officers will do a wonderful job in your stead. They know what big shoes they have to fill."

The admiral winked at Cook and patted Leo's shoulder as he passed out the door. "See you this evening, *Admiral* Webber."

Leo felt sick. Big shoes or not, they were his shoes, and he was the only one who could wear them properly. He didn't trust Cook to keep Shirley and Alma safe.

Yet he couldn't disobey orders. He left Admiral Hendricks's office with the need to throttle the first thing he saw. The stray cat that hung around base crossed his path, and Leo clenched his fingers. He looked to the sky and growled. He couldn't leave. He had to leave.

He had to tell Shirley. In person. Had to hold her one more time. Kiss her one more time. Now that he'd been reassigned, he had the freedom to do so.

He ran to his room for a coat and hat and informed Ensign Blanche he was taking out a boat. Lubec was just eight short miles, but it felt like eight hundred.

In Johnson Bay, he found the buoy and checked the trap for messages.

Nothing. He debated where the best place to moor the boat would be without garnering attention. He drove up and down the shoreline to no avail. He finally decided it best to go to West Quoddy and see if Alma could deliver a message to Shirley to meet him there.

An hour later, he stood inside the small kitchen of the keeper's quarters, cradling a mug of coffee Mrs. Geddy had made him. He cranked the phone's handle, and a moment later Alma's voice asked where he'd like to be connected.

"This is CW. I need to relay an extremely important message to 752 Sunset Point."

"Go ahead, sir."

"WQ immediately. Leaving tonight."

"Is that all, sir?"

"Yes."

"Your message will be delivered right away, sir."

"Thank you."

Now all he could do for the next hour was wait.

≣ CHAPTER 35 ≣

Shirley and her mother stared at one another, a plop of gravy congealing on the floor between them. The words her father had spat before he'd left still rang in her ears. A lunatic or a spy. She chuckled, and her mother's eyebrows arched nearly to her hairline. Willingly putting herself in this situation made her guilty of both, she guessed, though she wasn't about to admit to either.

Frustration mounted, and she wanted to scream but instead kissed Mama's wet cheek. Her parents had been caught in the cross fire of this mission at the worst possible of times, and their emotions were justified. She hated doing wrong to do right. But they couldn't let the evil in the world prevail without ruining the nation for future generations.

A house divided could not stand.

Yet she was dividing hers daily with every deception.

How was she to continue leaving messages when she had no boat? Why hadn't they caught the culprits after nearly two months of spying?

Shirley cleaned the floor while Mama stood frozen and continued staring.

Mama, who perfectly represented her gender role. The role Shirley had tossed aside in the selfish name of wanting more from life. Well, she'd gotten her more, and keeping house and scrubbing floors was definitely the less taxing of the two.

By the time Shirley went upstairs to dress, the initial shock of Daddy's accusation had faded to downright irritation. She was restless in both mind and spirit. Pacing her bedroom floor wasn't going to do anything except breed more negativity, so she wrapped herself inside James's flannel shirt and her overalls and left for the post office on foot to give Alma a message to relay to Leo.

The morning was crisp, but the presence of sunshine gave the day the energetic hope of spring. Mud season was in full swing, and soon the yearly plague of black flies would arrive to usher them into summer. Until then, every day graced with sunlight would be treasured by all.

She focused her heart on the light and the comfort of knowing that Leo would know exactly what she should do.

With a sense of confidence and peace tinged with trepidation, Shirley walked into town, greeting everyone she passed, the way she'd always done before she'd been branded a Jezebel.

A woman dressed in a gaudy purple skirt and white blouse rushed to the other side of the road, as if Shirley was exposing the town to a deadly disease. Feeling cantankerous, Shirley plastered on the sweetest smile she could muster and said, "Good morning, Mrs. Flagg."

The woman looked around. "Good morning," she mumbled and walked as fast as her snooty legs would carry her.

The Flaggs had always been too stuck up for their own good. Just because their ancestors founded the town, they thought—

Shirley stopped in her tracks. A history lesson from her freshman year of high school came rushing back. The town of Lubec was originally founded as Flagg's Point and the name later changed around the War of 1812.

Flagg's Point—the name of the location the German spy claimed his informant lived in.

She had to tell Leo right away. A telegram would be much faster than walking to the lighthouse to use the Geddys' phone.

She stepped onto the curb by the newspaper office and inhaled the familiar scents of town, hope buoying her spirits. Other than the red coat, this was her first real clue. She'd finally make a contribution to this mission.

The alley between the bookstore and the bakery was the fastest route, so Shirley turned in between the two buildings, ducking her head against the wind whipping through the small space.

A pair of boots aligned in her vision.

She startled and looked up at Mr. Fischer, blocking her path. Her heart skipped a beat, but she worked to keep her features as neutral as possible. "Beautiful day, isn't it, Mr. Fischer?"

"It is." The robust man had his hands in his trouser pockets, and he stood with his legs spread, as if blocking her from going around.

Mr. Fischer made no initiative to move, and his grave stare did nothing but make the encounter more awkward. Had Daddy confided in his good friend about the scribbling he'd found?

She smiled. "Well, I was just off to the post office and thought I'd take the shortcut. Sorry if I've disturbed you."

His mustache twitched into a smile. "Actually, you were just the person I was coming to see. Step inside and sit a spell. We're glad to see you're on the mend."

He pointed to the side door that led into the bakery.

She glanced at the building. "It's closed."

As it had been every Wednesday afternoon since she'd returned home.

"*Ach*, Schmidt won't mind you coming in to join us."

Us?

"We're still unsure what caused such a high fever. I'm doing much better but would hate to make anyone sick."

He shook his head. "We're not a bit worried about catching a fleeting sickness. Please, humor me and step inside."

Her intuition was shouting for her to run. This man who'd always been like a second father suddenly felt like a complete stranger. A potentially dangerous stranger.

"I wish I had the time, but—"

He grabbed her arm, gently but firmly, and ushered her inside with his bulk behind her, blocking any escape.

The door led straight into the kitchen that smelled of sugar and vanilla. He continued leading her through the doors that led to the display cases and seating area. Men clustered around one of the tables, and they turned as she walked into the room.

"Look who I found, boys," Mr. Fischer said.

Ernst, Mr. Schmidt who owned the bakery, and another man she didn't recognize greeted her. The curtains had been drawn, blocking any view of the street and any view that passersby would have inside.

Mr. Schmidt took a mug sitting upside down on a nearby table and turned it upright. He poured coffee into it from a pot on the table. "Join us, Shirley. Glad to see you're feeling better."

Ernst moved chairs, leaving an open seat for Shirley next to him. Everything inside her told her to run as fast as her legs would carry her, but she also knew she wouldn't get far with four men to stop her, should they try, and it would be best if she didn't let on that she was afraid. Whatever was about to happen could be the break they'd been searching for, and she had to find out all she could.

She sat and took the offered mug, letting the warmth seep into her fingers. Mr. Schmidt then offered her a pastry off the heaping plate in the middle, and she placed one topped with cherries on a napkin to be polite.

"Thank you." She took a sip of bitter coffee. "You gentlemen act as if you need to speak with me about something. How can I assist you?"

"Well, Shirley," Mr. Fischer said, "there's a matter of importance we've been wanting to speak to your father about; however, given the. . . delicate nature of the subject, he's naturally closemouthed in regard to it. Even to me."

"Oh?" She picked up the pastry and nibbled the edge, despising the slight tremor of her hand. "I can't imagine Daddy would keep anything important from his oldest friend."

"It's about your indiscretion."

"Oh." She looked at her lap, her face aflame. Her earlier confidence shrank to one inch tall.

Mr. Fischer cleared his throat. "Normally I wouldn't bring up such a topic that involved anyone outside my own family, much less in front of mixed company. But seeing as Ernst has discussed his intentions with your father and, well, we think you might be in danger, I felt it best to broach it, no matter how awkward."

She swallowed. "I know I disappointed everyone terribly, and I offer my sincerest apology. I made a stupid and grave mistake I'll regret for the rest of my life. I'm not sure how it puts me in danger though."

Something was amiss, and she played as naive and innocent as her limited actress skills would allow.

Mr. Schmidt sat. "There's been talk for the last year of spies infiltrating the United States through our coast. We believe someone or someones have infiltrated our beloved town."

Mr. Fischer poured himself coffee. "As male citizens and the protectors of this town, we decided we weren't going to stand for any trouble. We went through town telling anyone who'd listen, trying to get all the men to come together and stand against such, but no one took us seriously."

"So I've been closing the bakery early every Wednesday for us to meet in secret to discuss what we've learned and what we plan to do about it."

A secret society had been meeting in the bakery this whole time? "This news is most distressing. None of the other men are concerned? Not even Daddy?"

Ernst sat on the edge of his seat, tapping his thumb against the handle of his mug. "We serious because we know what government was left behind to come here. We no want our America to be dirtied as well. If no America, then no hope for any other country."

She agreed. If America faltered, where would people from other countries look to find integral democracy? Where would they see a land of opportunity where dreams could be pursued and obtained?

"Daddy really wouldn't listen to you?"

Mr. Fischer shook his head. "Your parents have suffered greatly from the loss of your brother. Losing a child is devastating, and he's just trying to make it through the grief every day."

She thought a moment. They'd danced around her question. "How does any of this put me in danger?"

Ernst put one hand on the back of her chair. "We've seen a man following you."

Shirley nearly choked on air. Leo said he watched her from afar. Had these men noticed him?

"Really?" Not the most intelligent of responses. . . "Me? Why? Are you sure?"

Mr. Fischer nodded.

"I no stand for a man to follow you." Conviction laced every one of Ernst's words. "I no stand for a man to throw you away too. I find him and make him pay."

She squirmed in her seat. She wanted to throttle Ernst for threatening Leo, even if it appeared as if Leo had done her wrong.

"I. . ." She rubbed the end of her nose, conjuring tears. "We loved each other. Things would've worked out if he hadn't been reassigned overseas."

The stranger sitting next to Ernst mumbled something in a language she didn't understand. Ernst chuckled.

"What?" She didn't like anyone in this party saying things she wasn't capable of translating. These men were into something, and she needed to know exactly what. She set down her mug and glared at Ernst.

Ernst's sternness softened. "Your lover stays in military while you send home shamed. Not fair. Government not right to tell people who they can and can't love."

"I agree." She held her chin high. "However, it's a man's world, and I know this. I knew how it would turn out if we were caught, and I made the decision anyway. I'm the only one to blame."

"No, Shirley. This Capitan Webber must pay." Ernst hit his fist against the table. Coffee sloshed over the rim of her cup and trickled down the white ceramic.

Mr. Schmidt cleared his throat. Shirley's skin turned clammy. She hadn't revealed Leo's name to anyone when she'd returned besides her parents. They were so ashamed of her they wouldn't have told anyone. How did Ernst know his name?

They all stared at her as if waiting for her reaction. None of this was making sense, but she needed to play along, find out as much as she could, and get out of here safely.

She pinched the inside of her leg beneath her clasped hands. Tears sprang to her eyes. She allowed her chin to wobble and the tears to fall.

"He. . .he took advantage of me. I've been denying it this whole time but. . .I can't any longer. It isn't fair that he gets to move on with his life while mine is ruined. No one will ever look at me the same way again. He should pay. They should all pay!"

The false outrage and conviction in her voice surprised her.

Mr. Schmidt looked to the other men and smiled.

She wiped at her tears. The entire mood in the room changed, and the men seemed to relax. Relief ran through her. She'd said the right things.

The man she didn't recognize finally spoke. "They should. We can help with that."

She clasped her hands tighter, heart racing.

Mr. Fischer laid a giant hand on her arm. "Our government is corrupt, my dear. Our families immigrated for a chance at a better life, and now the leaders are doing everything they can to squelch those liberties."

She swallowed. "What do you mean?"

Mr. Schmidt scratched his chin. "There are some of us—well, many of us—who believe the leaders in this country are taking us down a path that will soon make us the minority."

Leaders. The Roosevelts.

Mr. Fischer continued. "They are fighting a war that's not their own while giving land and jobs to those less deserving of it."

Sweat beaded the back of Shirley's neck. "The New Deal."

"The *Jew* Deal." The stranger lit a cigarette.

Mr. Schmidt yanked the cigarette from the man's mouth and dropped it in his coffee. "The Roosevelts are making laws to prosper all. Negroes, Jews, Irish. They are working hard on bringing them in, especially that *woman*."

The stranger withdrew another cigarette but held it unlit in his fingers. "She thinks that by writing some stupid articles in a newspaper she can change our minds. Too many are stupid enough to listen."

The motivation behind the threat against Mrs. Roosevelt pinged like a fork against crystal.

"You see, my dear," Mr. Fischer continued, "the Depression left us all nearly six feet underground. If they give what little jobs, land, opportunities to *them*, there isn't enough for us. *We* are the superior race."

Shirley's insides quaked. Where Mr. Roosevelt supported his wife's efforts for the most part, it was Eleanor who fought hard for what she called the underdog. For the oppressed, the segregated, the poor, the handicapped. That was why Mrs. Roosevelt was dear to Shirley's heart. The First Lady saw all people as humans with hearts and hurts, not as commodities or a skin color or a superior gender. She wanted everyone to have a voice—women and children included, every nationality included.

They were all created by God for His glory and His pleasure. No one was superior but Him.

Sitting tall, Shirley braced for war. "What can I do to help?"

Another round of pleased smiles went around the table. Mr. Schmidt stood. "Join us. Your knowledge of the military will help us gain ground."

She nodded. "And what about Joan?"

Shirley held her breath, praying her friend who was more like a sister was not involved in this underground society.

Mr. Fischer swatted her question away. "*Ach,* my daughter is too busy pursuing other interests."

Thank God.

She stood, ready to bolt.

Ernst rose beside her and grabbed her hand. "Let us join our families together and rise to power."

She was going to be sick. She didn't want to accept this man's proposal any more than she wanted the smallpox, but the evil going on within these walls warned her that if she refused, they'd have to kill her for revealing all the information they'd just exposed.

"I. . ." She cleared her throat. "I accept."

The lines around his mouth curled as he smiled. A smile that mirrored what she'd always imagined a villain's in a book would be. He leaned forward as if to kiss her, and bile rose in her throat. Then as if remembering she'd recently been raging with fever, he changed his mind.

She'd never been more grateful for illness.

Mr. Fischer embraced her. "My sweet girl. Now we will truly be family."

He let her go, and she smiled, though she feared it was more like a grimace. "Now," he said, "go home and tell your parents you've accepted. Ernst will be around this evening to discuss the matter further."

This was a nightmare she was afraid she wouldn't be able to wake up from. "Please, give me a few days. Daddy's temperament has been rocky since James's passing. It would be best if I told him tonight, and he had some time to get used to the idea."

Mr. Fischer considered this. "Maybe you're right, my dear. You know your father best."

Mr. Schmidt shook her hand, patting the back. "I will make the wedding cake."

Shirley coughed. The walls were closing in on her. She needed air. She apologized with a wave of her hand and fled to the door, gasping when she reached the alley. She sucked in cool air and the fuzzy blackness at the edges of her vision started to fade.

She started down the alley. The stranger from the bakery leaned against the brick, one foot propped against it, smoking a cigarette. He sneered at her as she passed. Too frazzled to care, she continued to the next street and to the post office, never so grateful to be outside and around other people in her life.

The post office was quiet. A sign at the counter read GONE TO LUNCH. Was it that late already?

Shirley reached through the bars and rang the bell. "Excuse me? I need to send an urgent telegram, please."

Someone stirred in the back, and Alma appeared. "I'll be right there, ma'am."

With every second that ticked by, the gravity of what Shirley had just experienced sank like an anchor in deep waters.

Alma returned, carrying a notepad and a pencil. "Ma'am, are you all right?"

Tears pricked her eyes. "I . . ."

The front door opened, and Mrs. Nettles walked in. The beak-faced woman nodded out of politeness but sniffed as she passed to her post office box.

Shirley straightened her spine. "I need to send a telegram to my sister-in-law, please."

"Of course," Alma said and slipped the paper and pencil through the bars. "Write down your message, and I'll get it sent right away."

Shirley made quick work of the message, her hurried writing close to illegible.

Need to see CW right away. I found them.

She slipped it back under the bars. Alma read the message, and her eyes widened. "Is this all you wish to relay in your message, ma'am?"

"Yes."

A metal box closed, and Alma eyed the woman as she passed behind Shirley toward the exit. "Very well, ma'am. That'll be two dollars, please."

Shirley dug around in her pocket until the door closed.

"You haven't seen the captain?" Alma whispered so quietly Shirley barely heard it.

"No, why?"

"Captain Webber's not here anymore."

What? Shirley mouthed.

Alma looked around and leaned close. "He called from West Quoddy not two hours ago to send you a message by courier. He wanted to see you before he left. I thought you'd gotten the message and had seen him by now."

Despair filled every nook and cranny in Shirley's being. "Left for what? Do you know what he needed?"

"To tell you that he's been promoted to admiral and was forced to leave on the evening train." Alma looked at the clock to their right. "Oh, Miss Shirley. He'll be gone from the lighthouse by now."

Gone.

Leo was gone.

Alma's warm brown eyes filled with sympathy. "We're to continue as normal under the supervision of Captain Cook."

Shirley hung her head. If there was ever a moment to feel complete and utter hopelessness, this was it.

"Then tell Captain Cook I'll leave a detailed message for him by buoy tomorrow morning."

⟩ CHAPTER 36 ⟨

Shirley jerked awake, breathing heavily. Sweat dotted the skin above her brows. She pushed her hair back and grimaced. The shower and fresh sheets last night were a wasted effort after such a vivid nightmare.

In the dream, Daddy's harsh words from the day before grated and echoed in her ears. *"That girl. . . Either Shirley has completely lost her mind, or she's returned home a spy."* With Shirley floating behind him through the air like a ghost, he'd walked to the Fischers' and personally hung the red coat on the clothesline. The rest of the Fischers and Ernst joined her father outside their home and simultaneously faced the ocean and issued the Nazi salute.

The strangle of fear had woken her in a panic. It surged through her still despite the early morning sun filtering in through the lacy curtains. The meaty scent of bacon wafted up the staircase and into her bedroom. The scrape of a metal spatula on a cast-iron skillet and the scuffle of Daddy's boots on the kitchen floor settled her frayed nerves.

She was home. Safe. Her father was not a Nazi. She had not married Ernst, and their families were not joined.

But Leo was still gone.

She leaned back against the headboard and closed her eyes. Hot tears ran down her face and dripped onto her nightgown. Leo had been her rock through this whole mission, and now that she was in the thick of the battle, he sat in an office somewhere enjoying his promotion, and she was on her own.

Despite the pretty words he'd said that day in the lighthouse tower, would she ever see him again?

She needed to leave a message for Captain Cook immediately.

Before she'd gotten a chance to tell Alma the details, Miss Middleton had returned from lunch. It had been too late to take Daddy's boat, leave a message, and return before Daddy came home from the mill.

Though she hadn't let on, she'd noticed the smoking stranger following her home. He'd probably been following her the entire time. No doubt he knew her routine and watched her bring in a haul nearly every afternoon.

Having pitied herself long enough, she dressed and joined her parents downstairs. She was ravenous, but her heart was too sick to eat. She needed coffee and reassurance that her world had not completely crumbled to pieces in the last twenty-four hours.

"Morning." She grabbed a piece of toast from a plate on the counter and coated it in butter.

"Good morning, Shirley." Mama stood at the stove, as far away from Shirley as she could get, stirring what looked and smelled like hollandaise sauce. Since the argument yesterday, Mama acted and spoke as if Shirley was a stranger who threatened their well-being.

Daddy said nothing. Typical. It cut her deeply, but she trusted that when the truth was brought to light, he'd see her as his daughter again and not as a disappointment. Though when he discovered she'd agreed to marry Ernst, the vein in his forehead that had been pulsing with ire the past several weeks may possibly burst.

Shirley ate her breakfast quickly, making no attempt at conversation. She wanted peace. She wanted her parents' love. She wanted normalcy.

She wanted Leo.

After washing her plate and fork, she kissed Mama's cheek before leaving, the way she always did. "Thank you for the meal."

Mama stiffened and glanced at her husband. Using his newspaper like a sturdy wall between them, Shirley bypassed the table and walked to the front door. She punched her feet into her boots, slipped into her coat, and reached for the boat keys hanging on the hook.

Gone.

She fingered through the other keys on the hook to see if they'd gotten mixed up. Nope. She checked her coat pockets, and then Daddy's coat pockets.

He was going to make her ask, and he was going to refuse. She hung her head and prayed for courage.

She padded back into the kitchen, humbled and agitated. "May I use the boat today, please?"

"No," Daddy said from behind his wall.

"May I please use the boat tomorrow?"

"No."

Her frustration mounted. "Next week?"

He lowered the wall. "Like I told you yesterday, you will not have access to that boat or any of my things again until you explain why you're using them for nefarious purposes."

Oh, how she wanted to yell every detail out loud. A part of her wanted to punish Daddy for rejecting and misjudging her.

The end of Shirley's nose burned from holding back her emotions. "Nefarious is extreme, don't you think?"

They stared each other down. Daddy's nostrils flared in anger, but his eyes were sad.

Don't be angry with me. I know you think you've lost a war hero while your other child has disgraced the family, but I haven't, Daddy. Trust me. Continue to love me.

He took his time folding the paper while Mama continued stirring the sauce, shoulders hunched. He sighed. "Nefarious or not? I don't know, Shirley Jean. Why don't you tell me?"

"I'm not in any way involved in criminal activity, if that's what you're asking."

"Then what are you involved in?"

Shirley bit her bottom lip. A part of her knew that if she told her parents the truth, they'd keep her secret. For her safety and theirs, they would. But she also knew Daddy wouldn't allow her to continue putting herself in danger, and he wouldn't hesitate to storm into the Coast Guard station and throttle them all for using her as a spy.

"I'm involved in lobstering and fishing the way I always have."

Daddy nodded. "Isn't that what I told you she'd say, Helen?"

Mama wiped a tear from her cheek and continued stirring.

"I don't believe you," Daddy said. "That is exactly why I've taken the boat keys and will keep them on my person from now on. Even while I'm sleeping."

He stood, making her feel tiny as his massive frame filled the small kitchen. "Your behavior is entirely my fault. I indulged you too much like a son and not enough like a daughter. I never should've relented by allowing you to join the SPARs, no matter how old you were. But it stops now."

The gulf between her and her father grew larger every day. And now she hadn't even a boat to cross between the two.

Shirley kept her voice low and controlled. "You won't have to worry about me much longer. Ernst proposed. I accepted."

Mama slapped her hand over her mouth. Daddy's face paled. He walked closer and met Shirley nose to nose. "I'm going to make something very clear, and you are going to obey if I have to lock you in your room. You are *not* marrying that man. Stay away from the Fischers. Don't involve yourself with them or in their business for *any* reason. I mean it, Shirley Jean. I don't care how old you are. I'll drag you out to the woodshed if necessary."

How many times growing up had he threatened a spanking in the woodshed but had rarely followed through with it? Judging by the murderous glint in his eyes, he now meant every word and, while he was at it, might make up for all those lost threats.

Well, at least it was a response. His concern for her had to mean he still loved her, right?

He leaned away, allowing her to breathe. She backed up a step. "The Fischers have been dear friends for years. Why would you say such things?"

He had to suspect the Fischers were involved in something horrid for him to turn his back on old friends.

"Helen." Mama jumped at his sharp tone. "Pack Shirley's bags. She's going to visit Charles and the kids. And pack plenty. This will be an extended visit."

Shirley's mouth opened in shock. "But—"

He waved his finger in her face, his cheeks turning a mottled purple. "Don't you *dare* try to defy me."

Shirley's shoulders, her will, her courage, collapsed right there on the kitchen floor. Daddy backed away, blinking, as if he was surprised at his own ire. A moment later, he stalked out into the morning sunshine.

Mama stood at the stove, weeping. A strange burning smell hit Shirley's nose, and she realized Mama had stopped stirring the sauce.

She went to Mama, removed the pan from the burner, and turned off the range. Something deep inside Shirley snapped. She had to finish this mission. Had to get that message to Captain Cook if she had to swim it to him.

Watching her mother sob into her hands made something rupture inside Shirley. This had gone on long enough. If she were to continue her mission and end this madness, she'd have to run away.

☰ CHAPTER 37 ☰

Leo walked the length of the navy yard, inspecting work on the fleet and assessing the progress of weapons. His chest ached at the sight. He could picture Lonnie and Donald here, hauling power tools and cutting steel.

The men working were either too old for the draft or had been sent home from overseas due to an injury. Many of the workers were female, which made him nervous when they handled the heavy machinery and explosives, but they were doing a fantastic job.

The zip and pop of rivets joining metal filled the entire yard. This was the rebuilding of the fleet after Pearl Harbor, and he was in charge. He'd gotten what he'd wanted at the start of this war, to serve his country at the highest capacity and to vindicate his brothers' deaths. What better way than to oversee the making of the weapons that would one day crush their enemies, ultimately ending this war?

And they would win this war. With allegiance and with their allies, they would end this war.

As he cleared the very end of the yard, he looked out over the water reflecting the orange glow of the sunset. How had Shirley taken the news of his leaving? He'd waited for her at the lighthouse as long as he possibly could. She hadn't shown, though Alma had assured him the message had been delivered in plenty of time. Whatever had kept her from him had driven him nearly mad. The entire ride to Washington, he'd felt like a caged lion on the verge of a good roar.

He wanted to call her but couldn't for fear someone would overhear their conversation. He wanted to check in with Captain Cook, but the Lubec mission was no longer in his jurisdiction. He wanted to contact Alma but couldn't for the same reasons.

So here he was, an admiral, gazing at the water with two stars and one golden band on his left sleeve and the title of Chief of the Bureau of Ordnance. Without Shirley, none of it brought him satisfaction.

His job was vital to the outcome of the war, and he'd dedicate his life to make sure this bureau flourished with the utmost care, skills, and vigilance. He was grateful. Truly. But it wasn't until after meeting Shirley that he began to see a life beyond this war, see himself as a husband, a father. A regular Joe.

Without Shirley, all his other dreams felt hollow. For the foreseeable future, he'd try to keep up with her when and where he could, pray for her without ceasing, and hope for a joyous reunion someday when all this settled down.

"Admiral Webber, sir!"

Leo turned to find a young woman saluting him. "Yes, Ensign?"

"We have a load ready to ship out, sir. It needs your signature."

"Very well. I'm on my way."

With one last look at the sunset, Leo cleared Shirley from his head. Later, he'd pray her sleep was safe and sweet.

Shirley wasn't sure if this was the greatest idea she'd ever had or the worst.

After a stern lecture from Daddy at the Central Maine depot in Eastport, she'd boarded the train while he'd stood on the platform and watched her every move. At the stop in Perry, she'd disembarked, retrieved her luggage, and used the public telephone to call Captain Cook's direct line.

No answer.

She considered calling the Coast Guard operator and leaving a message, but by the time the captain received it, she'd already be gone. Like it or not, she was finding her own way back to Lubec.

She'd have to do it quickly because her train was supposed to arrive in Aroostook at six o'clock, and when she wasn't on the train, Charles would immediately inform her parents. That alone would open a whole gamut of trouble, on top of staying hidden from Ernst and the group of men from the bakery. Word would spread, and then they'd all be looking for her for different reasons.

She picked up her suitcase and walked through the terminal, thinking of her transportation options. Walking was out of the question. She could hitch a ride, depending on whose path she came across who was willing to aid her.

A flyer on the wall made her stop. *Cobscook Bay Boat Tours. See St. Andrews Pendlebury Lighthouse, Mulholland Point Lighthouse, Lubec Channel Lighthouse, and West Quoddy Lighthouse. Tours run every Tuesday, Thursday, and Saturday at 10:30 a.m., weather permitting. $50.*

Shirley looked at her timepiece. Four thirty. She could find somewhere to board in town or doze on a bench in the terminal and ride the tour boat as close to home as she could get in the morning, but that was hours from now, and she'd rather stay with Alma if she could make it there.

She watched the passing patrons, trying to gauge their characters and their mode of travel. An elderly man walked in and glanced around. Little footsteps tapped the ground as a little girl around age four ran up to him and threw her arms around his legs. "Pappy!"

The man wobbled but held his ground. A woman who looked to be in her late twenties chased the girl and scolded her for plowing into her grandfather in an unladylike way. Shirley smiled. She remembered getting scolded in the same fashion when she was that age.

The threesome chatted for a few minutes and then started to leave. Shirley went after them. "Excuse me."

They turned.

"I'm so sorry to bother you." Shirley shifted her suitcase to her other hand. "My brother was unable to pick me up, and I'm trying to make it to Lubec in time for my father's birthday. Are you going that direction by chance?"

The adults looked at each other and back to Shirley.

"I'll gladly pay you, of course. I just. . .I really don't want to miss his birthday. He's been very sick, and I've been away training with the SPARs and haven't been able to care for him. I'm on leave and would love more than anything to surprise him on his special day."

The woman smiled and took her daughter's hand. "We can take you as far as Eastport, if that would help you. You'll have to take the ferry to Lubec from there."

Shirley looked at her timepiece. Quarter of five. "That should work. I believe the last ferry leaves at six."

"I'm sorry, miss." The man rubbed the back of his neck. "I drove the truck. There won't be enough room for all four of us."

The woman frowned.

"I'll gladly ride in the back if you don't mind." She couldn't lose this opportunity.

The man shuffled his feet. "It'd be a mite cold to ride in the back."

"Please, sir. I'll do anything."

The woman touched her father's arm. "You always keep a blanket behind the seat, don't you?"

Regret lifted from the man's face. "I do. Will that suit?"

"Perfectly." Shirley smiled. "Thank you so much."

After settling into the bed of the truck, she wrapped the blanket around her head and body and braced for a cold, bumpy ride. Thirty minutes later, the truck came to a stop at the ferry dock.

The man and woman got out of the truck, but the little girl stayed inside the warm cab. Shirley held out some bills. "Thank you, sir. I appreciate this more than you know."

He shook his head. "Keep your money, young lady. The pleasure was mine."

Shirley passed the folded blanket to the woman, who smiled and said, "Thank you for your service to our country."

"Thank you for your support." Tears of appreciation prickled Shirley's eyes. Not once had she heard gratitude for her sacrifice. Not that she was doing it for the glory, but she'd given up just about everything in her life for this mission, and it did her heart good to know someone was grateful.

She bought a ticket for the next ferry and waved to the sweet family as they drove away. She chose the most inconspicuous spot she could to wait and hoped no one would recognize her.

The ferry loaded quickly with only a few passengers and little cargo. Within fifteen minutes they were pulling up to the dock on Water Street. Her father's boat was not moored in its usual spot, thank goodness. By now, he was probably out searching for her.

Unable to be seen in the post office, Shirley wrapped her scarf around her head and left the docks as fast as her legs would carry her. If she could make it to the small building at the end of Menden Point and into Alma's apartment without being noticed, it would be a miracle. Alma would still be on duty, but this was the only way. Thankfully, the apartment was in the opposite direction of Shirley's home and there was a lot less traffic.

By the time she reached Menden Point, her legs were aching from the fast walking and her arm muscles burned from carrying the dumb suitcase. Relief filled her as soon as she entered the secluded area of buildings hidden within the trees.

She'd arrived. Breathless and weary, but unseen.

Menden Point was the part of town where the black fishermen and their families lived. Alma would still be working her shift, so Shirley would have to break into Alma's apartment without being noticed.

Keeping her head down, she was careful to hide her face as best she could with her scarf. Her hands were encased in gloves, so if she could keep her face from being seen, she was home free.

She entered the apartment building on a breath and a prayer. No one milled about, but sounds emanated into the hallway through the thin walls. Someone was cooking a meal that smelled so heavenly, she almost rerouted her destination. Especially when her stomach let out a mighty growl.

Alma's apartment wasn't on the main floor, so Shirley climbed the steps to the second floor. There were only two doors, and Alma's was on the left. Shirley looked around, placed her suitcase quietly on the floor, and took out a bobby pin from her hair. She slid it into the lock and maneuvered it around. Roxie sure had made it look easy.

After several attempts, a click sounded and the lock released, bringing a smile to Shirley's face. She picked up the suitcase and turned the knob to go inside.

A male growl sounded from behind her. "You step foot into that apartment, missy, and I'll make you regret it in ten different ways."

≣ CHAPTER 38 ≣

Alma closed the door behind her neighbor and spun to face Shirley sitting on the couch. Light from the oil lamp flickered from a nearby table. Shirley looked at her clasped hands and waited for a dressing-down from Alma.

The woman burst into laughter.

Shirley frowned.

Alma stepped away from the door, head shaking. "Miss Shirley, you is crazy."

Shirley shrugged. "I didn't know where else to go. And I couldn't stick around town for fear of being seen. No doubt Daddy has everyone in town looking for me."

"I understand." She sat next to Shirley. "But walking into Menden Point come as you please and then breaking into my house was just as risky. Not to mention the trouble it might bring me."

"I wasn't breaking in to steal anything."

"I know that." Alma leaned her head against the couch's back.

"It would've been fine had your boyfriend not been watching for you to get home."

Alma gave her a sidelong glance. "Micah is not my boyfriend."

"The way that man looks at you says there's a lot more going on than wanting to be a good neighbor."

Alma crossed her arms. "What on earth are you accusing me of, Miss Shirley?"

Shirley rested a hand on Alma's arm. "Nothing! I didn't mean it to come across *that* way. I'm just saying he's sweet on you. And it's...sweet."

Alma shook her head and stood but wasn't able to hide the grin on her face. "I don't have time for a man. We've got an assignment to finish, and then they'll be sending me back to DC. No need to go gettin' attached to someone I'm gonna have to leave behind."

"But sometimes love only comes around once, does it not?"

Alma looked away. "I'm probably the wrong person to ask about that, Miss Shirley."

"I suppose I am too."

Alma raised a brow. "You ain't fooling me. You and the captain done did fall in love."

"I. . ." Shirley flushed with the most delicious heat. "I hope that's what this is."

Alma giggled. "If I had to judge by the goofy look on your face, I'd say that's what it is."

Shirley laughed.

"Come on. I'll make us some tea."

Alma picked up the oil lamp, and Shirley followed her into the kitchen. She sat at the tiny table in the corner, feeling more relaxed here than she had at her own home. The edges of the wood were dented and chipped. While Alma put on the kettle, Shirley glanced at the rest of the kitchen. Broken tiles on the floor. Painted cabinets dingy with age. Thin shredded curtains on the one lone window above the sink. The apartment was clean and tidy but in need of attention.

"Is the government paying for you to live here?" Shirley hated to ask the question, but she knew the former telephone operator lived in a nicer place than this. A place with electricity.

"They are." Alma took two mismatched mugs from the cabinet. "I know it isn't much to look at, Miss Shirley, but I've lived in worse. What matters most to me is that it's safe and warm."

"I didn't mean to offend. I just. . ." Shirley paused to consider the right words.

Alma pulled out the chair across from Shirley and sat. "It's just that if I was white, they'd be more willing to pay for a nicer place?"

Shirley opened her mouth, then closed it. "Yes."

"It is what it is, Miss Shirley." The kettle began to steam. "Do I wish things were different? Sure I do. But we're making strides for equality, however small they might be. And there's white folk out there helping us fight for it too. Good folk like Mrs. Eleanor Roosevelt. We may not see it in our lifetime, but I believe in my heart that one day we'll not be looked at as different anymore. Won't be separate anymore."

Shirley put her hand on Alma's and squeezed. "I pray we *do* see it in our lifetime, Miss Alma."

The kettle squealed. "Maybe someday soon." Alma chuckled. "How about you tell me why you needed to break into my house."

"Do you think Micah will keep our secret?"

Alma took the kettle off the burner and poured steaming water into the mugs. "Oh, he'll keep our secret. Though I hated lying to him."

"It's awful, isn't it? I can't tell you how many lies I've told since this whole thing started. And I'm against lying."

"Oh, what a tangled web we weave." Alma placed tea bags into the mugs and handed one to Shirley. "I understand how you feel. I keep telling myself I'm doing the right thing by lying, but it still don't ever feel right."

Shirley lifted the string of the tea bag up and down, watching the herbs steep and the water turn a dark brown. "I'm a fugitive on the run. In the last twenty-four hours I've discovered a ring of German supremacists, accepted a marriage proposal from one of them, got kicked out of my house, put on a train to my brother's farm in Aroostook, and then hitchhiked back to Lubec."

Alma blinked. "My earlier assessment stands. You is crazy."

While they sipped their tea, Shirley updated Alma on everything that had transpired. When she finished, Alma shook her head. "The German American Bund."

"The what?"

"It was a popular movement that started six or so years back. Germans living abroad were encouraged to start groups to exalt German virtues and lobby causes for the Nazi party. They portrayed it here in the US as a patriotic way to blend the two cultures, but it was really Hitler's way of building an army of supporters overseas.

"They even took over Madison Square Garden a couple years before we joined the war. I remember being dead shocked at how many people followed, not even knowing what they was doing."

"Wow. I've never heard of them. Then again, I would've been in high school. I was guilty at that age of not being too concerned about things going on outside our town."

"As it should be, I guess." Alma stood and collected their empty cups. "Kids should be allowed to just be kids."

"The government is aware that communist parties are trying to overtake citizens and they're allowing it to happen?"

Water gurgled from the sink as Alma rinsed the cups. "They put a stop to it right after the war started. The leader was arrested for embezzling funds and deported back to Germany."

Alma turned off the faucet and leaned against the sink. "The authorities discouraged all future rallies, and things for the most part have calmed over the last few years. Especially considering how many eyes were opened to the Nazi party and what Mr. Hitler stands for. But as I well know, there's always a group of folks out there somewhere who wants to make life hard for the rest of us."

"I'm sorry for the way things are, Alma."

"Me too, Miss Shirley. You one of those good folks I was talking about." She took the lamp and exited the kitchen, plunging the room into darkness. Shirley followed with her suitcase.

They went to a small room at the back beside the washroom. Alma lit a candle and set it on a bureau while Shirley set to making a fire in the hearth. "I have a lamp in here, and I'll put this one in the washroom for you. The fire's good at keeping both rooms toasty. Micah goes to all the apartments and gets them heated up right before those who work get home. That's what he was about to do when you came along."

"Ah, now it makes sense. He doesn't like the idea of you coming home to a cold house. He wants to be the one responsible for keeping it warm." Shirley wagged her eyebrows.

Alma snickered. "Miss Shirley, you've got love on the brain. I'm too old for schoolgirl crushes, and Micah performs the same favor for ol' man Nikum right before he gets home from the mill."

"If you say so," Shirley teased.

"I do. Now you're welcome to have the bed. I'd offer you clean sheets, but there's just the one set. In any case, you should be comfortable enough."

Alma turned to go.

"Where will you sleep?" Shirley asked.

"On the couch."

"Nonsense. I'm not taking your bed. You sleep here, and I'll take the couch."

"No way. My grandmammy taught me that guests come first. I ain't wishing her ghost to come scold me in my sleep."

Shirley put down the suitcase and sat on the edge of the bed. "You're too old for schoolgirl crushes but not ghost stories?"

"Yes'm. And that's my grandmammy we're talking 'bout, so you best watch what you say."

If Alma only had one set of sheets, it was likely she only had one blanket as well. Shirley wasn't about to make her friend sleep on the couch without a blanket. "Nonsense. It's all settled. You'll sleep in here with me."

Firelight flickered across Alma's face, accentuating her frown. "Miss Shirley, you know that ain't the way folk be doing things."

"That doesn't make it wrong." Shirley patted the bed. "It's plenty big and sturdy enough for the both of us. It'll be like having a sleepover, like when we were girls."

"I ain't never had a sleepover."

"Well, then, that'll make it that much more fun."

Alma hesitated.

"We've been roommates before. It'll be just like then, only like the beds are pushed together. And then neither of us has to sleep on a cold couch."

Alma sighed. "Miss Shirley, you is *crazy*."

Shirley smiled at the acceptance in her friend's voice. "So you keep saying."

"It's true every time I say it."

The women readied for bed, then settled in. Shirley lay against the chilly wall, using a balled-up shirt as a pillow. Wood crackled and hissed in the fireplace.

"Miss Shirley, what do you plan to do from here?"

Shirley thought a moment. "I'll go to West Quoddy and use their phone to call Captain Cook."

"That's over a six-mile walk. Can you do that and not be seen? I expect the whole town will be looking for you by now."

"I don't see another way. There's too much to say in a telegram, and you can't call for fear someone in the post office will overhear. I have no boat to leave a message, so walking to the lighthouse is my only option."

"I guess you're right."

"I'm always right."

They laughed. "Like that time you accused Roxie of being a spy when she was sneaking love notes to her husband?"

"Yes, like that time."

"Or the time you thought the captain wanted to see you for romantic purposes when he only wanted to ask you to be a spy?"

"Yep."

With each example of Shirley being "right" they laughed harder and harder. Gratitude filled Shirley. Alma was an amazing person. A person the world might never get to know because of ignorance and prejudice. Yet Alma was the best friend Shirley had ever had.

Of course, Joan had always been like a sister. Despite how well they got along though, Joan had always pointed out things in Shirley that needed improvement. Her hair, the way she dressed, the things she liked. But there was never any judgment from Alma. Alma took Shirley as she was.

Alma turned her head to Shirley. "You got awful quiet over there all the sudden."

"Just thinking."

"'Bout the captain?"

"About what a wonderful friend you are."

"Oh Miss Shirley." Alma chuckled. "You is crazy."

☰ CHAPTER 39 ☰

Leo had only been at this job for three days and already a man had been seriously injured in a fall, the work on two ships was running behind schedule, and a train loaded with plutonium from his shipyard had failed to reach the Pantex on time, setting back the assembly of weapons to be shipped to the Pacific coast by almost twenty-four hours.

A lifetime in war.

He turned the page of his newspaper and folded it so he could hold it in his left hand while he finished his buttered toast with his right. It was the same news nearly every day—serve your country through scrap metal, ration updates, which battles had been or were being fought, and the ongoing death toll. The only relief on the pages were stories about celebrities or baseball players, which, while offering a temporary escape from reality, seemed insignificant in the grand scale. Unless the article told how they were aiding the war effort.

He swallowed his bite, brushed his fingers on a napkin, and flipped the newspaper around. Eleanor Roosevelt's "My Day" column was rather lengthy today and would no doubt stir hearts and conspiracies:

> Today marks the tenth anniversary of Hitler's burning
> of books—titles by beloved authors that challenged
> readers to think, to explore, to change. By doing so,
> Hitler believed he could murder the inspiration behind
> the authors' ideas. He may have succeeded in Nazi
> Germany, but in the rest of the world, it brewed interest.
>
> People who'd never heard of or read these books are
> now reading them. Their work is reaching people and

areas they never would have without Hitler's suppression.

I say that, not to praise Hitler for his actions but to say that humans have a natural born passion for freedom of speech and thought that only becomes stronger when there is an effort anywhere to squelch such. Enslaving people doesn't only come in the form of masters and whips and chains, but in making education impossible to obtain and hiding from them what is really going on in the world.

Enslaving people also comes by controlling other ways ideas are transmitted. By telling them how to live and where they can and can't go—outside the boundaries of moral law. Hitler will one day have to face the people he's enslaved and endure judgement. Knowing this brings hope to an otherwise dismal situation.

Access of freedom and thought of expression make great changes in people. Both are causes I fight passionately for every day. For everyone.

As such, I fight for those freedoms for myself also. Threats to my safety are not a new development. It comes with the territory and my bold opinions as a woman, I suppose. But I will not cower to those, like Hitler, who wish to control. There are those around me who ask me not to travel, to be a little quieter in my ways, but I will not. This weekend I will travel to our retreat on Campobello Island as we do every May, and I will do so without fear.

As Patrick Henry once said, "Give me liberty, or give me death!"

Leo dropped the newspaper, unsure which he desired most—to stand up and clap or visit the First Lady and scold her for painting a target on her back big enough for the whole world to see.

If only he could contact Shirley, but Admiral Grant had given strict instructions that Leo was to leave it in the Coast Guard's jurisdiction.

Leo ground his back teeth, his breakfast no longer appetizing. The matter may be in the Coast Guard's jurisdiction, but that didn't mean the separate branches couldn't share information. After all, he was an admiral now, wasn't he? That gave him leeway he'd not have as a captain.

He folded the paper, set his plate of scraps outside for the stray dog that always seemed to be begging, and rushed to his office. After holding while the operator made the transfers, Captain Cook came on the line.

"Admiral Webber, what can I do for you?"

"Have you seen today's *Washington Post*?"

"We're already on it. Secret Service informed us last night of the press release. They'll accompany the Roosevelts in separate vehicles ahead and behind them, though Mrs. Roosevelt has refused to have a guard inside their own car. They'll go as far as Rockland, then take a rented yacht up the Gulf of Maine and into Campobello Island by access of Lower Duck Pond, surrounded by armed agents in separate boats."

Leo studied the map on his wall, then released a pent-up breath. "Well done, Captain."

"I'm doing my best to protect both ladies, Admiral."

Leo hated his transparency. But when it came to Shirley, he felt inside-out. "Much appreciated, Captain."

They ended the call, leaving Leo to stare at the dot on the map where he'd left a part of himself. Did she feel as hollow without him as he did without her?

With everything running as smoothly as the captain had relayed, he could focus on his own mess with the knowledge that Shirley was being cared for and safe.

Shirley hadn't been able to get ahold of Captain Cook all morning. His secretary had offered to take a message, but there were too many details involved to jot down in a memo, and calling him back was out of the question since she had no phone.

She couldn't stay with the Geddys at the lighthouse because Mrs. Geddy was out of town visiting her new niece and an overnight stay would be too inappropriate. She wasn't allowed to tell Mr. Geddy the whole of it because she was to report to her superior, and only Captain Cook could relay information as needed.

Which meant that evading her brother's house, hitchhiking back home, and sneaking into Alma's house had gotten her no further than when she'd left the bakery.

Mr. Geddy had, however, lent her the use of his boat. Someone from the Coast Guard would patrol these waters today and check for a message, so she'd written a lengthy letter addressing every detail about the bakery, the names of the men involved, the German American Bund, and the admission of their plan to harm Mrs. Roosevelt. She'd addressed it to the immediate attention of Captain Cook. She explained to him what had transpired for her personally and that she was staying with Alma until he provided her with different instructions.

She stepped off the boat and moored it to the small dock a half mile from the lighthouse, double-checking the knot. She left the keys where Mr. Geddy had instructed and straddled the bicycle she'd rented from Micah that morning. The man was leery of her and her odd, secretive friendship with Alma. He had great intuition, and she was glad Alma had someone watching out for her.

Shirley had done her best to disguise her appearance. There weren't many people out on this side of the peninsula today, but she didn't want to take any chances. The oversize clothing and scarf wrapped around her face hid all but her eyes. It was the best she could do.

A strong southwesterly wind blew, making the bicycle teeter. Shirley corrected the contraption before it fell on its side. Mud splattered around the tires, and Shirley steered into the grass until she found a drier patch of road.

A tin can blew across her path. Tree branches swayed, and pine fronds stretched their arms out to sea. An ominous presence hung thick in the air. Invisible fingers of electricity hummed around her.

May storms were always the worst.

A voice deep inside her whispered that the sudden shift in weather was just the beginning of the shift to come.

☰ CHAPTER 40 ☰

Loud banging woke Shirley. It took a minute for her eyes to focus and her brain to register she was at Alma's house. On the couch. She glanced in the bedroom, but the bed was empty. Alarm shot through her like an electric shock. What time was it, and why wasn't Alma home yet?

The banging grew louder and more persistent. She shoved her feet into her slippers and tiptoed from the room. She thought maybe Alma had forgotten her key, but the pounding was too aggressive to be Alma. In fact, it was like a ravenous grizzly about to break down the door in search of food.

Had her father and the authorities found her? Had the GAB found her? She felt her heart race, unsure what to do.

A growl sounded from the other side of the door. "If someone doesn't open this door, I'm gonna break it down."

Micah.

Shirley blew out a breath. It was a bear of sorts. His huge muscular frame was exactly what she imagined John Henry would've looked like, had he been real. The gentleness with which he treated Alma, however, gave the impression that his insides were as mushy as oatmeal. Unless riled, of course, which he always seemed to be. At Shirley.

She opened the door and he barreled past, almost knocking her over. "Where is she?"

"Al—Gypsy? She hasn't come home yet."

"I *know*." In a match between Micah and a real grizzly, his scowl would make the grizzly tuck tail and run.

"Her shift ended at six, and then she was going to pick up groceries on the way home." Technically, Alma was staying late to contact the

Coast Guard station and report the list of daily calls, the same as she did every evening once she was alone in the post office. Alma was also going to make a call to Captain Cook, however, to make sure he got Shirley's message from the trap. Then she was going to pick up groceries on her way home.

Micah scowled. "It's almost midnight."

Shirley's heart dropped to her toes. She wrapped her arms around herself to ward off the chill of fear sinking deep within. She didn't realize it had gotten that late. She'd dozed off waiting and. . . Alma should've been home long before now.

"I wanna know what's going on right now." Micah stepped closer. His hulking presence was much like Daddy's, only scarier.

"What do you mean?"

"You know exactly what I mean. You showing up all sudden like, staying here like you's hiding out. Now Gypsy's gone. Tell me. Right now."

Shirley began to quake. If something happened to Alma because of her, she'd never forgive herself.

"Like we told you yesterday, my father kicked me out, and I have nowhere else to go. Gypsy has always been a close friend to me, and she's allowing me to stay with her until I find another place to stay."

"Gypsy ain't been around these parts long enough for you to be that good o' friends." Micah pierced her with intense eyes. "You think your papa is behind this?"

"Behind what?"

"Gypsy's gone. I waited one hour past the time she was supposed to be home 'fore I set out to walk her home. She wasn't at the office, there's been no sign of her on the road, and no one I ask has seen her."

No doubt Daddy had nearly burst a blood vessel when he'd found out that Shirley never arrived at Charles's house. Blaming Alma would not have been his method though. He'd have come here after Shirley first thing if he suspected she was here. And besides, Daddy didn't even know who Alma was or that they were friends. She went by the name Gypsy.

"No. I don't believe my father has anything to do with this. He'd have come for me, not her."

"Who you think is behind it then? Your fella?"

"My fella?"

"Don't be playin' coy with me, girl. The whole town knows why you got sent home from the military. I's guessing that's why your papa kicked you out."

Shame washed over Shirley. Not because of what Micah said but because until yesterday, she didn't even know Micah existed. Yet he knew all about her. How often did she go about life thinking only of herself and her own needs and responsibilities and ignore, even unknowingly, the lives of others? She didn't participate in the prejudice, but she didn't go out of her way to fight it either. Or to make them feel more included in the community.

She crossed her arms tighter. "It's not my fella. He's been reassigned far away from here and. . .it's complicated. He wouldn't hurt Gypsy."

"Then where is she?"

"I don't know. I love Gypsy as much as you do, and I would never put her in harm's way. You have my word on that."

He stepped away and continued to watch her, speaking clearly with his eyes that her word didn't mean much. Rightfully so, she guessed.

"I'm gonna round up a search party. If she comes here, send Isham out for us."

She nodded.

He walked through the doorway, then stepped back and pointed at her. "We's not done talking 'bout this. But Gypsy comes first."

"Yes, Micah. Thank you for looking. Please, find her."

For the remainder of the night, Shirley paced the apartment, praying, wondering what had happened, trying to decide whether or not to alert the authorities. If anyone could find her, it was Micah. If he didn't find her by morning, she'd call the Coast Guard for help.

———≈———

Leo tapped his pencil on the desk in a rhythmic pattern, turning the facts he'd learned from Captain Cook over and over in his head. They'd investigated the Fischers. They were from Germany, but nothing in their history or daily actions made them prime suspects. Their daughter Joan, Shirley's best friend and fellow SPAR, helped run the LORAN station. Joan's mother, Ingrid, was the woman Shirley had added to the suspect list for hanging a red coat as a signal, but the investigation had come back clean.

The coat turned out to be nothing more than a coat hanging on the clothesline.

Shirley had been sick that day and, from what Alma had reported, "raging with fever." That alone could cause a person not to have full grasp of their faculties.

Something he couldn't describe pestered his conscience like a hungry mosquito. Shirley would not accuse her friends and neighbors unless she really believed something was awry. Furthermore, she'd observed the coat several times before making the accusation the day of her illness.

He wished he could talk to her and learn more specific details. Wished he could see her face. Hold her.

Leo stood and threw off the thoughts. He couldn't do any of those things, so dwelling on them was pure torture. He walked to the wall map and stared at the Grand Maran Channel and the surrounding lands.

Supply ships between Canada and the US were dwindling, and he couldn't pinpoint why. Admiral Tremblay of the Royal Navy claimed their supplies were leaving on time, and Leo knew the supplies from the Washington Shipyard were as well, as he'd gone back over the logbooks to be sure. Several boats were either veering off course or returning altogether. They'd all suspected signaling issues, but they couldn't find anything amiss at the LORAN station. All the reports were perfect. Admiral Hendricks had checked.

That's when he realized they'd been questioning the mother of Joan Fischer, the SPAR who was supposed to accompany Shirley back home to Lubec. If Shirley really had suspected foul play with the Fischers, why hadn't she reminded him about Joan sooner?

Of course, she wouldn't have known about Joan working in the LORAN station because that station and the work done there were highly classified information. He wasn't exactly sure what went on there. However, letting him know her suspected neighbor's history with a daughter as a SPAR would've been helpful.

Last night, he'd called Commander Willis, who ran the LORAN station in Chatham, Massachusetts, where Joan was stationed, and offered enough information to earn the participation of the commander. Willis had reported that Joan was the most reliable and accurate worker there. All of her reports were punctual and her actions were accounted for. She was as clean as a blackboard after a good scrubbing.

Still, something didn't sit right. Especially where that Ernst guy was concerned. Leo had never been able to find any documentation on the man as a legal citizen or his name attached to any passenger logbooks before he'd been pulled off the mission. Captain Cook had yet to find anything on the man either. Two days ago, the man had disappeared, and the Fischers were claiming they had no idea where he'd gone, including Joan.

Joan had taken an oath to serve and protect her country. Leo was going to call upon that promise. Chatham was a good eight hours from here, but he needed to find out more about Ernst and what was going on with the supply ships.

Admiral Grant would skin him ten ways to Sunday if he knew Leo was still vested in this mission, but Leo was willing to take the chance. Captain Cook, while skilled and capable, didn't have any personal stakes at risk.

Leo did.

He had three days of leave. Captain Kane could handle things in the navy yard for the next twenty-four hours. Leo was going to Chatham to speak to Joan.

CHAPTER 41

The raw concern on Micah's face made Shirley's stomach twist. He hung his head and shook it with a defeated sigh.

Shirley was going to be sick.

She rushed to the wastebasket and dangled above it, sucking slow breaths in and out. Something was wrong. Something had happened to her friend, and Alma was in the worst kind of danger. Shirley could feel it.

Micah joined her side. "You really don't know nothing 'bout what happened to Gypsy, do you?"

His words were gentle. Surprised that she wasn't involved somehow.

"No." Tears slipped down Shirley's face. "But I have a theory."

"What's that?"

Shirley swallowed the vomit climbing up her esophagus and put her hand over her mouth. This was all her fault. Coming here had done nothing to help her cause, only to put Alma in danger.

She had to call for help.

Now.

She brushed past Micah to her coat hanging on a peg by the door and shoved her arms inside. Punching her feet into her boots, she opened the door only to be stopped by a beast of a man holding her back.

"Where you think you's going?"

Craning her neck until it hurt, she stared into Micah's dark eyes. She needed an ally. Someone besides the Coast Guard to help until they could arrive. She was desperate, and Alma's life was most likely in peril. She needed Micah's help.

Shirley closed the door and walked him to the middle of the room where it would be harder to be overheard. "This is going to sound crazy, but I need you to believe me," she said, voice low and even. "I need your help. Not for my sake but for Gypsy's."

He studied her for a few seconds. "Go on."

"I was not sent home on a dishonorable discharge. It's a ruse. I was sent home as a spy. There's a group called the German American Bund who've been holding secret meetings in the bakery. They plan to assassinate Mrs. Roosevelt, and it's my job to find out how and stop them."

He scowled, disbelief playing across his features. "If that's true, what's it got to do with Gypsy?"

"Her real name is Alma. We were roommates during SPARs training in Iowa. She was sent here to help me. She listens in on phone calls and telegrams and reports to the local Coast Guard."

He blinked. "And you think this group found out she's a spy?"

"I don't know. It may just be that they found out she was helping me hide. All I know is I need to get to a phone and quick."

She started to take off, but he stopped her again. "If you's really a spy, then why you telling me all this?"

"Because I believe you love Alma. If we're going to get her back alive, I need your help. And your silence."

"Gettin' her back alive is the only option I'll allow. How can I help?"

"I need to get to West Quoddy Lighthouse as fast as possible."

"Ol' Isham got a truck. It only runs on days it feels up to it, but we can try."

She followed him outside to a beat-up truck that looked as old as Isham, and judging by the man's white hair and wrinkles, he had to be in his midseventies.

Micah rushed to the driver's side and opened the door. "We need to borrow your truck, Isham."

Isham, who was standing by the woodpile, shuffled toward them. "I'll be happy to drive you anywhere you want to go."

Micah got inside, and Shirley followed on the other side. "No offense, Isham, but we need to get where we're going today."

The starter attempted to turn the motor and drowned out whatever Isham said in response. Micah hit the steering wheel with his palm. "Come on, truck. Don't be gettin' on my bad side today."

Shirley sent a prayer heavenward.

Another attempt and the motor fired. Micah punched the gas, and the truck jerked forward and sputtered, belching smoke and the smell of fuel as they trudged along. Either Micah didn't really know how to drive, or he was setting a record for how many ditches and potholes he could hit on the way there.

She instructed him to park outside the keeper's quarters, and she ran to the door and pounded as hard as she could. Mr. Geddy was probably in the thick of sleep by now, and she wanted to make sure he heard her. After several minutes of knocking, Micah joined her and tried the doorknob.

Locked.

"I don't think they's home." Micah looked in a nearby window.

Shirley didn't want to take his boat without permission, but this was an emergency. Since she couldn't get inside, she at least needed to see if the captain had received her message. She ran to the tower door to retrieve the keys, but that door was locked too. "No!"

She wanted to cry.

"What you be needing, Shirley?"

"Can you kick the door down?"

"Are you mad? A black man'll get hung for breakin' down the door to government property."

"I won't allow it. And no one will ever have to know you were here."

Micah stared at the door, torn.

"Please. For Alma."

He balled his hands into fists. "Many a man been killed over the love of a woman. Guess I'll be joining 'em."

He lifted his foot and kicked the door beneath the handle. It shuddered and cracked but didn't break. He tried again, and this time the crack was louder. Again, and the door split beneath his weight, flying open.

She ran inside and grabbed the keys and waved for him to follow her to the boat. They untied the rope and hopped aboard. The space felt small with him in it. "Sit there and hold on tight."

She started the engine and pushed open the throttle. The boat sliced through the water at top speed. She stayed in open waters, dodging buoys where she could to get to their rendezvous point in Johnson Bay.

As she neared where she'd set the buoy, she slowed their speed, careful to avoid the buoys of another fisherman. She looked all around for the solid red buoy with two thick yellow stripes, the signal for an emergency, but it wasn't there.

"What's wrong?" Micah frowned at her from the deck.

"It's not here."

"What's not?"

She briefly explained the buoy system to him, and she asked him to help her look for it. They drove around in circles, each one larger than the last in hopes of finding it.

"There!" She followed where Micah was pointing.

How had it gotten way out here? She let the boat idle then snatched the buoy with the hook. It lifted out of the water, bringing with it two feet of rope that had been severed from the rest. She examined the end and huffed. A clean cut. She'd seen it before when fishermen held trap wars over these waters, cutting each other's lines and causing them to lose their equipment at the bottom of the ocean forever.

Angry, she tossed the buoy onto the deck and watched it roll. Black markings flashed as it spun. She picked it up, and her breath hitched. The GAB's insignia had been crudely painted on one side.

Shirley's legs went weak, and she collapsed onto the washboard.

"What is it, miss?" Micah knelt beside her.

She held up the buoy, despair welling inside her and spilling out in the form of tears. "They know I'm a spy. The captain never received my message, which means help isn't on the way. They took Alma. I know it."

"We's gots to tell the police."

Shirley nodded. She had to keep her emotions under control so she could think. She had to think.

"I'm going to get a message to the Coast Guard if I have to swim there myself. I need you to alert the authorities of Alma's missing status and tell Mr. Geddy that I've taken his boat."

He agreed, and she sped them back to town. Hang it if someone saw her. She had some things she needed to collect from home before she set out to make a call. Like the gun she knew James had kept hidden with tape under the bed.

At the dock, they tied up the boat and ran to Shirley's house. Micah stayed outside to keep watch, and she burst through the front door and pounded up the stairs, her breaths coming hard and fast. She threw on warmer clothes, grabbed James's gun, extra ammunition, and a knife she tucked inside her boot.

"Shirley?" Mama put a hand at her throat. "Where have you been? We've been worried sick! Your father is out looking for you right now."

She looked down at the gun in Shirley's hand. "How dare you—"

"I'm sorry, Mama, but I've got to go."

"You aren't moving an inch until you tell me what's going on!"

Mama had never shouted at her before. Shirley couldn't waste any more time explaining things, but Mama had been through so much and didn't deserve any more pain.

She set the gun on the floor, grabbed Mama's arms, and guided her to the bed. Shirley knelt in front of her, keeping a tight hold on Mama's clammy hands. "Not everything in life is in black and white, Mama. For your safety and Daddy's, I can't reveal everything. Not yet. But the truth is I was not really sent home on a dishonorable discharge."

Mama opened her mouth, but Shirley laid a finger over her lips. "I need you to trust me, Mama. Please. I haven't disgraced you in the way I've led you to believe, but that's all I can say for now. I promise I'll tell you everything soon. For now, I just need you to trust me."

"Your daddy is afraid you've been taken. That's why he sent you away. The Fischers are tangled in some conspiracy, and he was afraid if you stayed and continued your meddling, you'd be harmed."

"I'm fine. But I have to go now." She kissed Mama's cheek.

"You're not marrying that man, are you?"

Shirley huffed. "Of course not. I never had intentions of going through with it. I only accepted his proposal to find out exactly what they were involved in. I have to go now. One of my dearest sisters needs help."

Mama yanked her arm. "I won't have it, Shirley Jean. Let the men take care of this. I won't lose another child. I won't. I can't."

"You're not gonna lose me, Mama." She hugged her tight and kissed her cheek. "Trust me."

Mama sank her face onto the mattress and sobbed a mournful sound that nearly tore Shirley to pieces. The worn, nubby Bible Captain Stratton had given her still sat on the bedside table where Shirley had left it last. She ran her fingertips over the faded gold lettering on the cover. "I love you, Mama. Daddy too. I'll make you proud."

Shirley joined Micah outside, and they ran toward the police station.

⟩ CHAPTER 42 ⟨

Jack's Joint was a swanky little club by the sea in Massachusetts not quite an hour from Chatham. Trumpets and trombones blared from the stage in the front, and puffs of smoke lingered above tables in the changing light.

When Leo had arrived at the LORAN station, Commander Willis had informed him that Joan's shift had ended three hours prior and that she frequented the club on Saturday nights. He'd asked the commander a few more questions that got him answers no further than what he'd known before arriving.

With Captain Cook's blessing, Leo only had a short amount of time to get his answers before he had to be back at the navy yard.

He'd get his answers.

The room reeked of booze and strong perfume. He weaved through the tables, scanning each female face. None of them so far matched Joan's picture ID on file. There were several couples dancing to "If You Please" by Bing Crosby. It was hard to tell in the dim light from this angle, but she could be one of the blonds plastered to an officer by the stage.

"Hey there." A middle-aged brunette wearing too much lipstick smiled at him.

"Ma'am." He continued scanning faces in hopes that she'd get the hint he wasn't interested in conversation, much less anything else.

She moved in front of him, attempting to block his view. Thankfully, he was taller than she realized. "That's a lot of decoration for one uniform. What's it all mean?"

Her fake Betty Boop voice grated, and so did her finger tracing the stripes on his arm. A blond walked out of the restroom smoothing a hand down her white blouse.

Bingo.

He shrugged off the stranger's touch and pivoted around her to cut Joan off. "Excuse me, ma'am."

A man stumbled into the aisle, slowing Leo's progress. Leo physically moved him out of the way and continued toward Joan.

"Excuse me, miss." She looked at him, a spark of interest lighting her eyes, and smiled. "Are you Joan Fischer?"

Wariness set in and sobered her flirtation. "Who's asking?"

"I'm Admiral Leonard Webber. I'm here on behalf of Shirley Davenport."

A knowing grin lifted one side of her mouth. "Ah yes. I remember you being there the night we enlisted. Shirley had her eyes on you even then. What can I do for you, Admiral Webber?"

He looked around the room. "Can we go someplace a little quieter? Outside, perhaps?"

"It's a little cold for a walk, don't you think?"

"What would you suggest, then?"

She looked above them. "Let me ask Hank if we can use the balcony. They only open it when there's a big crowd, but Hank owes me a favor." She winked and then fled to the bar.

Whatever that meant, Leo didn't want to know.

While he waited, he pretended to scope the joint. He threw glances to Joan at the bar. The big bartender looked at Leo, then nodded. A moment later, Joan returned. "Follow me."

They took a set of stairs to the balcony and sat at a table as far away from the stage as they could get.

Joan sat at an angle in her chair and crossed her long legs, revealing a shapely calf. She draped one arm over the back of the chair next to her as casually as if they were on a date. "Now what's all this about Shirley?"

He cleared his throat. "Well. . .we. . .uh, you see—"

"I know all about your relationship, Admiral—though I thought it was Captain?—and about the dishonorable discharge."

"You do?"

"I do. May as well release the elephant in the room now. Breathe easier, Mr. Webber."

Leo took a deep breath, acting like he was nervous.

"How is Shirley?"

"I don't know exactly. I was reassigned."

"And promoted?"

He nodded.

"Ah, how typical. The woman is ruined forever, and the man gets a promotion." She chuckled wryly. "Life is so unfair."

She had a good point, even if it was a ruse.

"I hate this for Shirley. I went to her home and tried to explain to her father that my intentions are honorable, but he wasn't having it."

This time her chuckle held amusement. "Knowing Mr. Davenport, I suspect not. How can I help?"

"Off the record, I've heard rumors that another man has proposed. A relation to you of some sort, I think. Ernst Schultzheimer?"

She blinked.

Twice.

"And you want me to what? Advise her to turn him down? Call him off?"

"I've written to her by way of a mutual friend, explaining my plans for us after I'm done serving. I have no idea what she'll say. I guess I wanted to talk to you to find out what my competition holds."

"Admiral Webber." She leaned her elbows on the table and clasped her hands, accentuating cleavage beneath a beaded necklace in that purposeful way he'd seen all too many times by certain kinds of women impressed by his uniform. "My father's cousin, twice removed, is many years Shirley's senior and isn't in the same atmosphere compared to you in looks. You've nothing to fear."

He feigned vulnerability, noting she didn't call him her uncle the way they introduced Ernst around town.

"I've heard stories of Captain Webber and his cold, fierce leadership. When it comes to love, it appears you're as insecure and awkward as a teenage boy."

He shrugged. "So this twice-removed cousin of your father's. . .can you call him off?"

Her eyes turned hard. "How did you know where to find me, Admiral?"

Smart little minx.

"It wasn't difficult. Shirley talked about you a lot during training. Said you'd trained in Florida with the other SPARs who'd excelled in science and mathematics. All I had to do was access your records to find where you'd been stationed."

"And what else did you discover?"

"That you're the most efficient and highly skilled worker Commander Willis employs. Your record is spotless, and you have an affinity for living life to its fullest."

She leaned back in her chair again, poised and confident like a queen on her throne. "Why are you really here, Admiral?"

Leo leaned back as well. Game time was over. "I believe your *uncle* is not only a threat to Shirley but a threat to our country. I came to learn all I can about him, as there's no record of his arrival into America. I have reason to believe he's a spy."

She blinked.

Twice.

"That's absurd. If you're so concerned about it, why don't you ask him yourself?"

"Funny thing is, he's disappeared."

"Oh?"

Now it was his turn to lean across the table. "You've taken an oath to serve your country and to protect it from all enemies both foreign and domestic. Where is your uncle, Miss Fischer? When did he arrive in America and why?"

Incensed, she looked away, then back at him. "His real name is Hanz Ernst Heinz. I'm sure that's why you found no documentation on him. He came to live with us just after Thanksgiving. After losing his wife, Germany held nothing for him anymore. My father talked him into living with us so he could start fresh. He's been learning English so he can secure a job and support himself. If he's left Lubec, it's likely because he's found a job. He is not a spy."

"Then why change his name?"

"Fresh start."

"And you're abiding by your oath with this information?"

Her eyes narrowed. "You're a strikingly handsome man, Admiral Webber, but I'm not sure what Shirley sees in you. Off the record, you're a terrible manipulator and your instincts are as off as Joe DiMaggio's fielding during the last Dodgers game."

"You're a strikingly beautiful woman, Miss Fischer. Off the record, you have a terrible personality and your necklace is hideous."

She fingered the coral beads at her sternum, somehow managing to flick open another button on her blouse for him to get a better view. "I agree, but it's a family heirloom that symbolizes strength and power."

The poor deluded woman thought she held both in spades. He stood. "Thank you for your time, Miss Fischer."

He left Jack's Joint and headed straight to the Coast Guard station.

Without Joan ever admitting a word, Leo had discovered the female informant the German spy had alluded to. The double-layer necklace with two adjoining brooches at the bottom did signify strength and power. But not because she'd inherited the heirloom. It was because the necklace had come from Eleanor Roosevelt's bedroom.

≡ CHAPTER 43 ≡

The post office came into sight, and Shirley stopped to catch her breath.

"You all right, miss?" Micah frowned, barely winded.

"I'm. . .fine." She wheezed, still weak from her recent illness and her attempt to keep up with the mighty sequoia running beside her. "You go request a missing person report with the police. I'll call the Coast Guard."

Micah took a step then hesitated, looking around. "You sure I should leave you? If all this is as you say it is, you in grave danger."

"So is Alma. Go, Micah. Do all you can for her. I will on my end too."

"Godspeed, miss."

"You as well."

The giant of a man took off toward the police station. Watching for cars, she ran across the street and into the post office. A line of customers stood at the window, impatient and frustrated. The ring of a telephone rang in the background only to stop and start again a moment later. Miss Middleton stood at the counter behind the bars, her hair disheveled and her voice frazzled.

Shirley cut straight into the line, mumbling an apology to Mrs. Hall. "I need to place an emergency call."

Miss Middleton's brows rose. "Well, you can't. Gypsy never showed up for work this morning. Lazy woman. I can't get ahold of Vicky to take over the shift either. I knew they wouldn't work out. I tried to tell the telephone company as much when they transferred Miss Earlywine. I said—"

"I don't care what you said," Shirley barked. Miss Middleton leaned back as if Shirley had slapped her. "When was the last time you saw Gypsy?"

"Why does that matter?"

"Answer me."

"Yesterday when I left the office, same as always. Now, go to the back of the line. I was helping Mrs. Hall."

Mrs. Hall once again stepped up to the counter, but Shirley mumbled another apology and bumped her out of the way. "I need to place an emergency call. Surely you know enough about the switchboard to get it started for me."

"If you have a true emergency, see the authorities. Now go to the back of the line."

As if the authorities would take her seriously enough to allow her to place a call from their station. Shirley looked around the room and saw the doorway Alma had come out of a few weeks ago when they'd talked privately. She went to it and stepped through into the postal workroom.

"Hey! You can't do that. This is government property." Miss Middleton skirted the counter and rushed toward Shirley. "This part of the building is for government workers only."

Shirley ignored the woman and continued to the little room in the back corner where Alma worked the switchboard. Her chair was empty, but her sweater still lay draped across the back as if she planned to return any minute.

Shirley's heart sank. Had she been snatched from this very room? Nothing looked amiss.

"Get out, Shirley Davenport, or I will have you arrested."

Shirley looked at the large box with flickering lights. A mass of tangled wires protruded from the back, and the contraption wouldn't stop ringing. Shirley had no idea where to begin.

"You have until the count of three to leave this building or I'm fetching the sheriff. One. . .two. . .thr—"

"Stuff it, Middleton. Stop acting so high-and-mighty for once and notice there's a world out there with people in it who need help. Not everything in life is as it seems, including whatever you believe about me. If Gypsy didn't show up for work today, it's because something happened to her. Now, I need your help. Lives are at stake."

Miss Middleton's mouth hung open. Her cheeks turned a blotchy red before her mouth twisted in a hateful scowl.

"As if I'd believe anything that came from the lips of a tramp."

Shirley considered slapping the woman but couldn't spare the time. She studied the switchboard and noticed numbers above each hole where a wire could be inserted.

"That's it. I'm fetching the sheriff."

"Have a safe trip."

Shirley didn't spare a look to see how incensed her comment had made the woman. She sat down in the chair, the ringing of the switchboard blaring through her head. A headset with a microphone rested beside the switchboard. Shirley put it on and stared at the wires.

Which one would connect her call?

She fingered through the cords until she came to one that wasn't connected to the others. She picked it up and studied the numbers on the box. The Coast Guard station was Waterville 2693. She ran her finger up and down until she came to that number.

Shirley stuck the wire inside the adjoining hole, but nothing happened. She only had seconds to spare before the sheriff returned to kick her out. She had to place this call.

She banged her fist on the table, shooting pain into her pinkie. A metal toggle switch had rammed into her finger. A small light flashed above it.

She flipped the switch and sound blasted into Shirley's headset. Startled, she released a noise.

A man's voice came on the line. "Finally. I've been trying to place a call for the last forty-five minutes."

"I'm sorry, sir, but you'll have to try again later." Shirley flipped the toggle switch down, and the light turned off.

Supposing that ended the call, Shirley flipped the switch back up in attempt to place her call before someone else called in. She placed the wire into the hole, but nothing happened. Oh, how she wished it were Vicky's shift, but Alma was the lead SPAR at this post and otherwise stayed at the Coast Guard station in Eastport.

Shirley spotted a lever on the side of the switchboard that looked like it turned. She gave it a good spin, and a moment later a woman's voice sounded in her ears.

"Coast Guard, Waterville, 2693."

"This is Petty Officer, Third Class Shirley Davenport. I need to speak with Captain Cook. It's an emergency."

"I'll transfer you."

Three rings sounded before someone picked up.

"Captain Cook?" Shirley stood and looked out the door to watch for Miss Middleton to return with the sheriff.

"This is Seaman Apprentice Ally McNeill."

"Shirley Davenport. I need to speak with the captain right away. It's an emergency."

"The captain is on his way to see you now. They've made an arrest in the case. A. . ." The sound of papers being shuffled sounded in Shirley's ears. "A Joan Fischer."

Breath left Shirley's lungs and her vision grew fuzzy at the edges.

"She was found in possession of a necklace stolen from Mrs. Roosevelt's bedchamber, as well as a secret signaling device she had built and was using in the basement where she was stationed. That's all we know at present."

The noise of the crowd in the lobby grew louder, and bodies parted to reveal the sheriff rushing in with Miss Middleton behind him.

She had to hurry. "Write this down quickly. I've infiltrated an underground ring called the German American Bund. They meet in the bakery every Wednesday. Felix Schmidt, Olaf Fischer, Ernst—I don't know his last name, but he lives with Olaf Fischer—and a stranger I don't know. Alma, the switchboard operator in Lubec, is missing, and I believe they've taken her. Send help immediately."

She spied the sheriff rounding the counter to the switchboard room. She ripped off the headset and looked around, then dashed out the door at the back of the room. It opened to the back side of the post office.

She sprinted toward the dock and Mr. Geddy's boat. The water was the safest place for her now. She untied the rope, the sound of frantic people in the distance. She jumped aboard and started the engine. The sheriff chased her down the hill to the dock. People standing nearby pointed at her and gestured with their hands, retelling the story.

Opening the throttle, she pulled away from the dock as fast as she could, nearly bashing the stern into Mr. Klink's boat. It wasn't until she reached open waters that she began to relax. Her heart slowed its speed, and she headed for the Coast Guard station.

A shadow loomed in the doorway of the cabin, and Shirley jerked to the side. Ernst grinned, evil and victorious, before he grabbed her and clamped his hand over her mouth and nose. Her world spun and then went black.

☰ CHAPTER 44 ☰

Leo stood from his crouched position after inspecting the signaling machine Joan had resurrected from parts in the basement of the LORAN station. She'd been sending practice signals for weeks, sending ships off course in preparation for the Roosevelts' journey to Campobello Island.

The woman was highly intelligent, he'd give her that. But overconfidence led to arrogance, and arrogance always led to stupid mistakes that could be tracked. Case in point, boldly wearing a necklace stolen from the First Lady, assuming everyone she'd come into contact with would be too ignorant to recognize the piece of jewelry.

His report to the JAG had led to Joan's arrest, and an inspection of her room revealed a folder taped to the underside of a dresser drawer no one would notice unless it was disassembled. Papers inside the folder contained notes she'd taken on how the signals worked and what supplies she'd used to repair the machine in the basement.

Flirtation with an officer had garnered access to the basement key, which she'd copied before returning. She'd studied duty schedules enough to know who would be in the hallways at what time, in order to slip into the basement unseen.

It all led up to the moment the Roosevelts' yacht would be escorted to the island. Signals would be sent to reroute American ships just before the entourage went through so that the waters were clear when the German U-boats attacked the Roosevelts' yacht. The expected end was to murder the First Lady, along with several members of the Secret Service, bringing the United States to its knees by ripping out the heart of the country.

The whole thing was disgusting and genius, and her plans had come so close to fruition it made Leo's stomach turn. Had it not been for Shirley's tip about the red coat—the red coat signaling to German U-boats—they might never have known until it was too late.

Joan was refusing to give up the names of any others she was working with, still holding out that the plan would somehow play out anyway. What she didn't know was that the Coast Guard had detained the Roosevelts' yacht in Rockland right before they'd left the dock.

"Who would've thought." Commander Willis shook his head in awe. The man had been apologizing all morning, feeling responsible for Joan's actions. It wasn't the man's fault. The woman was a professional con artist.

"Don't blame yourself, Commander. She passed every exam and all her training with flying colors. There's no way to test a person's heart. That's out of your control."

What a shame it was too. She could've made a good life for herself and her family. Now, she'd be tried for treason.

Commander Willis nodded, but shock still played across his features. They left the basement and made their way to the commander's office so Leo could call Admiral Grant and let him know he'd discovered the cause of the dwindling supply ships.

Admiral Grant would be livid that Leo had overstepped his bounds, but he'd also be grateful.

An ensign stopped them in the hallway and saluted. "At ease," Leo said, resisting the urge to rub his tired eyes. He hadn't slept in almost thirty hours.

The ensign handed Leo a paper. "Captain Cook of the Eastport Coast Guard station called for you at the Washington Navy Yard, but he was told you were here. I took down his message for you."

"Thank you." Leo unfolded the paper.

German American Bund discovered. Two suspects are in custody. One is Joan's father. A signaling device was found in the home. Two suspects are still unaccounted for. Both female officers on the case have gone missing. Come right away.

Shirley and Alma were missing?

Were they together? Or had their disappearances been separate?

Were they alive?

Leo crumpled the paper in his fist. They had to be alive. He couldn't live with himself if they weren't.

Pain split through Shirley's head. She cracked a swollen eye open. The room bobbed up and down. She coughed, and liquid sprayed out of her nose and onto her lip. The metallic taste hit her tongue. Her nose was bleeding. She struggled to sit up. Her hands were tied. Every bone and muscle ached.

Forcing herself upright, she looked around, trying to place where she was and why she was banged up. Fishing equipment, ropes, an anchor, and nets. She was on a boat. She thought back to what she last remembered. She was on Mr. Geddy's boat. She looked around again. But this boat was too large to be his.

A sharp twinge zinged up her back. She winced and rolled in the other direction to relieve the pressure. Alma lay crumpled in the corner, clothes ripped, skin bloodied.

Dear God, was she alive?

"Alma?" Shirley's ankles were tied together, which made wriggling over to her friend difficult.

Alma's skin was cold. The blood mostly dried. Her skirt and shirt were ripped in places that indicated she'd been brutalized in other ways as well. Shirley leaned to the side and lost what was left in her stomach.

She took a deep, shuddering breath and nudged Alma's clammy arm. No movement. Shirley felt for a pulse. Present but thready. Alma had been missing for almost twenty-four hours. How long had she lain like this, exposed and bleeding?

God, why is this happening?

Ernst's face flickered into her memory. His evil sneer right before Shirley passed out. Or was knocked out.

He'd obviously transferred boats and was likely driving this one. If it was just her on this boat, she might think he planned to force her into marriage. Since that wouldn't require Alma, the only reasonable explanation was that he'd found out they were spies.

What did he plan to do with them?

"Alma. Alma, you have to wake up." Shirley shook her friend harder. "Wake up."

Alma groaned and tried to look at Shirley, but with two black eyes, one completely swollen shut, she probably couldn't see.

"Alma, it's me, Shirley. Are you okay? What did they do to you?"

Alma ran the tip of her tongue over the split in her lip. The skin on her forehead tightened in pain.

"I'm so sorry, Alma. This is all my fault."

Alma rasped, clearing what sounded like gravel from her throat. "Don't you worry 'bout me, Miss Shirley." Her words were soft and garbled. "Ain't the first time I's been beat on."

A tear slipped down Shirley's face. Why did God allow the evil in this world to run rampant? Why didn't He stop it?

"Who did this to you?"

Alma's eyes rolled back in her head, and her head tipped forward before she caught herself. "Those fellas with the GAB. They been followin' you. Heard 'em say they watched you get off the train."

Shirley leaned her head back against the wall. Stupid! She suspected someone would be following her, but she hadn't counted on them getting on the train to follow her to Charles's house. She'd been so careful to make sure no one saw her.

Or so she'd thought.

The boat slowed and the engine sputtered. A shiver stole through Shirley. Did Captain Cook get her message? Did anyone know they were missing?

Ernst stepped into the hold, followed by the stranger from the bakery. The stranger set to collecting items hanging on the rack while Ernst loomed over the women. "My betrothed turns out to be a dirty little spy."

His broken German accent was gone.

"And what a pitiful spy she turned out to be." He bent, grabbed Shirley by the lapels of her open coat, and hoisted her to her feet. She teetered, finding it hard to stand with her ankles tied. "Wonder if you're any better at other things."

He pressed his face close to hers, and his rancid breath made her want to vomit again. She might've, if she'd had anything left to toss.

The stranger pushed Ernst aside, knocking Shirley down in the process. "That's no way to treat your fiancée, Ernst. You're supposed to be gentle-like. Hold her close." The man yanked her up and against him, grinding his body against hers. "Show her how much you appreciate her."

His hand trailed up her shirt, and she squirmed to get out of his hold. He pressed against her tighter, his hand continuing its journey. She reared her head back and head-butted his nose.

He let go, and she fell backward, banging the back of her head on the wall as she fell. Now her skull pounded all around. The man let out a string of curses, holding his nose. Blood spewed from around his hand.

Now they were even.

"I told you she'd fight back." Ernst uncoiled a rope from the wall.

As best as she could with bound hands, she patted her pocket for the gun. "Looking for this?" Ernst asked. He pulled the gun from his waistband and waved it to taunt her.

The stranger yelled a few more expletives at Shirley before going back outside. Ernst emptied the bullets, and they pinged on the floor, then he tossed the gun into the corner.

Shirley's hope plummeted. She looked to Alma, who'd drifted into unconsciousness again. Ernst walked over to Shirley, dragging the rope behind him. "Stand up."

"No."

He yanked her up by the lapels again. "I said, stand up."

Shirley glared at him through her one good eye. "What happened to your accent?"

"It appears we were both living lies, *Petty Officer* Davenport." He wrapped the rope around her waist. "I admit, you had me going for a while. The whole dishonorable discharge thing, that captain coming and then leaving, your heartbreak. . . I'd almost bought it. But you made one mistake."

"What's that?"

"The day at the post office, when Maxwell ran into me and I dropped the letters. You saw the one written in German in Joan's handwriting. The look on your face. Then your quick refusal to allow me to see you home. That told me you suspected something, and that made me question why that would bother you. I took a closer look and noticed your captain following you at times. So I dug deeper to see what you really knew."

Dug deeper? "What do you mean?"

"I needed you in a vulnerable state so you would answer my questions." He went over to the anchor and muscled it closer. He grabbed the other end of the rope and began tying it to the anchor.

"What questions?"

He chuckled, proud of himself. "I'm a research scientist at the University of Maine. Well, I was. The peaches in the basket you ate before you started feeling sick? They're my special recipe I created just for you. They contained the perfect amount of botulism. Enough to make you delirious and your mind weak but not enough to kill you. And if it did, oh well."

He'd purposely infected her with botulism?

Ernst yanked the rope on the anchor end tight. "That's when you revealed your knowledge of a red coat."

While her brain worked to process what he'd revealed, he hauled Alma to her feet. He tied a different rope around Alma's waist but tied the end to the same anchor.

"Is that how you came to know Joan, through the university?" She wanted to plug her ears so she didn't have to hear his answer.

"Intelligent girl. And beautiful. She was the perfect specimen to mold into carrying out my plan. Our passionate natures got the better of us, however, and she was forced to leave the university. But we kept in touch."

Maybe she did have more to retch.

"What are you doing with us?" Shirley asked.

Ernst, if that was even his real name, tipped his head to the side and mocked her in his fake broken English accent. "I trust you Americans call it sleeping with the fishes."

He laughed.

They were going overboard.

They were going to die.

Shirley would join James in heaven.

She looked over at Alma, who could barely stand. "Why kill us?"

He dragged the net over to them. "My protégée has been caught and arrested. She's loyal enough to never give up our names though. We were able to intercept your lengthy note for the captain, so we don't have to worry on that front. The only thing left to do is kill you. That way we can scatter elsewhere unscathed."

She closed her eyes, and Leo's sweet face filled her memory. For years she had discredited the roles of wife and mother, craving excitement and adventure in their place. She'd gotten what she wanted, only to realize with the dishonorable discharge those roles would be harder to obtain. With that, a greater appreciation for the God-given roles had made Shirley regret chasing her freedom.

Then Leo had kissed her, declared his intention of courtship, and made those underappreciated dreams possible once again. She'd thought for a few sweet weeks that she could have it all.

Amid the excitement and adventure, she was going to die serving her country and never know the sweetness of the marriage bed, the precious gift of a newborn babe. The honor of growing old with someone. Captain Stratton's speech about Amelia Earhart rose to the forefront of her mind. *Amelia had a purpose, and she fulfilled it. Now go. Fulfill yours.*

As long as Mrs. Roosevelt remained safe, then Shirley had fulfilled her purpose.

"What of Mrs. Roosevelt?" she asked between chattering teeth. She was going into shock.

Ernst threw the net over her and Alma and cinched it tight, squeezing both women together face-to-face. Shirley prepared her mind for death.

"The signals never came. That dog-faced woman escaped. Don't worry. You can be sure we'll get her next time. Karl! I need help," he yelled.

The man came into the hold, pinching his nose with a hand-kerchief. "My hands are tied. The stupid"—he rattled something in German—"broke my nose."

Ernst shoved him. "I'm gonna break your neck if you don't put that down and help me. We can fix your nose later. *After* we dump these two and get to safe ground."

Mumbling more German, Karl threw down the bloody fabric and helped Ernst wrestle the women to the deck. "Why didn't you wait to tie them up once you got them outside?"

"I didn't think of that," Ernst snapped.

"Too busy yappin'."

"Unless you want to join these ladies, shut your mouth and help me." Ernst spit and dragged the ladies a few feet more. Twice the men had to stop to catch their breath and scoot the anchor behind them.

Shirley pressed her forehead to Alma's. "I'm so sorry."

"Don't you go being sorry for me. You's a good woman, Miss Shirley. I was honored to know you, and I'm honored to die with you."

Fear and tears nearly consumed Shirley. "You're the best friend I've ever had."

And boy, it was the truth.

"Quiet with the sentiment over there," Ernst said. "You'll have forever for that."

Unwilling to die, Shirley dragged her feet and off-centered her weight as much as she could to make their progress difficult. Despite it, she was at their mercy, and they weren't giving any.

They reached the back of the boat, where they pressed the women as close to the end as possible. A roar sounded in the distance. The men stopped shoving and looked around. "What's that?" Karl asked.

Panic washed over Ernst's face. "Let's hurry so we can get out of here."

The men worked together lifting the heavy anchor to the ledge. They grunted and rested it on the lip of the boat. The roar grew louder.

The roar of a boat.

Karl panicked. "They're heading straight for us."

Hope buoyed Shirley's heart. The boat sped along the top of the water so fast it seemed to fly. A glimmer of a flag flashed.

The Coast Guard. They were going to be rescued!

Karl dropped the anchor on the deck with a thud, then darted back and forth, unsure what to do. He'd arched his arms over his head to dive into the water when Ernst shoved him over, cursing.

With a barbaric growl, Ernst lifted the anchor and shoved it overboard. Faster than Shirley could blink, the rope uncoiled, and they were yanked overboard and into the frigid water.

CHAPTER 45

Leo burst through the hospital doors and ran to the nurses' station. "Shirley Davenport, please."

The woman picked up a clipboard. "Are you family?"

"Admiral Webber, United States Navy. Miss Davenport is under my care."

"Right this way." The nurse walked through a set of double doors and down a long hallway full of rooms. "The doctor has given her a small amount of sedative to help her sleep and heal. Since her lungs were compromised, however, we're keeping a close eye on her to make sure the sedative doesn't hinder her airflow."

She gestured to the dark room on her right. "One of us stops in every few minutes to check on her, but I'll let the other nurses know you're here. Please let us know if you need anything."

"Thank you. Have her parents been informed?"

"I can't answer that. I'll see if I can find out."

"And the other lady? Alma Evans?"

Her brows crinkled. "She's in our intensive care ward. Her condition is. . .precarious."

"I understand. Thank you, ma'am."

Leo stepped into the dark room and his heart broke. Shirley was stretched out on the bed, her closed eyes and pale skin reminding him of a corpse. His insides trembled. This sweet woman almost died at the hands of Nazis. Bold and brave for her country.

What if he'd lost her?

Death played outside of his hands. Whether it was his brothers' lives or Shirley's, he had no control.

238

He looked away. Emotions clogged his throat and built pressure in his cheekbones. He loved this woman. Without doubt or reservation, he loved this woman. And he'd almost lost her.

Reining himself in, he scooted a chair next to her bed and wrapped her cold hand in his, careful of the IV. He pressed his lips to her fingers and thanked God for keeping her alive. For not sacrificing another person he loved to this blasted war.

Shirley twitched, and a tiny cough escaped her lips. The action created a snowball effect, and she opened her eyes, coughs continuing to rack her body. He helped her sit up and patted her back. Was she ever going to stop? "Nurse!"

A moment later, a different nurse walked in carrying a towel and a shallow bucket. "Good girl, Shirley. If anything comes up, spit it in here."

Leo held back her hair, stiff with dried saltwater. Shirley spit a few times and caught her breath. When the reddish hue in her face began to fade, so did his fear.

"This is good," the nurse said, dabbing Shirley's lips with the towel. "The more she can clear her lungs, the less likely pneumonia will set in."

"If it does?" Leo asked.

The nurse set the towel aside and eased Shirley back down on the stack of pillows. "Penicillin is working wonders for our soldiers overseas. Dr. Larabee mentioned trying it should her condition worsen. I believe that's what they've given Miss Evans to help combat bacterial infections."

Leo nodded his thanks, and the nurse left the room. He tucked Shirley's hair behind her ear. "Are you okay?"

She lifted her eyes and stared at him, as if in a fog. Then something registered and she tried to sit up again. "Leo?"

"Lay down." He sat so she wouldn't have to strain to see him. "Don't work on my account. You need to rest."

She swallowed, and tears poured from the outer corners of her eyes and ran down into her ears. "Shhh." He eased onto the edge of her bed and placed his hands on both her cheeks, brushing the tears with his thumbs.

"Oh Leo." She clung to his arm with the hand that didn't have needles protruding from it. His sweet Shirley had been through hell and back, and that judgment was made only from the facts he knew about. He had a feeling there were many more he didn't know about, which made his stomach turn.

He kissed her forehead, allowing his lips to linger. "I'm here now, sweetheart. It's all over." He leaned back enough to look into her eyes.

"Well done, Petty Officer Davenport. You served your country well."

She shook, and he pulled the blankets higher. "Did they—" Her voice broke.

"We got them. Ernst is in federal custody. The other man is dead."

Had Karl Rossilini not been standing in the coil of rope when the anchor was dropped, it wouldn't have wrapped around his legs and torso and pulled him against the railing, cutting him nearly in two. The rope held against his body and the railing long enough for a Coast Guard diver to jump into the water and cut the rope from the anchor. The other officers hauled the net of women up from the deep.

The horror of it made him sick. How that rope managed to climb high enough to cinch the man's torso, Leo would never know. The only reasonable explanation was that the good Lord wasn't ready to take those women home yet.

And Leo was grateful.

He sat on the edge of the mattress, holding her, never wanting to let go. He wouldn't relay the ugly details of it all unless she asked, and even then, he wouldn't do it here.

"Alma?" Her whisper was barely audible. Her eyes rolled in sleep, the sedative taking control once again.

"She's alive."

A small smile touched her lips before she succumbed to sleep. Leo pulled the blanket up to her shoulders, careful not to disturb any needles or tubes.

Her beautiful skin was marred and purple and her lip was cut.

He swallowed his anger, sat in the chair, and watched her sleep. His mind raced in a thousand different directions. No matter how far he chased those thoughts, they all led back to Shirley.

His future started with her.

Three weeks later, after a wonderful roast beef dinner, Shirley sat in her living room on the couch next to Leo. Daddy rested in the armchair in the corner, and Mama sat perched on one of the arms. Charles and his family had come for a visit. Little Jack and Roseanne played with blocks on the floor.

Alma had been staying with them ever since she'd been released from the hospital. Shirley insisted on seeing to her care. After dinner,

Alma and Micah had sneaked away for a private walk. The man had been at Alma's side every moment he could spare. Alma seemed to take comfort in the man's presence, but the ordeal had made Alma shrink within herself even further.

Shirley prayed Micah could draw her out.

Leo scooted to the end of the couch, reached inside his uniform jacket, and handed a folded paper to Daddy across the coffee table. "Official documentation. Shirley's service to our country, and letters from Captain Stratton and Admiral Hendricks clearing her name."

Her father opened the papers, and her parents read them. In the quiet, Leo reached for her hand, entwining his fingers with hers. It seemed as if a lifetime had passed since her parents had stood in the hospital room while Leo and Captain Cook had explained everything to them. Her father had wept and apologized for days. She didn't hold anything against him. What else was the man to think when all the evidence pointed to one thing?

When her parents finally looked up from the papers, Leo looked at Shirley and said, "Mrs. Roosevelt is planning a ceremony to honor you and Alma, along with the SPARs, WAVES, and other females serving their country."

Nervous energy ran through Shirley. "I'll get to meet her?"

"You will."

Jack toppled sideways and began to cry. Jessalyn, Shirley's sister-in-law, picked up the baby and bounced him gently. "I'm so jealous," she murmured.

Leo squeezed Shirley's hand. "We need to keep it quiet until the ceremony, if possible, as the incarcerated individuals are still under investigation. Then the paper is free to mention Shirley's service to clear her name publicly."

They all knew, even then, there'd be those who refused to see Shirley as anything other than a floozy. Those who felt a respectable woman wouldn't be willing to put her reputation at stake for her country. To put herself in danger for everyone.

Shirley couldn't care less about those people. She had her family, she had Alma, and at least for the foreseeable future, she had Leo.

Daddy wiped his eyes. "This calls for a celebration." He patted his wife's knee. "Did I smell a chocolate cake in the oven?"

They laughed. "Indeed, you did," Mama said. "And it's as chocolatey and sweet as it should be, thanks to Admiral Hendricks, who gave me the Fischers' ration booklet for the month."

They all smiled, trying to make light of the comment, but there was nothing light about it. They'd all been deceived by friends they'd held dear, and the hurt would linger for years to come.

Around the time they'd finished eating their slices of cake, Alma and Micah returned. "How was your walk?" Mama asked.

Micah dipped his head. "'Twas beautiful at evenin' time, same as always, ma'am. This part of the country never ceases to amaze me with its wonders."

"Well said," Shirley whispered. Tears threatened, as they'd done a hundred times a day since she'd woken in the hospital. All her life, she'd wanted to leave this town in search of something more. Now, she realized, this place already held what she'd been looking for the whole time.

Jessalyn passed the baby to Charles. "Would you both like a slice of chocolate cake? It's wonderful."

Micah looked to Alma.

Alma pulled her shawl tighter. "No, thank you, Miss Jessalyn. I'm tired after such a walk, as delightful as it was." She gave Micah a gentle smile to soften the blow. "I'm just gonna go ready for bed, if it won't be offendin' you all."

"Not in the least," Mama said. "You rest as much as you need."

Micah reached an arm out as if wanting to embrace Alma but with her still-healing injuries not sure how to touch her without hurting her. He put his hands in his pockets. "Night, Alma. I hope you sleep well."

Alma tossed him a doubtful look followed by a smile, then made her way down the hallway and up the stairs to Shirley's room. They'd offered her the use of James's old room for privacy, but the nightmares that haunted Alma every night were too frightening for her to face alone. They'd moved James's bed into Shirley's room instead so they could bunk together like when they'd been in Iowa.

Micah watched Alma disappear up the steps, the tenderness and love on his face so precious Shirley almost cried.

Again.

"Poor thing." Jessalyn took Charles's plate from the mantel and stacked it on her own. "Is she doing any better at all, Micah?"

Mama watched him as she gathered the other empty plates as well.

Micah shrugged. "'Bout the same."

Shirley stood and walked toward him. "Keep being patient," she whispered. "She's a strong woman. She'll get through this."

Micah bobbed his head.

"Stay for a piece of cake?" Shirley smiled wide, coaxing him. It was hard to believe a few weeks ago, he'd held such animosity toward her.

Micah sighed. "I don't claim to be a smart man, but I know better than to turn down a piece of cake."

They laughed, and Mama went to fetch him a slice. Shirley patted his arm, then stood on tiptoe and kissed his big, teddy bear cheek. Micah's eyes grew wide, and she giggled.

Leo stood. "I think I need a walk myself to help digest that wonderful meal, Mrs. Davenport."

Her mother had walked back into the room, carrying a plate and a look of scolding. "As I told you earlier, Admiral Webber, call me Helen."

"Thank you for the fine meal, Helen." Leo winked. He helped Shirley into her sweater and offered his arm as he opened the door.

Shirley snuggled close to his side, and they walked past the barn to the edge of the plateau where the sun was setting on the horizon. Waves sparkled like diamonds. The breeze stirred her hair, but at least it grew warmer as they passed into June.

Leo moved behind her and wrapped his arms around her waist. His scratchy jaw tickled her cheek, but it was glorious torture. Even though she had a lot of things to work through, she'd never felt more loved or safe with her family, and especially with this man.

She closed her eyes and rested the back of her head on his shoulder. Peaceful and content.

Leo grumbled low in her ear. "You really shouldn't do that."

"What?"

"Expose that soft part of your neck like that." The desire was evident in his voice. "It makes it awfully hard for a man to keep his thoughts pointing north."

Despite what he'd said, his lips traced a hot path down her neck and played with the skin where it met her shoulder.

She wanted so badly to spin around and get lost in him. To get caught up in something honest and forget there was evil in the world.

"Shirley." He turned her around to face him. She wrapped her arms around his neck, closed her eyes, and prepared to fall.

"Look at me."

She blinked her eyes open.

He tightened his hold on her back. "Will you marry me?"

She stilled. Had she heard him correctly?

"I know it's not all that easy with me in Washington and you here, but one day this war is going to end, and life is going to go on, and I want that life to include you. I want it centered around you." He touched his forehead to hers. "I want *you*."

Her heart swelled until she thought it might burst. "As long as I get to do boring things like keep house and cook and change diapers."

The tension in his forehead eased. "Sweetheart, I'll let you do anything you set your mind to."

"Then let's get married tomorrow."

He laughed. "I like your enthusiasm."

"You ain't seen nothing yet, Admiral." She pulled him down and sealed his lips with hers, kissing him as if it would be their last. Blessedly, it would be the start of many.

Looked like she'd get to have both dreams after all.

CHAPTER 46

Shirley cracked open her bedroom door and peered inside, not wanting to wake Alma had she managed to find sleep. Sleep would elude Shirley tonight for sure, after Leo's proposal and that kiss that only managed to leave them both wanting more.

The full moon cast the room in a silvery glow. The form on the bed still, Shirley tiptoed inside the room and closed the door behind her. Soft snores sounded from the bed. She unbuttoned her dress and let it fall to the floor, then yanked her nightgown over her head and punched her arms through. Slipping into bed as gently as she could, she frowned when Alma stirred.

Alma startled, hand to her chest.

"I'm sorry, Alma. I didn't mean to wake you."

Alma lay back down. "It's all right, Miss Shirley. I'm in and out of sleep anyway."

Shirley adjusted her pillow. The women rested in silence for a few minutes. "Leo proposed."

Alma's head turned toward Shirley. "Congratulations, Miss Shirley. I'm happy for you."

Shirley sat up on her elbow and faced Alma. "I suspect Micah is wanting to do the same, but he's biding his time."

Alma sighed as if she'd dragged the breath clear from her toes. "Micah is a *good* man. But I'm not ready to go marryin' anyone."

"Why not?"

"Been on my own too long, I guess."

Alma crossed her arms over her chest the way Shirley noticed she'd done several times lately. A subconscious defense tactic, perhaps.

Whether or not it was wise to brave the question, Shirley did. "Did those men hurt you? In a...carnal way, I mean?"

Alma squeezed her eyes shut and turned away. "They tried to. I fought 'em as best I could."

"How did you stop them?" Though it was painful to recall the details, it helped Shirley to talk them out. Like an ounce of the heavy weight got lighter each time she spoke aloud. Alma was maybe not that way, and Shirley would be respectful of that. If Alma told her to mind her own business, she would.

"They...well, they took one look at me underneath my shirt and was repulsed by what they seen. Same as any man would, I guess. It worked in my favor though."

"What do you mean?"

"Miss Shirley, I ain't never told no one this."

"It's okay, Alma. You don't have to tell me anything you don't want to."

Alma was quiet for so long Shirley assumed she wasn't going to answer. "I've kept it to myself all this time, thinking it would protect me. All it's done is eat me alive." Her voice crumbled with emotion.

Shirley reached out and held Alma's hand.

"I was born in the Greenwood district of Tulsa, Oklahoma, where tensions were high between the white folk and the black. My parents owned a little shoe store on the main thoroughfare.

"Some story 'bout a black man on an elevator with a white woman got blown up in a newspaper, and the next thing I know, folks on both sides is lootin' and shootin' one another. A group of white men burst into the office where my parents told us girls to hide and they..."

Alma's breath hitched. "After they was done with us, they took a knife to our chests. Cut us all up. Marked us forever."

Shirley's stomach turned. "How old were you?"

Tears slipped down Alma's cheeks. "I was seven. Elverly was five. She didn't survive all those cuts. Lost my mama and daddy that same day too."

Shirley started to say she was sorry for the losses, but the word was so insufficient.

"So you see, those men took one look at all that mutilation and changed their minds."

Keeping hold of Alma's hand, Shirley lay back down on her pillow.

"Watching you break that man's nose was one of the highlights of my life."

Tears took hold of Shirley. "Knowing a woman as strong and brave as you are, who's gone through all you have and is still willing to serve her messy country, is the highlight of mine."

"Don't puff me up, Miss Shirley. I joined the SPARs thinkin' I was just going to be a secretary or telephone operator and make a better wage. I never thought to be no spy."

"Why did you, then?"

"Mrs. Roosevelt, she's against crimes against people like me. She does her best to be our voice. To fight for our equality. She's worth serving for."

"Leo said she's planning a ceremony to honor us specifically, and all the women who serve."

"Don't that beat all? I've never been honored before."

"Micah tries."

"You've got love on the brain, Miss Shirley." Alma rolled onto her side, facing the wall.

"Give him a chance to love you, Alma. He wants all of you. Scars and all."

⫶ CHAPTER 47 ⫶

Washington, DC
October 1946

The audience stood and a roar of cheering and clapping thundered through the mall. Never had Shirley seen so many people in one place. The entire stretch of green between the Washington Monument and the Lincoln Memorial was a sea of faces and red, white, and blue bunting.

Captain Stratton stood at the microphone clapping, her body turned to the servicewomen standing behind her. The captain was the one they should be clapping for. Her service to this country was just as great as theirs. It was a pure shame that the SPARs were being decommissioned now that the war was over.

Shirley hoped for another chance to speak with Mrs. Roosevelt, but she was the former First Lady with important responsibilities and very little time. Still, receiving a hug from Mrs. Roosevelt and personal gratitude for saving her life three years prior was a high point in Shirley's life. Not as high as her wedding night or the birth of her sweet James, but close.

It was difficult to spot her handsome husband in the mass of people. If she could find Micah, she'd find Leo. As massive as Micah was, even he was hard to spot.

Ceremony completed, Shirley found Alma, and the women descended the concrete steps and made their way to the Smithsonian Arts and Industries Building where they'd planned ahead of time to meet up in case they all got separated.

Shirley loved this city. The beauty, the opportunities, the patriotism. She wouldn't mind living here a little longer if Leo decided to reenlist.

"There." Alma tugged her around a group of reporters. Sure enough, Leo sat on a park bench bouncing James on his knee. Micah was too large to join him on the bench, so he stood nearby, looking smart in his new suit.

"Hey." Leo stood and propped James on his hip. "Here come the most decorated ladies in all of Washington."

He approached and fingered the Legion of Merit award pinned above her right breast.

Micah said nothing, just leaned down and kissed his fiancée without reserve. Shirley and Leo passed a knowing look between them.

After almost three years of courting, Alma had finally agreed to marry Micah. Their wedding was scheduled two weeks from now in Lubec, where Alma had been working as a yeoman for the Coast Guard station in nearby Eastport.

James pushed at Leo's shoulder. "Down."

"I don't think so, little man." Leo bounced him up and down. "Those toddler legs are faster than they look, and there's too many people around to risk unleashing you."

Shirley kissed her son's sticky cheek, then made a face.

Leo shrugged. "He got hungry during the ceremony. I gave him the jelly sandwich left over from lunch."

"Ah, that explains it." She tickled James, who giggled with delight.

Leo looked back at the kissing couple then back to Shirley. "Those two may not make it to the wedding."

"Says the man who almost didn't make it until his."

Leo shrugged. "Can you blame me?"

Shirley put her lips to his ear. "We're married now though."

He chuckled. "Yes, we are."

She smiled and turned to look back at the city, a hand cradling her lower belly. She was expecting again but hadn't told Leo yet. The doctor believed it was twins. While the idea of two newborns at once intimidated her, she prayed the doctor was correct. And that they were boys, so they could name them Lonnie and Donald after Leo's brothers.

"Are you two done yet?" Leo asked over his shoulder. "I'm growing old over here."

Micah pulled away and looked around, as if he'd forgotten they were in public. "Life's too short to rush things, Mr. Leo."

Alma winked at Shirley.

As they walked home, the men talked about some new car the Ford Motor Company had released called a De Luxe something and how they'd been built with leftover parts from before the war.

Such talk bored Shirley to death, so she reached for James and walked beside Alma. "Let's talk about something that matters."

Alma laughed. "Like what? How you's keeping a secret from your husband?"

Shirley's mouth dropped open, and she grabbed Alma's arm to pull back from the men. "How do you know? I haven't said a word."

"Miss Shirley." Alma laughed. "You glowin' like that fancy new lamp they put in the lighthouse. You couldn't be more obvious."

Shirley twisted her lips. "Do you think Leo knows?"

"No." Alma continued walking. "He's a man. He doesn't notice things like that."

Shirley followed. "Good. I want to surprise him."

"Oh, he'll be surprised."

They walked a few steps before she nudged Alma's arm. "Maybe come Christmas, you'll be glowing like that fancy new lamp in the lighthouse."

Alma's eyes bugged. "What? Nah. I'm too old." She bit her bottom lip and looked at Shirley as if she was scared silly.

It was Shirley's turn to laugh. "You are not. In fact, if I was a betting woman, I'd put money on it. Yep, I predict by Christmas."

Alma rolled her eyes and put her arm through Shirley's. "You is crazy."

⊒ EPILOGUE ⊑

Present Day

The forward to *Always Ready*, a biography written by Lucy Webber-Shaw:

It is in the midst of tragedy when Americans bolster their courage and rise from the ashes to protect their families and possessions. Sometimes that courage comes from a natural-born dogged determination, and other times it's inspired by the words and actions of others. Eleanor Roosevelt was a master at inspiring others through her example, her accomplishments, and years of writing her acclaimed "My Day" columns.

She inspired children to serve their country by collecting books to send to soldiers overseas and scrap metal to aid the war effort. She inspired women to take off their aprons, set their pots and pans aside, and join the workforce, to not only help their men but to keep the economy running during war. She inspired men to realize that women were capable of such tasks and to see them as equals.

It was Eleanor who helped inspire the first female-only reserve of the Coast Guard known as the SPARs—an acronym for their motto "Semper Paratus, Always Ready," so named by their strong and courageous leader, Captain Dorothy C. Stratton.

The reserve was established eighty years ago to free able-bodied men working the home front to join the war effort. Dorothy Stratton, Purdue University's former dean of women and lieutenant commander of the WAVES, was the first woman accepted into service and asked to direct the SPARs. Others told Miss Stratton she couldn't afford to do it. She responded, "I can't afford not to."

It was women like Dorothy Stratton and Eleanor Roosevelt who inspired hundreds of other women to enlist. Women like my great-grandmother, Shirley Davenport, who was looking for a way to serve her country and live as an independent woman.

When she enlisted, she never would have guessed her journey to independence would lead her into espionage, where she'd willingly offer to sacrifice her life for Mrs. Roosevelt's.

Thankfully, my great-grandmother survived to tell the tale that captivated her many grandchildren around the supper table. Let me share it now with you—the story of saving Mrs. Roosevelt.

AUTHOR'S NOTE

I hope you've enjoyed the tale of *Saving Mrs. Roosevelt*. While this story is purely fiction, including the biography in the epilogue, there are some real-life events and characters I threw in for fun.

The SPARs who trained at Iowa State Teachers College really were trained by naval officers and not Coast Guard instructors. However, former WAVES turned SPARs trained as captains at Oklahoma A&M University in Stillwater alone as a group. I thought it would be fun to mix them up for the sake of my story, giving you characters like Bridgette, Lucy, and Roxie.

Captain Dorothy C. Stratton traveled from SPARs training site to site and didn't stay in one place throughout the entirety of a group's training. She made it to the graduations every six weeks, however, and usually brought another female of importance along, such as US Congresswoman, later US Senator, Margaret Chase Smith, known as the "Lady of Maine."

Dorothy Stratton really did have a Bible that she found in a desk from the former dean of women at Purdue, Carolyn Shoemaker. It was passed from dean to dean over the years, but I thought it would be fun for Dorothy to pass it to Shirley for the sake of the story. In reality, the Bible was passed down to Captain Helen Schleman, who became the dean of women at Purdue after Dorothy and her time serving in the military. Read more in Angie Klink's biography *The Deans' Bible: Five Purdue Women and Their Quest for Equality*.

Captain Stratton's friendship with Amelia Earhart was real, and she was quoted using the Lewis Carroll poem when asked by a reporter years later what kind of things they talked about when they visited one another outside of work. Dorothy told them, "Of cabbages and kings"— her smart, ladylike way of passing off his question.

Alma Evans's character is very loosely based on Olivia J. Hooker, the first black woman to enlist in the SPARs and a survivor of the 1921 Tulsa Race Massacre, who later became a psychologist and professor. This amazing woman died at 103, and her life and sacrifices are still touching the hearts of people today.

Botulism is an often-fatal disease of the nervous system caused by neurotoxic proteins. Several nations produced botulism toxins during WWII as a potential bacteriological weapon. I used it in this story as a way for Shirley to compromise the mission and to tie Ernst's and Joan's relationship at the college.

Eleanor Roosevelt really did have a double-brooch coral necklace given to her by her mother, Anna Hall Roosevelt, that Eleanor passed to her daughter, Anna Roosevelt Halsted, in the 1940s. The necklace was never stolen except in fiction. The piece is on display at the Franklin D. Roosevelt Presidential Library in Duchess County, New York.

Several dates and ship names were altered to fit the timeline and mood of the story. I hope for entertainment's sake you'll overlook some of my tweaking, such as the timeline of the Doolittle Raid and the "My Day" column by Eleanor Roosevelt that I referred to in chapter 39. The last few paragraphs were added with my own words to mold the column to the events of the plot.

I encourage you to learn more about Dorothy C. Stratton, Olivia J. Hooker, and the SPARs. These brave and honorable women paved the way for the advancement of women.

ACKNOWLEDGMENTS

Without my agent Linda S. Glaz from the Hartline Literary Agency, this book would not exist. She encouraged me to submit a proposal for the Heroines of WWII series, and twenty-four hours later I had fleshed out the entire novel. The rest is history (pun intended). Linda, you are my constant cheerleader and, most of all, my friend. I'm blessed to take this journey with you.

A huge thanks to the sisters of my heart—the Quid Pro Quills—Robin Patchen, Pegg Thomas, Kara Hunt, Jericha Kingston, and Susan Crawford. Your support, prayers, wisdom, and honesty push me to be a better writer. I couldn't survive my fictional worlds without you.

To Becky Germany and the Barbour team for this fantastic cover and your amazing editing skills. You ladies rock!

Thank you to Nikki and Mahendra Jatindranath for helping me with all things military. Without you both I would've been lost. I appreciate you! Any mistakes found in the story in regard to the armed forces are accidental and entirely my fault.

Adam, not only do you provide inspiration, but your patience and encouragement during the entire process keep me going. Thank you for walking this journey with me. Can you believe we just celebrated twenty years?! Having you by my side is an honor.

To Levi, Silas, and Hudson—thank you for your patience and support as I write in nearly every spare moment. Holding the title Mom means more than all. Though the dynamics of our family are changing quickly as you take your first steps into the world as men, I will *always* love you to the moon and back.

Above all, I thank my Lord and Savior Jesus Christ. All honor and glory are His.

Thank you, dear reader, for taking time out of your busy life to spend it with my characters. Until next time. . .

⊒ HEROINES OF WWII ⊑

They went above the call of duty and expectations to aid the Allies' war efforts and save the oppressed. Full of intrigue, adventure, and romance, this new series celebrates the unsung heroes—the heroines of WWII.

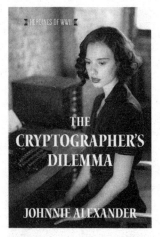

The Cryptographer's Dilemma
By JOHNNIE ALEXANDER

FBI cryptographer Eloise Marshall is grieving the death of her brother, who died during the attack on Pearl Harbor, when she is assigned to investigate a seemingly innocent letter about dolls. Agent Phillip Clayton is ready to enlist and head oversees when asked to work one more FBI job. A case of coded defense coordinates related to dolls should be easy, but not so when the Japanese Consulate gets involved, hearts get entangled, and Phillip goes missing. Can Eloise risk loving and losing again?

Paperback / 978-1-64352-951-6 / $14.99

A Picture of Hope
By LIZ TOLSMA

Journalist Nellie Wilkerson has spent the bulk of the war in London, photographing pilots taking off and landing—and she's bored. She jumps at the chance to go to France, where the Allied forces recently landed. She enlists Jean-Paul Breslau of the French underground to take her to the frontlines. On the journey, they come upon an orphanage where nuns shelter children with disabilities. Can they help save the children before the Nazis come to liquidate it?

Paperback / 978-1-63609-019-1 / $14.99